SAVING COTTONWOOD

LISA PAGE

JUPITER MOON PRESS

To the Ancestors, the Allies, and the Crow Clan of the Rio Grande Valley.

Until one is committed, there is hesitancy, the chance to draw back, always ineffectiveness. Concerning all acts of initiative and creation, there is one elementary truth, the ignorance of which kills countless ideas and splendid plans: that the moment one definitely commits oneself, then providence moves too.

All sorts of things occur to help one that would never otherwise have occurred. A whole stream of events issues from the decision, raising in one's favour all manner of unforeseen incidents, meetings and material assistance which no man could have dreamed would have come his way.

I have learned a deep respect for one of Goethe's couplets:

Whatever you can do or dream you can, begin it. Boldness has genius, power and magic in it. Begin it now.

-William Hutchison Murray

CHAPTER 1

Who locks themself out of their own house, dummy?

Iris shook off the thought as she scrolled through her phone and called the first locksmith she could find: Cottonwood Pop-a-Lock.

"Pop-a-Lock," a sing-songy female voice said.

Iris pressed her forehead against the cold glass of the front window. "Uh, hi, I seem to have locked myself out of my house. I had a really hectic morning, and I forgot my house key, which I know I should have on the same ring as my car key, but, well, I took it off one day when I didn't want to carry all those keys walking through the neighborhood. But you don't want to know all that. Anyway, now I'm locked out and need a locksmith." *You sound pathetic,* whispered the mean voice in her head.

She caught her reflection in the glass— silver wisps of hair that had apparently sprouted at the moment of her divorce were coming loose from her bun. But hadn't she earned a few gray hairs?

"Your name?" the efficient operator asked.

"Iris Barnes."

"What's your address, hon?" Iris cringed at the endearment. She must sound as pathetic as she felt.

"I'm at 208 Silver Avenue." Looking down the tree-lined street of historic Craftsman and Victorian homes and across the street into the green park, she noted that the elm trees were starting to leaf, and a pair of Cooper's hawks were building a nest. The constant whoosh of highway traffic had scared away other buyers and made this beautiful, hundred-year-old, probably falling-apart house almost affordable on her librarian's salary.

A lower leg caress and a chirp let her know the familiar stray cat had arrived. Because of the cat's long black hair and Iris's soft spot for strong females making it on their own, she began calling her Xena the Warrior Princess. But she did not want a cat. She most definitely did not want a cat. She had inquired with the neighbors, but so far, no one had ever seen her before.

"I'll radio the van, and they'll call to let you know when they can arrive. It shouldn't be too long."

Iris hung up and sank onto the front steps, absentmindedly running her fingers through the cat's silky fur. The thought of calling a friend crossed her mind, but who? Six months in a new city hadn't yielded the sort of friends she could reach out to because she was having a rough day. Honestly, most days over the past year had been rough since her seven-year marriage had ended when she heard the words, "I never really loved you."

With all the time alone she was suddenly experiencing, she had stumbled upon the voice in her own head. And it was not very nice. Maybe she had coexisted with that same voice when she was married. She wasn't sure. If so, the volume had definitely increased since her divorce. *You'll never make real friends here. You'll never belong anywhere.*

She hated that her divorce had knocked down her confidence and stolen her future life. The kids, grandkids, and secure golden years fell straight into a file marked *Not So Fast*.

Straightening up, she gave herself a pep talk. After all, she was holding her own. In the past year, she had uprooted her life, moved to a new city, started a new job, and even bought a house entirely on her own. Well, along with the bank.

"Yes, I am a competent grown-up, thank you very much," Iris said defensively to the fluffy cat. "That's right. You understand," she said, scratching Xena's ears as the cat purred.

Looking around at the blooming purple lilacs and yellow forsythia in the front yard, she felt a muted version of the uplift and optimism she usually experienced in spring. Her inner optimist had called in sick since the divorce, but she needed to turn a corner soon. She wanted her life back. Taking a deep breath, she inhaled the scent of the lilac flowers. They were lovely, she admitted.

Iris was a gardener and a homebody, and this hundred-year-old craftsman-style house was her post-divorce refuge. *If I could just get inside already.* She looked at her watch and gazed down the street.

She recalled the first time she walked into the house as a homeowner only a few months ago. On top of the built-in bookshelf, the previous owner had left a vase of yellow daffodils. *Which, come to think of it, still looked fresh. Weird.* Next to the vase was an unusual note. Although Iris had never purchased a house before, she didn't think this kind of thing was customary.

WELCOME HOME!

For the past 21 years, I have found this house to be a peaceful and nurturing resting place. This home is the container for a strong, positive, energetic force, but of course, that's why you are here. We are all just caretakers of our dwellings for a short time. May this home give you what you need.

Here are a few things you should know: From April through October, the hummingbirds expect to be fed. It's four to one, water to sugar. You won't regret it, I assure you.

The three Afghan pines in the front yard are friendly and make good conversation partners if you enjoy talking to trees. You can ask them anything. Any changes to the house should go through them first.

Almost all the plants here are medicinal or edible. Expect a mushroom bloom in the northeast corner of the backyard in early spring. Be careful of these. They are strong. Well, that's about it. Oh, and remember,

A WHITE VAN slowly approached her. The driver noticed Iris sitting on the porch and pulled the van to the curb. Iris spotted the "Pop-a-lock" logo on the side, which featured two antique skeleton keys crossed like bones on a pirate flag. A young man stepped out; he was lanky, possibly in his early thirties, about 5'10" with long, curly black hair pulled back into a ponytail. In fact, he kind of looked like a pirate. His most noticeable facial feature was his dark, thick eyebrows. He wore a faded blue T-shirt depicting double-bunned Princess Leia, finger to her lips, saying, "Read. It's our only hope."

"Iris?" He held out his hand. "Ezra. I would have called, but I was nearby."

Shaking his hand, Iris said, "I love your shirt! I'm a librarian. I can't believe I've never seen it before."

He smiled. "Huh? What are the odds I'd meet a librarian on the day I chose to wear this shirt? The Force must be alive and well."

Iris giggled.

Ezra opened his bag and retrieved a tool that looked nothing like a key. He inserted the tool into the lock of the old black metal doorknob and immediately opened the door. "There you go."

"Wow, that was... suspiciously easy."

"Yeah, these antique locks are basically just for show."

Concern flickered across his face. "You might want to install something more secure."

As she reached for her credit card, a thought stopped her. "Wait, how do you know this is my house? I mean, you didn't ask me for ID or anything. What if I'm a burglar using you to make my breaking and entering easier?" Even as she said it, she realized how unlikely a burglar she appeared, wearing what passed for professional attire in Cottonwood, New Mexico—an untucked button-down blouse with stretchy straight-leg pants that had seen better days.

"If you were a burglar with any skills, you could pick this lock."

"Okay, fair."

"But also," his smile turned enigmatic, "you were sitting on the front porch with your cat."

"Oh noooo, that cat's not mine. She's a stray," Iris said quickly. She had no time or inclination for pets.

The locksmith's face softened, and he smiled patiently as if explaining something to a child. "Actually, that cat is yours." He nodded toward the black feline, which was then performing an elaborate figure-eight around Iris's ankles.

His smile suggested he knew something she didn't. He left through the front door with a slight twinkle in his eye. A pleasant waft of desert sage followed in his wake.

"Hmmph." Iris was accustomed to feeling like an outsider when it came to jokes. Today it was more annoying than usual.

But relief washed over her as she stepped back into the house. The floor creaked beneath her feet as she crossed the threshold, and she could still smell the lingering scent of fresh paint. The room glowed with warm light, which she had noticed the first time she walked in. She looked around, appreciating the original hardwood floors, scratched and nicked, but that gave the place character.

A large Navajo rug filled the center of the room. Iris

purchased it in Santa Fe after her divorce. Its vibrant rows of colors and geometric patterns in red, black, brown, and cream made the room feel cozy. A sizable stone fireplace with a dark wood mantel and built-in bookshelves separated the living room from the dining room. The ceiling beams were polished and dark brown.

Sitting down, Iris felt the comfort of regaining access to her home and, like it or not, the locksmith said something she needed to hear. She brushed cat hair off her slacks, let out a breath she didn't know she had been holding, and felt her heart unlock to the fluffy cat. *My cat, huh?* She shook her head, returned to the solid front door, and opened it.

Immediately, Xena the Warrior Princess strolled inside, lay down like royalty on the living room rug, and began grooming herself. Xena's green eyes caught Iris's brown eyes and blinked one slow time. Iris sighed. The cat was obviously in on the joke, too. It did feel right to stop resisting. She heard the words in her head, "Your first step."

The words didn't feel like her own. It was as if they had been dropped in from somewhere else. She shook off the momentary strangeness and supposed that, yes, it was a first step—another first among many in her new life. Maybe opening the door to the stray was a step toward healing her heart.

Iris glanced back at the strangely written note from the previous owner, which sat next to the still-fresh-looking daffodils. She had left the note out because it seemed like it might illuminate something important if she could only grasp it. She reread the end of the letter, perhaps for the twentieth time.

OH, and remember, there is always help available if you need it. You have allies, seen and unseen, who are just waiting to assist. Don't hesitate. Your burdens are not yours alone; they are meant to be shared.
Joan Flores

Iris always felt a bit defensive while reading this part. Who says that to someone moving into a house? She listed her burdens: a broken heart, tight finances, anxiety about pretty much everything, and, since the divorce, a loss of confidence in her judgment. These were her burdens alone.

What did that even mean, seen and unseen allies? How could anyone help her with these things? She was on her own and needed to pull herself together and figure it out. *But what if there was help out there for the asking?*

Iris set the letter aside and moved to her meditation chair. Since the divorce, meditation had become a new habit and an effort at self-care. Xena leapt onto her lap.

"Oh, so we're doing this together, huh?" The cat had no response but to curl up, her tail covering her face.

Iris began to focus on her breath and the warm weight of the big cat resting on her lap. Before long, the mean voice in her head started its relentless monologue. *You're always going to be alone. You're not lovable. You're going to grow old in this house and die alone.*

Oh my God. Really? Enough was enough. That voice was full of crap. Iris had read more than a few self-help books in her day. She made a conscious decision right then and there not to contribute to her suffering with a narrative that was so ridiculous.

Joan's note echoed in her mind: *You have allies, seen and unseen.* She wasn't sure about this, but she had nothing to lose. She spoke aloud, "Allies, seen and unseen, please help me with my burdens." The light coming through the window hit a small quartz vein in one of the fireplace stones, making rainbows glint on the wall.

Saying the words brought her an unfamiliar wave of comfort. Xena looked up at her, meeting her eyes with confirmation and affection.

"Hmm. That actually works." Iris returned to following her breath in and out of her nose. As thoughts arose, she brought her focus back to her breath, until the purring, the traffic noise, and the birdsong all became one big ebb and flow.

She settled into a sense of rightness, as if she were in the right place to learn and grow. Maybe this move, this new job, and this new city weren't a colossal mistake after all. Perhaps it was the beginning of something new and good.

And then the daffodils lit up in flames.

Xena

I am here as a helper; well, more than a helper. I just got a promotion. Now, I'm a bodhisattva. You know, filled with love and light and ready to apply skillful means to end suffering and bring awakening. Kind of like a warrior princess, but no.

This is my first assignment. I think I may have overdone it with the daffodils. I'm still getting my bearings in this dimension. Iris doesn't know it yet, but she has a big job coming up. A saving-the-planet sort of job. It all snowballs, as things do. The butterfly flapping its wings causes a tsunami somewhere else, and all. You know the drill.

The world is like that. Interconnected. Anyway, I am here to help Iris wake up and ensure this crazy situation with a million moving pieces goes smoothly. I'm pretty sure I can handle it, well 72% sure.

So, something you should know about me: I am beyond time. Time is not linear; well, to you, it is. But I'm no longer subject to that rule. I graduated. Many restrictions that apply to you no longer apply to me. It's cool. Well, it would blow your mind, so we'll take this slow.

Anywho, I perceive all of time, all at once. It's a tapestry, and I see the threads connecting Iris to those who came before and those who will come after. This house has been around for a long time. Now, it's Iris's turn to weave her story into the fabric of this place.

Like all humans, she has an insecure, fearful monkey brain that constantly tries to avoid the pain of life and pursue the things that feel good, or at least safe. Honestly, it's exhausting to watch, but it's also endearing. Like most of her human tribe, she believes this monkey brain is all she is. My job is to help her realize her true nature and save some trees in the process. I know she doesn't see it yet, but I am her ally—along with good old Ella from over a century ago- don't forget time isn't real. But you'll see.

CHAPTER 2

*I*ris looked at her alarm clock. It was 6 a.m. She could have slept another hour, but sleep eluded her. She had spent half the night searching online for why daffodils might spontaneously combust. *What was that? There is something strange about this house.*

After her quick morning routine that now included feeding a cat, she pulled into the parking lot of Trifecta, the local coffee shop. Noting the dark circles under her eyes in the rearview mirror, she vowed to start prioritizing sleep. But she shrugged it off when she smelled the freshly ground coffee beans mingling with the scent of warm pastries.

Looking around the industrial-chic space, she took in the vining potted plants hanging from the high ceiling rafters, glowing pendant lights, and a chalkboard menu of drinks above the ordering counter. Morning sunlight streamed in through the high clerestory windows.

A few young men, casually dressed in black T-shirts and jeans, worked on their laptops at the wooden picnic-style tables. The tattooed barista with pencil-tip-short black hair expertly poured her favorite double-shot latte.

Iris found a seat and opened her iPad to continue working on a grant for more computers at the middle school where she worked. Then she noticed Ezra, the locksmith, standing in line at the counter. He wore a black Batman shirt and jeans, and today his curly hair cascaded loosely around his shoulders.

Her fingers hovered over her laptop as her mind began its familiar process of crafting excuses to avoid conversation. Maybe he wouldn't notice her. Introverted, she contracted, wishing for an invisibility cloak. *As soon as they start making those I'll be the first in line.*

At work, she was confident and in control. However, out in the world, she felt hesitant to reach out to others, especially since the divorce. Additionally, she looked a bit disheveled this morning. She pushed her hair off her forehead, just in case, but kept her gaze intently focused on her screen.

"Ahh, the cat lady."

Dammit. Iris looked up, already bristling at the label, but Ezra's easy smile disarmed her. "Iris," she said, recovering. "And you were right. Xena is my cat."

"Yes, she told me." He winked. "Every witch needs a cat."

Under other circumstances, she might take offense at *cat lady* and *witch*. But somehow, coming from Ezra, it felt respectful and gently teasing at the same time. Iris laughed her lovely laugh. It was one of her best features. Her ex-husband said it sounded like bells.

The caffeine was kicking in, and she managed to come up with a retort. "Perhaps a cat lady, but definitely not a witch."

"Ah, well, there's still time," Ezra volleyed back easily. Changing the subject, he said, "Hey, I know the woman who lived in your house before you."

"Oh, really? Joan Flores?" The city had a population of 300,000, but it felt smaller.

"Yeah, she's living closer to the river now. I help her out around her place with odd jobs, carpentry work, and with her bees in the fall. She spent years living in Tibet when she was younger, before living in your house. She's a unique character; she's worth getting to know."

Maybe that explained the note? Iris hesitated. This was not typically something she would bring up. She blurted it out, unable to censor herself. "Joan seems a little crazy to me." She immediately regretted her bluntness.

"Crazy? No. She's free."

Iris lost a beat. She thought he would say "free-spirited," but he stopped at free. She didn't understand. "Free," Iris echoed, the word hanging between them like a question. She wasn't sure if she believed it. Iris could feel her contrarian nature rising. "Well, we're all free. It's not like we're slaves." This was another reason Iris avoided conversation: the inevitable conflict that arose. Her ex-husband called it her "rebuttal brain."

Ezra was unperturbed. "Hmm. Most people are at the mercy of their thoughts. Not Joan."

Iris remembered her recent epiphany during meditation, to not contribute to her own suffering, but it would sound too much like bragging, and like another rebuttal to mention it. Instead, she pivoted. "So, Joan left me this note. It was kind of peculiar."

His eyes flashed interest. "Was it about the mushrooms?"

"Well, yes, about the mushrooms and other things." Iris paused momentarily to gather her thoughts. *Who else knew about the mushrooms?* She chose to focus on what had piqued her interest in Joan's letter. "She said something about how there are allies, seen and unseen, that are, well, ready to help. To help with our burdens. I just thought it was… odd."

Ezra sat down across from Iris with his coffee. This was apparently worth an extended conversation. "Ahhh, and what are your burdens?"

He seemed so relaxed and open, curious, and kind. She felt wound up and stiff. She recognized the contrast. And she couldn't help the familiar feeling of not-enoughness. Her breath felt stuck in her chest. *Why did she bring this up?*

Iris stood at the fork in the road, torn between being vulnerable and projecting a facade of confidence. She took a breath, inhaling the scent of sage. She had never known a man who smelled so good, and Ezra truly seemed kind; he wasn't making fun of her.

She tried to smile, but it came out more like a tight grimace as her face refused to relax. "Well, I just thought it was odd. But I can't seem to stop thinking about it. We all have trials, and that's part of life. I guess it just intrigued me a little."

"That's true; we all have trials." Ezra looked down at his coffee, the clouds of cream thick in the white ceramic mug. He seemed in no hurry and did not appear uncomfortable. Perhaps he looked slightly amused. His breathing was relaxed, and his chest was open. Iris felt how her shoulders were up around her ears and let them down. Her body wanted to mirror the relaxation she saw in him. It would be such a relief, but it was also so unfamiliar.

"I think the first step," he said slowly, still looking down into his coffee cup, "is to let the burdens be there. The pain is in resisting. There's a phrase," he looked up toward the ceiling as if pulling the words from the high, light-filled space. "What you resist persists. The mind isn't up to the task of managing our burdens. You know, the big ones."

He nodded slowly and continued to speak, as if addressing a wild squirrel he didn't want to frighten away. "For me, allowing and being curious gives grace some room to infiltrate." He smiled, looking pleased to express that thought.

Iris believed she could use some grace infiltration, and she liked his smile. But something he said stopped her. *The mind is not up to it. What does that mean?*

He continued, "And then in allowing what is to simply be, God, or Love, or your allies, or whoever can do the heavy lifting."

Iris did not believe in miracles. Or God in a traditional way. Or some divine grace infusion. But she could use some peace. Or simply to feel more comfortable in her own skin would be a relief.

Ezra spoke more quickly as if the difficult ground had already been covered. "I can introduce you to her, to Joan, if you want." He let the invitation hang in the air, looking at Iris.

He received no immediate response and tapped his palm on the table as if something had been decided. "Hey, I need to leave for work. I'll see you later."

"Yeah, see you later," Iris said a beat too late, the smell of sage wafting into her nose. She hoped she would see him later, a half smile playing on her lips. While the social interaction was taxing, its aftereffect left her feeling a bit lighter, as if a weight had been lifted.

Home in the early evening after a long day of work at the middle school library, Iris set down her laptop case and sank into the couch. She loved her job but looked forward to summer as eagerly as the kids did. Her mind wandered back through her day, and stopped at her interaction with the locksmith at the coffee shop that morning.

She was sure it was nothing. He probably had a girlfriend. The sun hit one of the quartz veins again on the fireplace, and this time, she watched as a rainbow made its way across the wall. She took a breath and felt an unfamiliar sense of well-being. She decided this house did have good energy. The daffodil incident had been forgotten.

Xena jumped up on the couch next to her and meowed. Taking the hint, Iris got up to prepare the cat's dinner. As she stirred the cat food and set it on the floor, Iris recalled how Ian, her ex-husband, had always been dismissive of her intuition until she stopped mentioning it and subsequently ceased to experience it.

"You're being ridiculous," he'd say with that condescending smile. He'd twist her perceptions when she confronted him about his late nights and constant texts until she doubted herself. This dismantling of her self-trust made her question the very instincts that were warning her about his betrayal.

Iris listed her recent feelings that could count as intuition and decided to trust them. *The house had good energy. The cat was a positive addition. And that locksmith seemed like he could be a friend. Yes. That's a good start.*

XENA

Iris, dear, sweet Iris, you have no idea how much your life is about to change. Together, we will rebuild your trust in yourself, stronger than before, because there is no moving forward without it.

Soooo, let's get back to time. Time is like paging forward or backward in a book. I can sense the page in the book that is most connected to this time. The page that opens contains Ella, the first owner of this house from over a hundred years ago. Her black hair is pulled up in a bun, and she's wearing a long dress and boots, walking out the front door to meet a carriage pulled by horses. A different version of me is there, here, actually, or here in a different time. It's complicated.

She is determined to preserve the forest. She set this whole thing in motion and cast a silver thread through time—an insurance policy that is now coming due. Iris will gradually understand some of this, but for now, I hold the big picture, along with the Fae, who might honestly have a wider lens than I do.

As I mentioned, the Fae are involved. They are always involved. Meddling, gossiping, protecting, poking around, and creating drama. They're everywhere: in homes and gardens, the wild places, in the soil and the sky. The Fae of the wider bracts of land are called Genii Loci. You'll meet one. Then there are the elementals, not Fae exactly, but close. They are the embodiments of the natural forces: the cloudmakers and rain bringers, the fire starters and mountain builders. And I can't forget, of course, there are the Queens. You'll meet them too, in time.

CHAPTER 3

On her way to work, Iris drove past a band of protesters on a downtown corner. Their signs swayed angrily in the wind as they chanted, "Hands off our forest!" She slowed down as she passed the group. A young man's glare met her eyes. She quickly turned her head, and her hands tightened on the steering wheel.

What was that about? The fervor in their chants and the man's uncomfortable stare tightened her chest.

She swung into the Trifecta parking lot for a quick cup of coffee. It was far superior to what they served in the teacher's lounge. Waiting in line, she overheard two men talking behind her.

"F'ing developers."

"Yeah, that sucks. Cutting down trees is legit uncool."

What was all the buzz about? Something was brewing in Cottonwood, and she could feel the tension.

Feeling uneasy, she pulled out of the parking lot with her to-go cup. As she went to take a sip, she suddenly hit a bump and splashed hot coffee across her shirt. Cursing under her breath, "Dammit, dammit, dammit," she reached for some napkins on the passenger side while trying to drive and salvage her shirt for the workday. *Well, this is on brand. Caffeine and chaos before 9 a.m.*

IRIS SWUNG OPEN the heavy metal door of the middle school. She ducked into the faculty bathroom to assess the damage to her blouse, blotting it with a damp paper towel. She noted the same circles under her eyes from yesterday. *Great.* She needed to pull herself together. She took a deep breath.

As she walked through the quiet halls, the distant hum of the HVAC system was the only sound breaking the early morning silence. The scent of chalk dust, floor wax, and gum permeated the air. She entered the library, her library, where she felt most at home, and momentarily settled into the comfort of being surrounded by books.

Large windows allowed ample light, small nooks featured comfy chairs, with rugs scattered around. Row upon row of books rested on low shelves. A cardboard rocket capsule, crafted by the kids, hung from the ceiling, while books about space exploration lay spread out on a table.

Before the kids arrived, the school's silence felt almost alive. This quiet pause was like an in-breath before the halls filled with children posing, running, teasing, laughing, confiding, and posing. She loved her job. Sure, there was some bureaucracy and too many meetings to deal with, but this was her sphere of competence.

She understood the power of books for people, children especially. Her superpower? Finding the exact right book to spark a new interest or open up a new world. It was the one part of her life where doubt did not touch her.

At college in California, she majored in library science because the young people in her classes seemed like her—nerdy, serious, informed, and tech-savvy. Librarians were relentless researchers, and Iris excelled at tracking down information. She could have been an investigative journalist, but the thought of making a difference in kids' lives kept her working in the school setting. Well, that and her social unease. Both her parents had been educators, so perhaps that contributed too. It was in her genes.

The only problem with being a school librarian was that they were a dying breed. With school budget cuts, culture wars, and book banning, librarians were being let go at an alarming rate. Most people didn't realize their value. Librarians supported teachers with current technology and provided children with opportunities they wouldn't otherwise receive. Most importantly, they served as a safety net for at-risk children. Iris took this part of her job very seriously.

She settled into her desk and did a word search for "drone," trying to find the email from a month or two ago from a Forest Service scientist. He wondered if her students might be interested in learning how drones were used in the forest. He volunteered to do a drone demonstration and then a summer school drone computer coding workshop. It was time to write him back. If she was right about this idea, it could be a perfect fit for Federico, a student she was concerned about. He was a good kid, but lost and susceptible to bad influences.

After reviewing and responding to the email, Iris sorted through the stacks of nature books to find something new for Annabelle. Annabelle was a quiet, diligent student who often went unnoticed by teachers preoccupied with managing the disruptive kids. However, Iris saw Annabelle and was determined to nurture her passion for understanding and protecting nature.

After finding the book she was looking for, Iris scanned the news headlines of the local paper online. The front page headline read: Bosque Sold To Developer

What? Is this what the protestors and the guys in line at the coffee shop were talking about? This was a big deal. Reading the article, Iris felt a heaviness in her heart. A developer was offering the city fifty million dollars for the cottonwood forest by the river. Shops, brewpubs, and condos were planned. The ancient cotton-woods would be cut down. *Wasn't the area next to the river a preserve or some sort?* Cynically, she wondered: *But could it be bought? Something needs to be done. Kids need nature. Everyone needs nature.*

Her fingers flew across the keys as she searched online to learn more about the preserve. She leaned in closer and closer to the screen. An article she found linked the start of the preserve to Ella Ross in 1919. *Why was that name familiar?*

Iris's pulse quickened. *Ella Ross? Wasn't that the name on the historic plaque by my front door, along with the date 1911!* Many of the historic homes in the neighborhood had those plaques. She had intended to research the name but hadn't had a chance since moving in.

She read quickly, "Ella Ross, the first female attorney in Cottonwood, at 208 Silver Ave, Cottonwood, NM, set up a preserve of 6,000 acres of land next to the river to protect the Rio Grande Cottonwood ecosystem in perpetuity." Ella Ross created the Cottonwood Bosque preserve almost a century ago and was the first owner of her house. The coincidence was astonishing.

She wanted to rush to the city records office immediately to investigate. A ball of anxiety tightened in her chest. The logical part of her knew she should stay at work and follow the rules. But she had accumulated a lot of leave, she reasoned. The internal dialogue wavered back and forth a few more times, but finally, she found herself in Principal Lovage's office, manufac-turing a fever. The coffee stain helped sell it.

"Go home, dear. Something's going around."

GUILT MIXED with exhilaration as she drove downtown. This felt important. Freed from her work responsibilities, she drove her used Subaru to the city offices. There, she remained holed up all day, sifting through musty public information files. How could a developer buy preserved land along the Rio Grande River, she wondered. She also wanted to learn more about Ella Ross and how she established the preserve.

Iris noticed the clerk behind the counter watching her. She returned to her research, but when she looked up, he was on the phone and still staring at her. When she stared back at him, he quickly averted his gaze. She shook off the prickly sensation of discomfort.

As Iris sifted through records from another century, the smell of aged paper and ink surrounded her. Each document she uncovered felt like a puzzle piece. She discovered that Ella Ross was the first female attorney in Cottonwood. *Wow. She was definitely a go-getter.*

Iris found out that when taxes were not paid on preserved land for three years, the land would be returned to the city. *Hmmm, who had been paying the taxes on that land since 1919?* Iris uncovered the records that provided the trail. Ella Ross paid the taxes until she died in 1955. Then, the preserve was turned over to Eric Sutter, Esquire, an attorney specializing in land trusts.

Then, in 1990, Eric Sutter Jr., Esquire, began paying the taxes. She reasoned it must have been a father-son law firm team, and when the father retired, the son took over. *Well, what happened to Eric Jr.? Why hadn't the taxes been paid for the past three years?*

Continuing to follow the trail of paperwork, Iris found a newspaper article stating that Eric Sutter Jr. was killed in an automobile crash three years ago. His car was discovered at the bottom of a ravine off a forest service road in the Sandia Mountains. The weather was clear at the time, and the accident was attributed to driver inattention. And that is where the breadcrumbs ended.

Why wasn't there someone to take over the tax payments after that? Were there records missing? Iris's eyebrows scrunched together as she tried to fit what she had learned into a cohesive story. She tilted her head left and right and rubbed her neck. Then she closed her eyes, resting her forehead in her palms with her elbows on the table. Her stomach growled. It was time to go home.

As she left the city offices, she felt the clerk's gaze following her. Before the feeling of unease could take hold, she became distracted by the swirling thoughts in her mind about Ella Ross and how extraordinary it was that the woman who lived in her house a hundred years ago had helped establish the Rio Grande Bosque Preserve.

After opening a can of food for Xena and eating some cheese and crackers herself, she made a pot of chamomile tea and settled onto the couch. Something about the situation felt off. *Why didn't anyone take over the tax payments after Eric Junior died?* It bothered her.

She peered into her laptop, tapping away in search of any information. A newspaper article from three years ago appeared, detailing an office fire at the address listed for Eric Sutter Jr., Esq., two days after the fatal car accident. Details of the fire were sparse, and the investigation into the cause of the fire was inconclusive.

Car crash. Mysterious fire. And now, the looming sale of the preserve. Could these things be connected? She had a feeling they were. *Had anyone else connected these dots?* She looked up from her screen and let out a breath.

If she were a journalist, she would investigate the site of the car crash and the office fire. She would call Eric Sutter's widow, the fire captain, and the police to gather more details. However, that would require speaking to people she didn't know. *No, best to not get involved.*

Fighting for things that could not be saved was exhausting. She thought about her marriage, doomed, despite her efforts to make it work. A familiar hopelessness began to settle in.

Xena jumped onto her lap, purring and gently kneading Iris's thigh. Iris stared at the wall in front of her, petting the cat and reflecting on the past. She caught herself. No, she needed to move forward into this new life and embrace what the future had in store.

She turned back to the article she had photocopied at the city offices about Ella Ross. Iris smiled, thinking of the first owner of her house, a female attorney in the early 1900s. It was admirable that Ella cherished the cottonwood forest along the river enough to start a preserve to protect it. She was a woman ahead of her time.

She imagined Ella walking on these same floors, looking at these same walls, and cooking in the kitchen. She could almost see it. Almost. She envisioned Ella sleeping and dreaming here, creating a scheme to save the forest. Iris imagined herself and Ella as friends. Ella would be the bold friend, and she would be the nerdy, quiet tag-along.

Iris asked aloud, "Ella, what would you have me do?" Then she shook her head. She was spending too much time alone, and this was silly.

But she couldn't let it go. In her research of the city records, she had found a black-and-white photo of Ella from an old New Mexico Bar Association newsletter. She brought it up on her laptop and gazed at the picture. Ella was wearing a black dress, with her black hair styled in a bun and a few stray tendrils framing her face. Her eyes were brown, and she wore a hint of a smile as if she were in on the joke. *Of course, she would be in on the joke. She was smart and savvy.*

Iris printed the photo and then rummaged through a closet to find an empty picture frame. The frame's wood felt warm in her hands, as if Ella was reaching out to her across time, guiding her toward something she couldn't yet see. She placed the framed photo of Ella on the fireplace mantel. Iris decided it didn't feel spooky; it was more like having an old friend around.

· · ·

XENA

Well, now we're in the thick of it. Now that Iris knows about Ella, Ella can have an even greater impact on this time and place from the Otherworld, and the real work begins. The silver thread is strengthening. Iris will sense this as a boost to her inner knowing and an increase in her resolve. Ella is bold, but Iris is more than a tag-along friend. She has her own destiny to fulfill.

Unfortunately, this also brings the dark forces of greed and corrupted power out of the shadows. I wrap Iris in a spell of protection. The forces gathering against her are strong, but I am stronger. I understand that there is no good or bad in the ultimate infinite. However, we are living in the relative here, folks. This world revolves around good and evil, and the battle between them is all-important in this world. Without it, there is no story.

CHAPTER 4

*A*nnabelle, tall and willowy at 11 years old, stood on a tire swing tethered to a giant Cottonwood tree. Her long hair, the color of light brown sugar, hung straight down her back. She swung out over the mostly dry ditch bed, leaning forward and back while gripping the old rope tightly. Swinging helped her think, and seeking solace in the trees calmed her worries. She considered going to visit her Aunt Joan for a chat, but ultimately decided she'd rather be alone with her thoughts this afternoon.

Swinging, she seesawed between the view of the sky through the cottonwood canopy and the white flowers of the yerba mansa plant covering the ground. The rustling leaves above her whispered a reminder that she was never truly alone. The yerba mansa plant helpfully enveloped Annabelle in its earthy, warm scent, wrapping her in the familiar presence of the forest. Annabelle loved how yerba mansa carpeted the forest floor with white flowers in summer and red leaves in fall.

Annabelle had a never-ending curiosity about the forest. From the plant walks she'd taken during school field trips, she learned that yerba mansa was antimicrobial and could help with colds, flu, and even some cancers. This information delighted her. There were so many secrets hidden in the forest that most people didn't see or understand. Her desire to uncover these secrets often led her to great lengths, like spending an entire day watching ants, trying to piece together the intent of their intricate activities, or lying on the ground for hours looking up to observe how the porcupine managed to sleep high in the cottonwood branches without falling.

Through her regular observations, her bond with the forest deepened. She knew where there was a coyote den and watched from a distance as the pups came out to play in the spring. She knew the tree where a pair of crows nested year after year. At this time of year, she was aware that the fledglings were out of the nest, soaring independently while still shadowing their parents, begging for food handouts. She knew many of the forest's secrets, but now, for the first time, her knowledge felt like a burden. It was a painful reminder of what she couldn't protect.

She thought back to the recent morning that changed everything. Her mom had dropped her off early for school, and Annabelle made her way to the library, her favorite place in the building. She hoped for a new book recommendation from the librarian, Ms. Barnes.

Annabelle was an only child and generally felt more comfortable around adults. Children could be unpredictable and sometimes mean. She appreciated that adults discussed important, serious topics. Ms. Barnes had recommended what turned out to be her favorite books: books about nature, crows, and fantasy stories about kids saving the world. Annabelle smiled, anticipating a new book to read.

When she arrived at the library, Ms. Barnes was oddly nowhere to be seen. Annabelle glanced at the computer screen on the librarian's desk. The news headline, BOSQUE SOLD TO DEVELOPER, jumped out at her. *What?* Her eyes widened. She felt a sharp pang in her heart. *Could this be true? No! It couldn't be!*

What would happen to all the animals if the trees were cut down? The inevitability of the forest's loss was like a physical blow, made worse by the feeling of powerlessness. *If only I could do something, if only I were grown up!*

Since that day, Annabelle carried the burden of loss in her chest. She shook her head and jumped off the tire swing and walked slowly home, her mind filled with thoughts of the forest's uncertain future.

Suddenly, she felt the sensation of being watched. She looked in every direction, but no one was there. Looking down at the path, she saw a large black feather on the ground, likely from a crow. She picked it up, feeling her heart lift a little. She had admired crows for as long as she could remember. Unseen by Annabelle, two crows watched her from high in a cottonwood tree. What Annabelle didn't realize was that while she knew the forest creatures, they also knew her.

BACK AT HOME, Annabelle lay on the living room floor, her feet resting on the couch. The unrelenting summer heat had set in, and only a few weeks remained before school would be out. The book "Bless Me, Ultima" by Rudolfo Anaya rested on her stomach. SparkPuff, her small white dog, lay beside her on his back, paws pointed upward, enjoying the fan's cool breeze on his belly. She stared up at the twirling ceiling fan. It was late, but she didn't feel tired. A sense of unease wouldn't let go of her.

She could hear her parents talking in the kitchen. She overheard her father say loudly, "Fucking developers. Who do they think they are?" Cursing meant her parents didn't realize she could hear them, so she listened intently, lying still on the living room floor, wanting to find out whatever was not meant for her ears.

"I know. I can't believe they are even talking about this. Cutting down trees for condos and brew pubs? It's disgusting,"

Annabelle's mother, Maria, said. "There'll be a protest. We should go, as a family."

"It's not going to do any good. We're so close to finding a mycelium strain at the lab that will protect the forest against climate change. But this," Nate threw up his arms, "there's no protecting the bosque against this."

Annabelle continued to listen. She knew her father researched how mushrooms could aid trees through myco-restoration. *So the forest development was truly going to happen.* Her heart sank.

"I hate feeling powerless. I think we should go to the protest. We can make signs," Maria said. "It's this weekend at Robinson Park. We need to do *something.*"

Annabelle's heart raced. *Yes, do something! A protest!* The forest was in danger, and she had to do everything she could to protect it. She shot up and marched into the kitchen.

"We should go to the protest. I am going to the protest." She crossed her arms over her chest, fixing her stare on her father, whom she perceived as the main obstacle. Annabelle watched as her parents glanced at each other. She knew they were silently communicating, but she wasn't sure what they were saying.

Maria looked at Annabelle with her lips set in a way that Annabelle knew meant she was putting on a brave front. "Honey, we will do everything possible to stop it. And we will all go to the protest."

Annabelle looked at her father and could tell by his expression that he believed protesting was futile. *Did that mean the forest couldn't be saved?* "Dad, you said you're trying to save the forest." Annabelle bit her lip, formulating her argument and holding back tears. Her sadness was not just for the trees that might be lost but for the life that thrived under the forest's protection: the coyotes, the birds, and all the residents of the bosque.

Nate said gently, "That's right. I'm working hard to find a strain of mycelium to make the cottonwoods more hardy in the face of global warming. But if these developers cut down a bunch of the old cottonwoods..." He paused, looked away, and ran his hand through his slightly thinning hair. "Well, those trees are irreplaceable. The forest needs those old trees to function. They have the most mycorrhizal connections to the younger trees. Those old ones share resources that help the smaller trees survive." He shrugged. "It's how the ecosystem works." Nate looked at Annabelle and shook his head. "I don't know."

Annabelle watched as her father seemed to morph from a scientist feeling hopeless, to a parent responsible for his daughter's well-being. He took a breath and sat up a little straighter. "But if the city wants to develop that area, all we can do is speak up. We can go to the protest and the public hearings about this development and voice our concerns."

Annabelle sensed from how her father said this that these things would not be enough. Reading adults involved constantly teasing out the truth, and right now, it seemed the truth and what she wanted to believe were at odds.

As her mother hugged her, Annabelle felt her anger dissipate and helplessness take its place. She began to shake, and then came the tears of grief, as she imagined the animals losing their homes and the personal loss of her forest sanctuary, the place where she felt most at home. Her chest ached. The last time she cried this much was when her Grandpa Frank died.

As the sobbing slowly ebbed, Maria said gently, "Querida, I'm going to make some tea. Who wants some?"

As they all sat together on the couch, quietly drinking tea and lost in their own thoughts, Annabelle volunteered, "I miss Grandpa Frank." Her mother put her arm around her.

"Me too. Sometimes new sadness brings back old sadness m'ija."

Annabelle pondered this, and though she didn't have the words to explain it, she felt that when she looked back to the time before her grandfather passed away, things didn't feel so hopeless. There was an ache for that time in her heart—the time when her grandfather was alive and the forest seemed like it would go on forever. Exhausted, with her eyes half-closed, she said, "I'm going to bed. Good night."

"Que suenes con los angelitos," her mother called out to her.

LYING IN BED, her father's words percolated to the surface of her mind. *All we can do is speak up.* But was that all? Wasn't there more they could do? She squeezed her eyes shut and spoke directly to the living forest. *I will do everything I can to save you. Just let me know how.* She imagined the trees and the animals, and in her mind's eye, she saw two crows high in an old tree. She heard a single crow call into the night before the soft fog of sleep came for her.

THE QUEEN

The High Faery Queen of Mycelium observed the family scene involving Annabelle, Nate, and Maria. She had come to influence Nate's dreams, just as she had for many years.

She watched over the human world with the patience born from millennia. Her connection to the mushroom mycelial web of life that spanned the globe was deep and ancient. She felt the pulse of the forest, the ebb and flow of energy connecting every living thing. Now, more than ever, humans needed her guidance to combat the forces of chaos, greed, and short-sightedness threatening to irreparably undo the order and beauty of the earth's natural state.

She collaborated with the overarching planetary Fae to inform many humans, not just Nate, about the potential of utilizing mushrooms as alchemists to heal the forest and much more. As Nate dreamed, the Queen diligently planted ideas, images, and inspiration in his mind. She encouraged, nudged, and propelled him further. Tomorrow, he would awaken with a surge of inspiration and rush to the lab with fresh ideas to pursue better solutions, getting ever closer to something that could save the cottonwood forest.

She liked that after working in the lab, Nate was covered in mycelium spores. To her, they glowed blue around him, in his hair, and under his fingernails, making him easy to find in the vastness.

Nate took all the credit for his ideas, of course. The Queen sighed. A lack of appreciation or acknowledgment accompanied the territory of working with humans. They were lucky, oblivious recipients of the ideas that Fae muses carried back from the Otherworld, the Otherworld that contains the great field of potential from which all ideas and creativity bubble. *Ah, well, working behind the scenes suits me.*

There were times, long ago, when humans actively sought counsel and teachings from the Fae. Perhaps hope lay with the Crow People resuming their bond with humans, she mused. She knew efforts were underway. *The crows and humans are so alike. Both are curious, social, quick learners who easily fall prey to their egos.*

Her job was done for the night. She traveled through the ceiling as if it were a pool of water, breaking through the surface into the cool night air. She flew through the starry sky, appreciating the view. The moonlight caused the floating mushroom spores in the air to sparkle with blue light. This view always revived her after her work.

She could also see something else—something she had been tracking for some time. It was a silver thread weaving itself ever stronger and thicker as it made its way through time. She recognized that her old friend, Ella, had sent this thread to create a bridge between past and present, between the Otherworld and the world of Iris and Annabelle, the Crow Clan, and Grandmother Cottonwood. She had not forgotten. The Queen smiled as the thread flickered a greeting and a quiet promise.

CHAPTER 5

Grandmother Cottonwood had summoned the Crow Elders, and with trepidation, the five eldest crows of the council arrived high in her branches. They waited in silence, reverent yet uneasy. Summons from her were rare and never casual.

The Fae were also present, but only visible in the sparkle of sunlight and audible in the rustling of leaves. They understood what was at stake and that the crows were the key to restoring balance. A plan had been architected in whispers between Grandmother Cottonwood and the Fae.

The mighty Cottonwood began to speak slowly to the crows. Trees always spoke slowly. "I have called you, dear ones, for a very difficult conversation." The crows waited patiently, tilting their heads.

Though the words came out slowly, the Grandmother's voice resonated through the grove. "Our time is ending. The river no longer floods. The soil no longer sings." There was a heavy silence. The crows shifted uneasily on their perches, feeling the gravity of her words. They had felt it too. Drought, heat, thinning roots.

The Crow Elders were quick thinkers, so conversing with trees was always an exercise in patience. Their sharp minds were already making connections and jumping ahead.

Grandmother Cottonwood continued slowly, "And there are plans among the Human People to cut down many of our old ones."

The crows recoiled at this. They understood that the Fae spoke to her, and the Fae were privy to everyone's business, human, plant, and animal alike. Living partially in this world and partially in the Otherworld, the Fae had access to a vast network of knowledge.

The Crow Clan also had connections to the Otherworld through their allies and ancestors. However, unlike the Fae, crows firmly inhabited the human world, residing in fields, cities, and forests.

Grandmother Cottonwood continued, "I have chosen to meet with you because of your ability to bring messages to the Human People. I believe our future rests with them. However, the chance of success is very small, and time is running out." The forest fell silent, and all rustling and birdsong ceased. "I ask that you send the Human People a message."

The Crow Elders' eyes widened. *It had been such a long time. The bond had been broken.* Doubts flitted through their minds. However, the crows quickly calculated and realized that helping Grandmother Cottonwood was essential for their survival. The thought of losing their beloved trees and their home near the river was almost too much to bear.

The eldest, Sarafina, thoughtfully responded, "We will help you however we can. Your branches are our sanctuary. We are most humbly at your service." She bowed her head, and the four other elders followed her example.

A cold wind swept through the grove, disturbing the elders' feathers and causing a chill. More beings listened to the old cottonwood tree than could be seen.

. . .

AFTER MEETING WITH GRANDMOTHER COTTONWOOD, the Crow elders convened a meeting of the entire Crow Clan. Hundreds of crows filled the branches of the cottonwoods near the Rio Grande River, loudly cawing greetings to one another.

The eldest crow, Serafina, raised her head to speak, and everyone fell silent. "Grandmother Cottonwood, now over 120 years old, has informed us that the Cottonwood Clan is dying."

There were audible gasps among the audience of crows. If that were true, it would mean the unthinkable. Their oasis in the desert, the thin ribbon of green along the river, their home for eons, would be lost. This had been their forest and river for as many generations as they could remember. The Cottonwood trees were the nexus between land and water, a necessary and irreplaceable part of the ecosystem.

"After some deliberation, the Crow Council of Elders has come to a decision. We must do all we can to preserve our home." Sarafina looked around at the group. "Now, I want to remind you of a history you may have forgotten. The Crow People and Human People have always been intertwined."

"In the long ago," Sarafina began, her voice carrying the legacy of centuries of knowledge passed down through the Crow People, "we were allies and wise counsel for each other. We were messengers between the Human People and the Otherworld. Our bond with the Human People was sacred, forged in trust and mutual respect. When they could no longer hear their ancestors and allies, we kept the world in balance by carrying messages between the humans and the Otherworld. But that trust was shattered by human betrayal, and the bond was broken."

The Crow People were surprised to hear the elder speak of this. The bond between the Crow People and the Human People had been essentially broken for many, many years. Only a few crows and humans kept the thread of it alive. And they were far outside the norm.

Roanoke received glances from some of the other crows. He gave gifts to humans, a vestige of the old bond.

The Elders knew only a small number of humans left on earth could, through ritual and trance, travel to the in-between place where humans and animals would still meet. But there simply were not enough of these humans to tip the scales. So, indeed, the world was now out of balance.

Sarafina continued, louder, "The break happened many moons ago, when the Human People, during a war long ago, betrayed the Crow People, using us to gain an advantage over each other."

All Crow People knew the story of the human soldier king named Terak, who had deceived one of their own, a crow named Talia, into believing he was seeking peace with his enemies. Talia informed the soldier king of the enemy's hiding place. The result was massive bloodshed and death. The human's deceit sickened the crows, and the bond was broken.

The Crow People then voted to suspend their role as messengers between humans and the Otherworld. Although the Human people had long since lost their memory of this time, the Crow People had not forgotten and even still felt the pain of betrayal, thanks to their meticulous passing of information from generation to generation.

Softer now, Sarafina said, "But the effects of our separation from the Human People have come to light. Our separateness has endangered the forests and the waters and the very Earth itself. The time has come to forgive the past."

And louder, her voice echoed through the forest, "We will again be messengers between the Human People and the spirit ancestors, the trees, the Fae, and the allies. Grandmother Cottonwood has called on us to help, and help we must. We have long carried wisdom from across the veil, bridging the seen and unseen worlds, and we shall do so again."

Sarafina took a breath and looked around at the tree branches filled with crows, searching for any clue about how her speech was received.

A muffled discussion began among the crows. Murmuring among themselves, their voices blended doubt and hope as they pondered whether they could genuinely trust the Human People again.

Marsilio, a very handsome crow, asked aloud what many were thinking. "But can we even talk to the Human People anymore? Wasn't that ability lost long ago? Hasn't the bond been broken beyond repair?" The crows whispered among themselves. Many thought this to be true.

The elder Sarafina replied, "This has been discussed by the elders. The Crow People have a long history as problem solvers. We feel the link may be weak, but it can be strengthened with our sense of purpose and a little help from Grandmother Cottonwood and the Fae. And it is the Human children we will speak to. We know they are better able to hear the voices of the forest. They have not yet taken on the full mantle of separateness, and their hearts more easily resonate with truth."

Sarafina looked skyward. "There is a child, for whom the forest is a friend and who retains her connection with all creatures. She will be the first to listen."

Roanoke shifted on his branch, uneasy. An old memory, maybe his first memory, flitted through his mind. It was of a human girl feeding him and his love for her.

The crows, again, spoke softly among themselves. This could work. They knew and respected the power of the Fae, and the Crow People, in general, held themselves in high regard and were never hesitant to rise to a challenge.

The Elder Serafina said, "If the bond is reestablished with children, the link between our peoples can become normalized again as they grow up. And there can be hope for a future of healthy forests and waters, for nature Herself to thrive again, and for balance to be restored." Sarafina knew this would not be easy, or even likely, but she retained her faith in the help from those unseen: the ancestors, the Fae, and other forces of goodness throughout time that would come to bear when asked.

She waited again for quiet. "But even a child cannot hear without a voice to guide her. So I am here to announce that the first Crow emissary will be... Roanoke." As the name *Roanoke* echoed through the grove, the crows fell silent, and their collective gaze turned toward their friend.

Roanoke was startled to hear his name. His wings twitched involuntarily.

Delphinia, his mate, looked over at him, her eyes wide. She knew the Human People had saved him as a young hatchlet after a fall from a nest—this sometimes happened. It made sense that the elders felt he could best convey such an important message. She understood the elders had chosen wisely, but would it put her mate in danger?

Roanoke looked around at the hundreds of crows. He felt the weight of destiny resting on him. This would take some time to sink in, but he stood taller, and with a deep breath, he spread his wings and stepped forward onto the branch. "I will do my very best," he said, his voice strong and steady, "to bring the message of Grandmother Cottonwood to the Human People." As Roanoke gazed over the forest, he silently vowed to do whatever it took to save the Cottonwoods and, in doing so, save the Crow Clan. This was their home. He could not fail.

After a moment of silence, as the entire forest seemed to absorb this new information, a few crows began to caw. Then, louder and louder, more joined in until a cacophony of noise from the Crow People filled the forest and the surrounding neighborhoods. Time was running out, but the scales had tipped toward nature due to the strength and wisdom of the Crow Clan.

. . .

PEOPLE WALKING THE FOREST TRAILS, and even those living in houses a mile away, heard the overwhelming sound of nearly a thousand crows cawing. What could all the noise be about? The humans tried to guess among themselves. Did an eagle show up? A young boy said it sounded like the crows were having a meeting. The adults smiled, unaware that their separateness from nature made them unable to hear the truth.

CHAPTER 6

The impulse of spring was fully empowered on this warm May day in the Rio Grande Valley, where the scent of blooming flowers mingled with the complex aroma of the soil. Iris knelt on the ground, pulling dandelions from her front yard, their stubborn resistance to her efforts mirroring her internal struggle.

As Iris weeded, her mind kept returning to the bosque. The thought of it being sold gnawed at her, and she couldn't shake the feeling that something larger was at play—something she didn't yet understand but was slowly drawing her in against her better judgment.

She looked up from the grass to see Xena, covered in dirt and leaves after rolling in a flower bed. Iris shook her head but felt a growing softness in her heart for this part-wild creature who had walked into her life.

Hearing the *ding-ding* of a bicycle bell, Iris looked toward the road. A woman on a bright pink bike, with short white hair and wrinkled brown skin, made her way to the curb. A woven basket attached to the handlebars was decorated with orange plastic flowers. Iris noticed that the basket contained full, brought-from-home canvas grocery bags, with celery peeking out from the top. *No doubt organic.*

"You know, those weeds are good medicine—they're edible. I hope you'll use them in salad or soup and not just put them on the compost pile," Joan said. Iris did not have a compost pile, and no, she was not going to eat the weeds.

"I'm Joan, by the way." She held out her hand. Iris knew immediately that this must be Joan Flores, the previous owner of her house and the author of the strange letter. She could be no one else. Free and a free spirit, it seemed.

Uncomfortable, nervous thoughts arose: *Will she like me? Will she disapprove of the changes I made to the house and yard?* The familiar question whenever she met someone new was whether she would measure up.

Iris got up from the ground and wiped her hands on her jeans, ready to face judgment. Instead, she noticed Joan's eyes sparkling with warmth. When she looked at Iris, she seemed to see everything.

The two women shook hands. As Iris took Joan's hand, she felt like she was being pulled out of a hole in the ground and into the blue sky—somewhere clear with an expansive view. Time momentarily stopped in the vastness. It was over in a heartbeat, but the feeling lingered, leaving her slightly disoriented.

Joan's voice brought her back. "It's looking great around here. I love the flowers. My mother was a gardener. I'm more of an herbalist. What I grow isn't always beautiful, but it is useful. And who is this?" Joan asked, looking down at Xena approvingly. Xena, still appearing feral from her roll in the dirt, seemed already enamored with Joan and was rubbing against her leg.

Iris felt her feet on solid ground once more. "This is Xena, the Warrior Princess. She showed up when I moved in."

"I see." Joan smiled broadly. "A warrior princess is good to have around."

"Ezra, I think you know him; he was the locksmith I called

when I got locked out. I didn't want a cat, but he told me Xena was my cat, and, well, it's working out." Iris wasn't sure if she was making sense.

"Oh yes, Ezra the magician."

Iris furrowed her brows. "He does magic tricks?"

Joan looked down to find the word she was looking for. "Ah, no, more like a wizard, I suppose."

The world tilted slightly for the second time in as many minutes, causing Iris to feel off-balance. Once again, it seemed that the people around her were in on something, leaving her to piece together the clues.

After a pause, Joan looked up as if she were receiving a message. "Would you be interested in joining a meditation group? I run a meditation class at my house, and I'm starting a new group next week."

Joan's offer caught Iris off guard. Her initial inclination was to make some excuse, to say she had plans. However, before she could articulate her resistance, her mouth betrayed her with the word "Yes!" On some level, she knew this invitation was not to be refused.

"Great, I live in the house at the end of Don Onofre Road by the river. See you Sunday at 11 am." Joan smiled and seemed to pedal away intentionally before Iris had any more time to think about what she just agreed to.

What just happened? Iris reviewed her sudden decision. Meditating on her own was going fine, and she detested new social situations. However, that short interaction with Joan surprised her. It gave Iris a taste of something she didn't know she wanted. Something that felt like freedom. True freedom. Her mind returned to what Ezra had said about Joan at the coffee shop. *Joan is free.* And that was what Iris had felt. And it was a revelation.

. . .

SHE ALTERNATELY FELT anxious and curious as the days counted down to Sunday. Many times, she attempted to talk herself out of attending. She imagined meeting strangers and having to engage in small talk, one of her least favorite activities. She worried that people would think she didn't belong, that somehow her inexperience and ignorance about meditation would show through in something she said or did.

Xena strolled by and rubbed against her legs. Iris felt a wave of calm and a softening in her belly. Her body said go. It was clear. This difference between her head's navigation system, consisting of doubts and competing thoughts, and her body's steady compass was familiar from her younger days but had atrophied in her marriage. She knew it had value, and it was time to start listening again to what her body was communicating. Despite some misgivings, she knew she would attend this meditation class.

ON THE APPOINTED DAY, Iris approached the warm brown stucco house, its soft edges framed by heart-shaped cottonwood leaves. The home appeared to grow out of the sandy brown ground. She admired the tall hollyhock flowers in various shades of pink that bloomed in front of the adobe wall, reaching toward the impossibly blue New Mexico sky.

The end of the street was quiet. A gentle breeze stirred the colorful Tibetan prayer flags that hung along the house. Brushing against a lavender plant allowed the scent to reach Iris's nose, prompting her to take a deep breath. She noticed her namesake flower blooming against the house, while vinca and rose vines intertwined chaotically near the front door. Iris could hear the hum of bees enjoying the flowers. The combination of scents and beauty soothed Iris.

She was on time and the first person to arrive. After living less than a year in New Mexico, she was still learning that being on time meant arriving early. The solid wooden front door with turquoise-blue trim had a metal knocker shaped like a giant bee. She knocked, unsure of what was in store, but she felt this decision, made outside her comfort zone, would lead her somewhere different—somewhere better.

Joan opened the door with a smile. "Iris, welcome."

Iris shyly returned the smile and was directed into the living room. She sat down on an old couch covered with reddish-pink fabric. "The others should be arriving soon." Joan went back to the kitchen to set out mugs for tea, giving Iris time to look around the room.

All the furnishings were well-used. Woven rugs adorned the floors and walls, while the hardwood floors, where they peeked out, showed wear from years of use. A large orange tabby cat sat in a patch of sunlight, grooming her face. A sizable Tibetan tapestry depicting a haloed goddess in vibrant colors hung on one wall.

A few bundles of herbs were tied to the ceiling beams, and the aroma of mint and lavender wafted through with the breeze from the open window. Books overflowed from the bookshelves and were piled on various flat surfaces. Iris, with her librarian's eye, looked closely. There were titles like Every Day Herbalism and Be Here Now. She saw books by Thich Nhat Hanh, the Zen Buddhist monk and author. Iris had heard of him and made a mental note to borrow one of his books from the library now that she was officially a meditator.

A two-foot-tall goddess statue sat on the thick fireplace mantel, seeming to preside over the room. The goddess was seated upright, surrounded by flowers painted in red, white, and yellow. She had one hand on her thigh and the other raised, palm facing outward. The statue's eyes seemed to be looking at Iris, who could not take her gaze away from it. There was an aliveness to it. When she thought she saw its arm move, she blinked twice.

Iris looked away, dismissing the strange visual experience.

She felt an unfamiliar calm in her belly, but was juggling a jumble of thoughts in her head. Her thoughts turned to her recent divorce, pondering whether listening to her body's wisdom more during her marriage would have spared her some pain.

Before long, people began arriving, many of whom knew each other and embraced warmly. Much of the conversation in the room focused on the recent announcement that the bosque was for sale. It was the talk of the town, and Iris listened closely to learn anything new.

An older woman with long gray hair, wearing a T-shirt printed with the word "Resist" above a clenched fist, said fiercely, "They're trying to push the development through the city council without public input. They're going to regret it."

Ezra ambled in, wearing jeans and a Spider-Man T-shirt. An air of ease surrounded him. His long black hair was pulled back in a ponytail. Iris was surprised to see him, but she smiled and waved in his direction. Surprise crossed his face as well, and he returned her smile. He sat down next to her on the couch.

With everyone seated, Joan struck a Tibetan singing bowl with a small wooden dowel, and a long, low tone sliced through the chatter. Silence followed as people closed their eyes.

Iris, unsure of what was expected, closed her eyes, occasionally peeking out until she eventually turned her attention to her belly to feel her breath there and allow her exhalations to slow. Her mental chatter quieted. In a profound way that had never happened before while meditating alone, a warm blanket of peaceful stillness enveloped her. After a time, her mind wandered, but returning to the stillness was effortless. It was as if the room was cradling her, supporting her in a new way of being.

Iris wasn't sure how much time had passed when Joan tapped the metal bowl again, a signal that the meditation was over, she assumed. The bowl produced tones and overtones that were a pleasure to follow to their conclusion.

When Iris opened her eyes, her gaze rested again on the

goddess statue on the mantel. The goddess's arms swayed, dance-like; then, a jolt of electricity shot from the statue's chest to her own, making her eyes widen. However, when she looked around the room, no one seemed to have noticed anything. *What was happening?*

Joan began, "Welcome, everyone." With her sky-blue eyes, she looked around at each person in the room. Iris noticed little purple and blue lights around Joan. She blinked. *Was it time for an eye exam?*

Joan continued, "We are here to do some important work. And by working on ourselves, we are tipping the world toward a better future. It all starts from within." This wasn't what Iris expected to hear.

"We begin by clearing away what prevents us from being our true selves. Your first assignment is to forgive. Forgive everyone who has ever hurt you, and wish them well. Then forgive yourself for all the people you have hurt, intentionally or unintentionally. Wish them well. And wish yourself well. Dig deep into this. Practice every day. Forgiveness points our lives toward freedom."

Wow, no pressure. Iris expected a quaint meditation class. *This sounds more like a superhero job—no wonder Ezra was wearing a Spiderman shirt. Ah, but he always wore something from the superhero genre.*

The short teaching ended, and chatting resumed. Joan called Iris to one of her overflowing bookshelves: "Iris, I saw you looking at the statue on the mantel. It's Tara, a divine being in Tibetan Buddhism. I thought you might enjoy a book about her." Joan pulled out a hardback book with a colorful, intricate picture of the goddess on the cover and handed it to Iris. "Keep it as long as you like."

"Thank you. That statue is… unusual." Iris wondered if the book would contain any explanation for her odd experiences. After putting the book in her bag, she went to the door to leave, falling in step with Ezra.

"Hey, how's it going, cat lady?"

Iris shook her head. She never imagined herself a cat lady. "Going good, except for the city trying to sell the forest along the river to the highest bidder."

"Yeah, that's bullshit."

With excitement in her voice, Iris shared, "I've been doing some research. Did you know the first owner of my house, Ella Ross, set up the Rio Grande Preserve?"

Ezra's face lit up with interest. "I thought that land was supposed to be in a preserve of some kind. And someone who lived in your house set it up?"

"Yup, a hundred years ago."

He tilted his head. "That's wild. Well, the mayor has shaken a hornet's nest on this one. He's going to hear from the people. I hope it's enough to make a difference." The look on his face made Iris think he had doubts.

"Me, too." Iris looked down at the dusty path. She felt the burden of secrets she wasn't ready to share as tension in her body. It seemed premature. She had no proof regarding her suspicions about the death of Eric Sutter. She reminded herself she had decided to let it go.

Yet her mind persistently returned to this topic. She had discovered something significant, something that tied her house, and possibly herself, to the fate of the bosque. But then, this was not her sphere. *Who do you think you are? Nancy Drew?* Anyway, she might be totally off base about her suspicions. *Best to stay quiet about them.*

IRIS FLOPPED onto the couch when she got home. Xena immediately jumped up beside her and nudged her forehead against Iris's hand to be petted. Iris absentmindedly scratched Xena's head the way she seemed to like it. *Ugh, forgiveness.* The thought made her stomach tighten. Forgive everyone who had ever hurt her? *What if they didn't deserve it? What if I'm not ready? Couldn't I start with something more manageable, like praying for world peace? But then, maybe if everyone could forgive, we wouldn't need to pray for world peace.* Yes, she guessed it made sense.

She looked at the picture of Ella Ross on the mantel. "What do you think, Ella?" she whispered, wistfully hoping for a sign to guide her. A refreshing breeze carried the scent of lilacs through the house; Iris barely noticed. However, Xena looked toward the picture on the mantel and swished her tail, then turned to Iris intently, her green eyes narrowing.

Xena

I'll tell you what Ella thinks. She thinks Iris has a job to do, and she'd better snap to it. Soon. I think so too. Time is running out. Enough of this pussy-footing around, Iris. The world is moving, and you must move with it. The time is now.

I am doing my best to send her a clear message to get involved. After all, this is her fight. Her fears and doubts often overwhelm her, but with my support, she will conquer them. She is much more powerful than she realizes. Ella's silver thread is here, weaving itself into this time and place, bringing to life a plan conceived long ago. And Iris doesn't know it yet, but she is central to the plan.

CHAPTER 7

Annabelle sat curled in a beanbag chair in the school library with her nose buried in a book.

"Hey, Annabelle, is your mom working late?" Iris asked gently.

Annabelle didn't look up. "Yes. She has a meeting."

Something about her tone felt off. "What are you reading?"

"About what animals do when they lose their homes. This one's about forest fires." She paused. "Our forest might as well be on fire." Her voice was flat. "They are going to cut it down."

A pang went through Iris's heart. "I heard about that. I'm upset about it, too." Iris sat cross-legged on the floor beside her, knees drawn in.

Annabelle finally glanced over. "There's going to be a protest. My family is going. My dad doesn't think it will make a difference, though. He says it's a done deal." Annabelle bit her lip.

"Well," Iris said slowly, "I guess you never know. I was planning to go to that protest, too. Maybe I'll see you there."

"We have to save the animals and trees. We *have* to save them." Annabelle looked at Iris, obviously trying not to cry.

Iris's chest tightened. "I'm so sorry, Annabelle. Some grown-ups are making really bad decisions. But other grown-ups are trying to stop them. We don't know what will happen yet."

Annabelle's sorrow pierced through Iris. She couldn't keep pretending this was someone else's problem to solve. The truth had chosen her. She held a piece of the puzzle that could change things. She almost wished she didn't.

Iris began to wonder if she fell into the category of grown-ups who were making bad decisions simply by staying quiet. The thought stung. She had led children on plant walks through the forest. She had exposed them to the wonder of nature. Didn't that count for something? But didn't that also mean she had a duty to protect it? Her body already knew the truth, but her mind was still in bargaining mode.

BACK HOME, Iris tried to lose herself in a book, but the words wouldn't land. Guilt buzzed at the edge of her awareness like a mosquito she couldn't swat away. She reached down and scratched Xena's head, her eyes drifting to Ella Ross's photo. Then Annabelle's grief-stricken face flashed in her mind. And the mayor, smooth-talking his way around destruction.

Iris exhaled sharply. No more hiding behind fear. She wasn't brave. She wasn't a leader. But she had a stubborn streak. Once she made up her mind, nothing could move her. That's what her ex had said. And for once, he was right. She wasn't going to let this stand. Iris opened her laptop and typed in the name Blair Sutter. *Time to let my inner Nancy Drew out of the closet.*

Iris had learned through a recent late-night computer search that Blair, Eric Sutter Jr.'s widow, still resided in town. Blair operated an online business selling gift baskets filled with New Mexico products, such as green chile jam, biscochitos, and red chile powder. She maintained a significant social media presence, making her easy to find. Iris took out her phone, inhaled deeply, and dialed the number.

"Hello?"

"Hi, my name is Iris Barnes, and I'm a librarian at the middle school. I'm researching the recent sale of the Bosque and discovered that your husband used to manage the preserve's finances. Would it be possible for us to meet for coffee?"

A FEW DAYS LATER, at the coffee shop, Iris and Blair sat at a sturdy wooden table facing each other. Blair was well-dressed, adorned with expensive jewelry and tastefully applied makeup.

Iris had always been a low-maintenance sort, never taking much to makeup, and her clothes fell more into the functional and budget-conscious category. No one would describe Iris as "well put together." Comfortable, maybe. Iris felt out of her league talking with Blair.

Deep breath and remember why you're here. "I was reading up on the history of the preserve," Iris began, choosing her words with care. "It's such a special place. I came across a few old articles that mentioned your husband... Eric." She glanced at Blair, who gave a small nod of acknowledgment. "They said he handled the finances for the preserve."

Blair's expression shifted almost imperceptibly. "He inherited his father's business, so I guess that may have been part of it. I didn't know all the details."

"I also saw something else... about the accident," Iris added gently. "I'm so sorry for your loss. And I read that just days after... his office caught fire?"

Blair exhaled slowly, her fingers tightening around her cup. "Yes. That's right."

Iris said nothing, allowing space for Blair to fill the silence.

"The police seemed to brush me off, and the fire inspector wouldn't even look me in the eye." Iris gave a small, understanding nod.

Her voice sharpened with practiced control. "I've been suspicious ever since it happened. It's too big of a coincidence, don't you think?"

Iris nodded vigorously.

"I don't know what Eric would have been involved in that would have made anyone want to kill him or burn down his office. It doesn't make any sense. I know with every bone in my body that he wasn't involved in anything criminal." The strength of Blair's conviction came through in her tone. Iris believed her.

Iris leaned closer. "Blair, I know this might be difficult to hear, but I've started wondering if his work on the preserve could have put him in the crosshairs of someone who wanted that land for other purposes."

A shadow passed across Blair's face, and then her expression became blank. "I read recently that the bosque is going to be developed. It's such a shame." Blair shook her head and averted her gaze.

"Yes, I agree." Iris had noticed the look that passed over Blair's face, but wasn't sure what it meant.

"Well, do you think that could have anything at all to do with Eric's death?"

Iris paused a beat. "Blair, I'm beginning to suspect maybe it does."

Blair's eyes locked onto Iris. "Iris, if there is anything I can do to help, please let me know." Her voice was firm but laced with underlying fear. "This whole situation has never sat right with me, but maybe it's beginning to make sense now. I need to know the truth. For Eric's sake."

The sincerity in her voice was undeniable, but there was an intensity in her gaze that Iris couldn't read. "Blair, I'm looking for evidence that maybe Eric was pressured or offered a bribe regarding the preserve," Iris said carefully. "Is there any chance he might have saved old emails or files on a hard drive at home? A calendar entry, maybe?"

At the word *bribe*, Blair fidgeted with her napkin, looking nervous. "I can look. I know he would never take a bribe. But… if someone tried to coerce him…" Her voice trailed off. "Who do you think it could have been?"

"I don't know yet. Someone who stood to benefit if the preserve changed hands. A developer, maybe. Or someone connected to the mayor's office."

Blair's eyebrows lifted. She took a slow sip of her coffee. "The mayor?"

"Or someone acting on his behalf," Iris said. "Even if we can't trace it all the way, anything unusual like dates, emails, or notes might help."

Blair nodded. "I'll look. And I'll let you know if I find anything. I want answers as much as you do."

As they gathered their things, Iris glanced up and noticed a man in the corner of the coffee shop, his gaze lingering on them a little too long. Maybe he was just looking at Blair, but something about him unnerved Iris. Even as she stepped outside and slid into her car, she could still feel his eyes on her through the window. A warning flickered in the back of her mind: *trust your intuition.* But doubt crept in just as quickly. She was probably just on edge from the meeting.

Iris tried to shake off the discomfort and concentrate on the facts as she drove. Eric's suspicious death, the fire, and the bosque sale seemed connected, but she had no proof, only a feeling. Talking with Blair about Eric's death validated her sense that it was no accident. Now, she just had to connect Eric to someone involved in the development. Then she would turn the information over to the police because the more she uncovered, the more dangerous this felt.

AT HOME, Iris opened her laptop to research the funding sources behind the Bosque development. She tried to focus on who stood to gain the most from the project. After some digging, she discovered the name Ivan Storic. He was a self-made multimillionaire involved in other riverfront projects in the Southwest and was financing most of the money for the Cottonwood project. Cynically, she thought they probably wouldn't let the minor detail of a one-hundred-year-old preserve stop them. It seemed that there were always workarounds for people with wealth and power. Iris sighed.

It was becoming a reflex to look up at the photo of Ella on the mantel, and as Iris did, a bolt of determination coursed through her. A message sent across a century sparked a memory to flicker at the edge of her thoughts.

Iris had meant to investigate the old trunk in the attic, but between moving in and unpacking, she hadn't found the time. She had only been up there months ago when she tagged along with the home inspector. The attic was accessed by a rickety pull-down ladder, and she remembered it being cramped, dusty, and filled with spiderwebs.

Still, what if that trunk held something important that could reveal more about the preserve and Ella's intentions? It was a long shot, but she couldn't shake the feeling that it might contain a clue. There was only one way to find out. It was time to open it.

She steeled herself, entered the hallway, and pulled the cord that lowered the ladder. As the door creaked open, a small cloud of dust puffed into the air. She looked up into the black hole and slowly made her way into the attic, rung by rung. Doubts arose; maybe it wasn't even Ella's trunk. But as she reached the top rung, it felt as if the attic had been holding its breath, waiting for her to arrive.

She felt the dry, warm air against her skin. The only light came from a small window. Taking a breath, she wrinkled her nose, trying to suppress the urge to sneeze. Iris stared across the low-ceilinged room at the trunk. It was only an old piece of luggage, yet she felt herself magnetized toward it.

The trunk was reddish and covered in leather, which was

peeling off the underlying wood in a few places. It was about two feet wide, three feet long, and tall. The wood beneath the leather was dark and weathered. The trunk's edges were reinforced with tarnished brass fittings, which had dulled to a muted greenish hue over time.

Iris appreciated the trunk's heavy metal lock, crafted long ago when even utilitarian items were made with care and attention to detail. She tried to slide the trunk across the floor to move it away from the wall. It was too heavy. She wouldn't be able to get it down the ladder—at least not by herself. She pulled on the old metal lock, but it held fast. She wondered if she could break it with a hammer.

She descended the ladder, feeling the cool air in the hallway, and retrieved the hammer from her small tool chest, a gift from her father when she moved into her first apartment.

Back up in the hot attic, the hammer heavy in her hand, she looked at the lock. *Okay, I can do this.* She swung the hammer and missed the lock, hearing the dull thud of hitting wood. She had never been good at hand-eye coordination, and she was too much of a bookworm to be interested in sports. *Oh well.*

She tried again. She knew she had hit the lock when she heard a metallic clang. But the lock held. She tried again and a third time. Iris stared at the old, stubborn lock in frustration. She could use some help. Then she remembered. *I know a locksmith.*

Xena

Time is a delicate weave. The threads of history and fate are beginning to pull more tightly together. The trunk is bursting with old secrets, ready to be unleashed upon this time. This is not done lightly. The extremes of dark and light in this period are driving changes that would have been unthinkable in another time. And Iris is closer than she realizes to unlocking the truth.

So here I am, folding through time again like it's casual Friday when- boom! Ella returns through the front door and sets her bag on the table. This sets something into motion, an arc of consequences that reaches all the way into the present. Stay with me.

Out of her bag, she pulls a skeleton key. This is no ordinary key. It comes straight from the Otherworld— the faery world. You might imagine that faeries lie around drinking mushroom lattes and critiquing human fashion, and, truthfully, they do, but they also mean business, and they want that key back. Yesterday.

The key will come to Iris; it has to now, and it will link her to Ella and the Fae. This happens through the magic of the Otherworld, and it is at the discretion of the Fae. And spoiler, it's not the only key. There are two! The Fae tend toward excess if you ask me.

At this stage, my job is to continue bringing Iris's clair abilities online. You know the clairs: clairvoyance, clairaudience, clairsentience, claircognizance, and my absolute favorite: clairolfaction. These abilities will allow Iris to fulfill her responsibilities. No problem. I can do this. I was born for this. And so was she.

CHAPTER 8

Maria, Annabelle's mother, sat at her work-from-home desk, but her eyes weren't on the screen. She gazed out the window, where a light breeze blew, and the day appeared idyllic on the surface. However, underneath, something was stirring that she didn't recognize. She could only feel it.

She had felt out of sorts all week. Not in a loud, dramatic way, but she found herself doubting and questioning her choices. Was it the changes on her doorstep, the Bosque development? Was it the pain of seeing her daughter's grief? Or was her own weariness causing a slow drift from meaning? Balancing work with being a wife and mother was consuming. It was easy to get caught up in the constant demands and lose touch with her own inner voice.

When she was about Annabelle's age, her own mother had taught her to read tarot cards, and it had become a touchstone in her life. Not to predict the future necessarily, but to help her listen to her heart. The cards guided her home when she felt lost.

She had begun teaching her daughter a bit about them, but so far, Belles was more interested in reading books about animals. In time, she told herself.

She reached for the old velvet bag in the bottom drawer of her desk, where she kept the precious things that mattered. She took her mother's deck out of the bag and shuffled it. Its corners were worn from her mother's fingers and now hers. The cards still smelled faintly of piñon smoke from the old fireplace in the house where she grew up.

She whispered, "What is moving beneath the surface?" It was always the right question.

She drew three cards and placed them carefully on the desk. She smiled. The first card was the Fool, symbolizing a fresh start, a leap into the unknown, and trust that the path would reveal itself step by step. She was fond of the Fool and believed it was a good omen. New beginnings were on the horizon for her, or perhaps for all of them.

The second card made her pause. It was the Hierophant, reversed. She murmured, "The rebel priest." This was her mother's interpretation. Her mother was Catholic, but her understanding of the reversed Hierophant made Maria feel there was room for more than just the church in her heart. Her mother used to say the reversed Hierophant was the priest who built altars in the woods instead of churches.

She combined the cards in her mind. This was an unconventional journey without the support of the established order. Or perhaps it was about an older, deeper order, from before the construction of churches. The order of nature and wild things. Maria glanced out the window just as a black crow swept across the sky, heading south.

The two crossed keys of the Hierophant card caught her eye. Usually at the bottom but in reverse position, they were now at the top of the card, the crown. The keys to knowledge of the self and one's own heart come from the inner journey. She thought of her daughter Annabelle and her nephew Federico, the young ones of their lineage, forging their own paths.

The third card was the Moon. This card placement represented resolution, but the Moon doesn't offer resolution or clarity. It was mysterious, ambiguous, and wild. With no tidy resolution, the Moon instead leads deeper into the mystery. *The Moon never answers; it only draws us in.*

She sighed and leaned back. Sometimes, the cards spoke clearly, while at other times, they only raised more questions.

OVERCOME with worry about the sale of the bosque, Annabelle decided to walk to Tia Joan's house on Don Onofre Street. "Byyyye, mom, I'm going to Aunt Joan's," she yelled down the hall toward her mother's closed office door.

Joan was her Grandpa Frank's sister; therefore, she was actually Annabelle's great-aunt. Unlike all the other adults in Annabelle's life, Joan spoke to her like she was an adult, not a child, for which Annabelle was forever grateful. She sensed that Joan would have the clarity and perhaps the comfort she needed right now.

Annabelle walked through the gate into the lush front courtyard. Through the window, she could see Aunt Joan sitting at her kitchen table. When she knocked, Joan answered, "Come in," all drawn out and sing-songy. Annabelle felt welcomed already. She opened the wooden door and received an enthusiastic greeting.

"Belles! There you are! I've just been thinking of you." Joan's whole face was a giant smile radiating goodness. The crystal in the window spun, scattering rainbows throughout the small kitchen. Annabelle wrapped her arms around Joan's waist, resting her head on Joan's chest.

"Sit down, sit down, m'ija. How did I get so lucky today that you stopped by for a visit, hmmm?"

As they sat by the window, Joan poured her niece a cup of spearmint tea and automatically offered her honey, knowing that Annabelle liked her tea sweet.

Annabelle's feet swung beneath the table, not quite touching the ground. She twirled some strands of hair around her finger, wondering how to begin. Then, with her elbows on the table, she pressed her forehead into her palms. Being in Joan's presence provided the safety necessary for the overwhelm to engulf her. When she looked up, tears filled her eyes.

Looking at Annabelle, Joan said, "What's this? Tell me."

"They're going to cut down trees, and animals won't have homes. Probably, some of them will die, and I can't stand it. I can't stand it." Annabelle made fists with her hands, her body tense from alternating between anger and despair.

Joan folded her hands in her lap. "This is serious. We need to look into it." Annabelle nodded, relieved that a grown-up heard her concern. And she knew her Tia meant it.

Joan went to the cabinets and rummaged around until she found what she was looking for. She pulled out a silver bowl, went to the big farm-style sink, filled it with water, and then set it on the table between them.

Annabelle looked up at Joan with wide eyes. Joan had only brought out the scrying bowl once before, and Annabelle vividly remembered it. It was after her Grandpa Frank died. She experienced looking into the water and feeling her grandfather's presence profoundly. She felt curious and a little worried about what the bowl would reveal this time.

They sat across from one another, gazing into the still water. Joan lit a match and brought it to the ends of some sprigs of dried rosemary from the garden, producing sparks and smoke. She moved the rosemary bundle in a circular motion around the bowl before setting it down on a small plate. "For clarity, m'ija," she said. The smoke lingered over them, creating a new space—a space in which to view the arc of time.

Annabelle inhaled the aromatic smoke. Something settled within her. This was what she needed. Her thoughts and breath slowed. Joan extended her hands from across the table, and

Annabelle took them. Almost immediately, a solid knowing arose within Annabelle.

"What is it, Belles?"

"It's going to be okay."

"Yes, it is. But let's see what else we can find out. Please tell me what you see. In the water."

Annabelle looked down into the bowl. It shimmered. Then, she closed her eyes. Her voice sounded like it was far away. "I see the crows all sitting in a big tree. Something has been decided. I'm going to help them." Annabelle scrunched her eyes shut, trying to find out more. She opened her eyes and looked into the water. "I'm not sure what else. Aunt Joan? What do you see?"

"That was very good, Belles." Joan smiled at her niece. She gazed softly into the bowl, and after a few minutes, she said, "I see that there are others involved besides the crows. It is the little people. And I see some shadowy figures. You are safe, but I worry about someone else." She whispered, "Iris."

Joan looked at Annabelle and said, "Iris Barnes. She's the librarian at your school, isn't that right?"

"Yes, Ms. Barnes. She's the librarian," Annabelle nodded.

"Ah, well. She bought my old house on Silver Street. And she's coming to my meditation class." Joan looked away, out the window, and almost to herself said, "But there's something about that old house, and…" Joan looked surprised. "And the key." A wave of regret passed over Joan's face. She looked back at Annabelle. "I need to think about it a little more." She smiled reassuringly at her niece.

Annabelle was curious but didn't pursue it. She got what she came for. She finished her spearmint tea, and with her hair swinging and one shoe untied, she walked toward the door. "I have to get home, Tia. Sparkpuff needs a walk."

Joan smiled, "Come back soon, Belles."

. . .

JOAN SAT down to reflect on what the scrying bowl had revealed. She needed to give the key to Iris. That much was clear. She had to trust that Iris would know what to do with it when the time was right. In retrospect, she should have left the key with the house. That was the instruction, after all. She shook her head. She knew better. But she had gotten too attached to it. It seemed that no matter how long she practiced, she could still fall into the trap of attachment.

Joan went to her living room and sat in a chair before the Green Tara statue on her mantel. She closed her eyes and said aloud:

"I forgive myself for all missteps past, present, and future. May it be so.

I call my power back. All that was taken from me, all I gave away, and all I lost. So be it.

I am deeply grateful to my allies and ancestors, the spirits of the woods and the river, the home and the garden, and the venerable divine Green Tara. Thank you for your protection and guidance.

Hear my request. Protect Iris Barnes and Annabelle Castillo from all forces that wish to harm them, now and always."

Joan brought her palms together at her heart. Unseen by Joan, the statue of Green Tara blinked once, making it so.

THE HOUSE WAS quiet when Annabelle returned from Tia Joan's. She dropped her bag by the door and wandered in, still in an altered headspace from the scrying bowl experience. She peeked into the kitchen and then walked down the hall. Her mother's office door was open. The office was empty, but she saw three tarot cards on the table. She moved closer. Her mind was open and ready for the symbolism of the cards.

She recognized the Fool, the first card of the tarot, the beginning. She felt the sense of faith the young man had in embarking on a journey. She recalled the emotions she experienced when she first closed her eyes at Aunt Joan's. She knew deep down that everything would be alright. The Fool card evoked that same feeling. *That card is me.*

The second card was trickier: the Hierophant, upside down. She didn't know much about that one, but she noticed the two keys crossed like an X. Tia Joan had just talked about a key. She smiled at the synchronicity, feeling in the flow of something.

The last card was The Moon. She grinned. That one, she liked instantly, partly because of the animals and partly because it was messy, magical, and half real and half not, like a dream.

Just then, her mother came into the room with a glass of water. She looked surprised. "Belles, I didn't know you were home. How was Tia?"

Annabelle turned, still smiling. "Good," she said simply.

Maria took in how grown-up her daughter seemed. She felt a pang of recognition that Annabelle was beginning to carve out her own life, and she might not be privy to all of it.

"I see you found the cards," Maria said, her voice soft.

Annabelle nodded. "Yes, they spoke to me today."

Maria looked at the spread, then back at her daughter. "Good, m'ija. I'm glad." Annabelle hugged her mother and went to the kitchen to find a snack.

CHAPTER 9

The boys in PE class started up again, their cruel chant echoing off the gym walls, emphasizing the first syllable of each word. "Turtle, humpback, turtle, humpback…" Each repetition further opened Federico's wound of being an outcast and broken.

Federico had spent his whole life being reminded to "sit up straight" by parents, teachers, and even strangers. But no matter how hard he tried, his back refused to obey. It curled inward like a shell, as if trying to shield him from the world.

In elementary school, it hadn't mattered so much. He'd had friends then, and kids were kinder. But middle school changed everything. He stopped trying to fit in and instead made a habit of disappearing, shutting his bedroom door and vanishing into the glow of video games, where no one commented on his posture and no one expected him to smile.

As the boys' cruel chanting grew louder, Federico's heart sank deeper into his chest. Each word seemed to crush any hope of belonging or being anything other than the *humpback*. No teacher came to help. He felt his face grow hot, and he gritted his teeth to suppress the tears. He longed to disappear, to be invisible.

Finally, he couldn't stand it any longer. His vision narrowed into a tunnel of rage and humiliation. Maybe he was a turtle, but he could run fast, he thought. His legs propelled him through the gym doors, past the laughter and taunts, until he found himself breathless and alone in the parking lot.

Why do I have to be like this? His heart was beating out of control from emotion and exertion. Out of breath, he leaned against a parked car and slid down into a squat, his back rounding into its shell shape.

"Hey, Rrrrico," a male voice called out. Federico unfolded himself and looked up. It was a boy from the high school. Federico recognized him as the older brother of a boy in his 7th-grade class. Federico tensed, expecting more mocking.

"Hey man, you okay? You're Federico, right? I'm Joey, Ben's brother. I think I met you once when Ben had a birthday party. It was a long time ago." Joey wore a ball cap low over his eyes. He dressed like the druggies at school, but he was smiling and engaging and seemed non-threatening, so Federico relaxed a little.

Without making eye contact, he said, "Yeah, yeah. I'm fine."

"Well, I'm just saying 'cause you don't look fine." Joey tilted his head.

"No, I'm good. I'm good," Federico mumbled.

Joey had the flash of an idea cross his face. "Hey, you should come out tonight with me and my boys. We're going cruising, man. You'd like it." Joey smiled, showing a silver tooth.

As Joey extended the invitation, a voice in the back of Federico's mind told him to say no and walk away. But the desire to belong was overwhelming. He was only twelve. He wasn't friends with anyone who drove. He felt trepidation, but there was also something thrilling about the invitation. Joey's smile emanated an easy camaraderie mixed with charisma that was very hard to refuse.

Federico's voice was barely audible when he said, "Yeah, okay." He ignored the warning bells going off in his head.

"I'll pick you up at your house around 8 o'clock. It'll be fun," the older boy reassured him.

FEDERICO WAS outside waiting at 8 pm. He told his parents he was going to play video games at a friend's house. They seemed happy that Federico had made a friend.

Joey pulled up, driving the sleek, sky-blue Chevy Impala that Federico had seen earlier. The car seemed too full of boys already, but one of the back doors opened, and Joey yelled, "Rrrrico." Federico felt a tiny seed of belonging, despite his trepidation.

Federico climbed in, and the car roared down the street, the bass thumping so loudly that he could feel it vibrating in his chest. The warm wind whipped through the open windows, carrying the scent of rain, sage, and fast food all at once. The car's speed felt like freedom—way better than a bike. The boys in the car were all older, but Federico recognized one of them from the class above him.

Sitting in the front with Joey, an older boy with facial hair who kept flicking ash from his cigarette out the window, completely ignored Federico. Another kid, stocky and with dark, intense eyes, kept glancing at Federico and then at Joey in the rearview mirror.

Amid the loud music, they offered Federico a puff from a joint. He took it and inhaled, then coughed several times, his throat burning. The boys laughed, but it felt like he was included in the joke, rather than being made fun of. Next, they passed around a communal bottle in a paper bag. Federico considered refusing, but the feeling of belonging to the group was more intoxicating than even the weed.

He took a swig and made a face as his tongue touched the roof of his mouth, his lips squeezed together, and his eyes squinted and watered. He had sipped beer before, but this wasn't beer. As the substances coursed through his body, his usual stiff, flat expression transformed into one of animation, and he laughed longer and louder than he had in a long time. He felt alive, and he liked it. The tight skin that usually confined him loosened.

They cruised through downtown, and the world outside the car blurred into neon lights and streaks of color. The boys catcalled and whistled at girls out the window. As the car sped through the night, Federico couldn't help but notice the sharp glances the older boys exchanged when they thought he wasn't looking. Something in their eyes made him uneasy, even as he laughed along with them. Yet the thrill of being part of the group drowned out the small voice inside that whispered of danger.

The long blue car pulled into the Dog House, the hot dog place at the end of Central Avenue that had been a teen hangout for generations. Joey's easy confidence was infectious. Federico carefully watched how Joey talked and commanded attention, finding himself trying to imitate the older boy's swagger. The boys ordered Frito pies with warm chips, red chili, and cheese served in a paper boat. Joey approached the window and pulled out a large wad of bills from his front pocket.

Gloria, an older woman with her name sewn onto her uniform and a hairnet covering her black hair with white roots peeking through, accepted the hundred-dollar bill. When she went to make change, Joey waved and said, "Keep the change," as he turned and walked back to the car. To his boys.

Gloria used to have two sons. Now, she had only one. That hundred-dollar bill would not buy her child back from the dead. The gangs roaming Cottonwood preyed on young boys, offering them a sense of belonging before turning them into servants of the drug dealers. Too many boys died in that transaction. Gloria understood what she was witnessing. Her mind raced back to the son she had lost, his bright eyes dulled by the lure of drugs and easy money. Seeing young Federico, she whispered, "Dios mio," and her hand instinctively went to the cross around her neck. "Please, not another one." She watched as the car pulled away into the night.

Federico leaned back in his seat. The warmth of the Frito pie was temporarily comforting, but the thrill that had initially surged through him was starting to fade. He felt a growing knot of tension in his chest and a sense of being small and out of place. He began to wonder if perhaps this evening had been a mistake. He looked out through the window as they left and saw the cashier from the Dog House looking at him with sadness in her eyes.

CHAPTER 10

On her way to work, Iris decided to stop by Trifecta. She couldn't make this a habit on her limited librarian paycheck, but their coffee was too good to resist. Plus, it was the last week of school, so it was time to celebrate a little. As she pulled into a parking space, the familiar double skeleton key Pop-a-Lock logo on a white van caught her eye.

Stepping into the cafe, she scanned the room for Ezra. There he was, tucked into a corner, absorbed in his laptop. She noticed the Spider-Man sticker on the laptop case and the black Yoda T-shirt he wore. She shook her head slightly and smiled, a slight flutter of excitement in her chest at the sight of him. It was silly, she knew. She got her latte and walked over to where Ezra sat. "Hey, Ezra. What are you up to?"

He grinned and looked up at her. "Oh, hey, Iris. I was looking for a geocache to do after work tonight. It's supposed to be nice out, and the wind is finally dying down."

"Hmm, I guess I wouldn't peg you as a geocacher." She vaguely understood the concept of treasure hunting with GPS or something like that. In her mind, she had always linked it to the same group of people who used to obsess over that Pokémon Go craze everyone was doing a few years back.

"Yeah, some friends are doing a series of Cottonwood geocaches in the bosque to help people appreciate the beauty there." He shrugged casually. "Plus, it gets me and Molly outside after work."

Iris felt her heart sink a bit. Hmm, Molly. Of course, a guy like Ezra would have a girlfriend. Still, she reminded herself that friendship was all she was ready for right now, anyway.

"Oh, hey," she said, suddenly remembering the trunk, "I actually have a locksmith question for you."

"Shoot," Ezra said, closing his laptop slightly, his attention fully on her now.

"There's an old trunk in my attic, and it's locked. I was wondering if you could help me open it. It looks like it could be from the original owner of the house. I'd love to know what's inside."

Ezra's eyebrows drew together, and Iris could tell he was intrigued. "An old travel trunk, huh?"

"Yeah, it's large, leather-bound, and looks ancient." Iris observed Ezra's face carefully.

"Sounds interesting. I'd love to help."

"Oh, I was hoping you would say that!" She clapped her hands together.

"You know, it's probably empty, but it could contain treasure." Ezra had a playful glint in his eyes.

"I'm definitely voting for treasure," Iris shot back. Though she thought it was most likely to contain nothing valuable, she felt thankful that Ezra was willing to help.

"Maybe Saturday afternoon?" he said.

"That would be perfect. Really, thank you for being willing to do this. I'll pay you for your time."

"No need. I'm happy to help out my friends." His words were casual, but the warmth in his voice lingered.

. . .

IRIS SLIPPED into her car with the realization that she had been friend-zoned. He had a girlfriend. That was that. And really, it was fine. She could use a friend. She wasn't ready to date anyway. She was finding her way as a single person. Her heart had not healed from the divorce. Even if he had been available, she wasn't. Not yet. The hamster wheel of her mind continued to spin on this topic until she pulled into the school parking lot.

Then, in a leap of understanding, she caught herself. *Ahh. There are those looping thoughts again.* She knew what she needed to do: get into the present moment. She began by noticing her breath. Then she scanned her body on the exhale. She felt the tension in her heart, jaw, and shoulders release a bit with the simple act of noticing.

Look at me, having epiphanies in the school parking lot. She smiled in a silent nod to her own growth. Then, she grabbed her to-go cup and headed into the school.

While walking toward the library, Iris saw Fedrico. He had dark circles under his eyes, and his clothing looked disheveled. "Hey, Federico," she called out.

He looked up at her sleepily. After going out with his new friends last night, he was weighing the draw of belonging versus danger. So far, the scale tipped toward belonging. But at the end of the night, he had seen one of the boys flash a gun from a pocket, and that gave him pause. But it felt good to have people to laugh with. *They seemed like nice guys. They were just having a good time.*

"Federico, walk with me," Iris called. Federico obliged, and together they headed toward the library.

"So, I was wondering if you could help me with a program I'm starting. It's about drones."

Federico's eyes showed some interest. He used to have friends with drones, and they were cool. He managed to fly one a few times. However, they were small toy drones that often got taken by the wind and lost. He recalled getting yelled at by an old man after climbing a wall into his backyard to retrieve a lost drone. Federico tried to explain, but the man kept shouting, "Get out!" He felt uncomfortable after that experience and hadn't flown any drones since.

"George Miller from the Forest Service is coming to show us some drones they are working with and also to see if anyone is interested in a summer drone computer coding class. Iris continued, "The drones he works with are big, and they do over-head surveys of the forest. But anyway, I need someone to help me set up next week after school. Could you be available?" Iris felt Federico's flash of interest and thought he might take the bait.

His hands were deep in his pockets, and looking down, he said, "Yeah, maybe I could do that."

AT HOME THAT NIGHT, Iris wondered if she would hear back from Blair. Her mind kept circling back to Eric Sutter's death. Maybe she should contact the police, but the thought made her stomach knot. She wasn't a detective; she was just a librarian with too many suspicions and not enough evidence.

What if I'm wrong? What if I'm not? The weight of the decision pressed down on her, making her nostalgic for the simple days when her biggest worry was overdue library books. She had decided to take this on, but it was stressful.

She sat in her living room, surrounded by her books and plants. The large stone fireplace made the room unique. She imagined workers over 100 years ago building it stone by stone. She lit a few candles, anticipating the darkness. Dusk settled on the neighborhood, casting a light that silhouetted the trees across the street in the park in pink and gray, accentuating their beauty.

Xena took her place against Iris's thigh on the couch, a slight purr emanating from her soft black body. To relax, Iris opened Joan's book about the Tibetan divine being, Tara.

A breeze blew through the room. *Did I leave a window open?* She set the book down on the coffee table in front of her. The candles flickered. The breeze concentrated on the wooden coffee table, turning the pages of the open book. Iris felt a shiver run down her spine. She glanced around the room, half-expecting to see something. But there was nothing—just a lingering feeling that she wasn't alone.

Iris got up and checked the living room windows. They were closed. *It's an old, drafty house, and this whole thing with Eric Sutter is making me jumpy, that's all. I'm still getting used to living alone.*

Returning to the couch, she looked at the open page of the book. She had already read that there were twenty-one different forms of the goddess Tara. The wind had turned the page to the chapter on Green Tara. Her eyes fell on the goddess's image. The serene expression was almost comforting, yet there was something in her gaze. It was powerful.

She read, "Green Tara is an enlightened bodhisattva associated with compassion, wisdom, and the element of air. She manifests as wind that quickly comes to people in times of danger or need. Green Tara helps people overcome their fears. She protects plants and forests, is associated with nature, and is often depicted with flowers."

Iris hesitated. *That's strange. The element of air... Manifests as wind... Could the goddess be here?* The thought seemed ridiculous, yet Iris felt a chill accompanied by goosebumps. Her body sensed the truth, but her mind didn't trust it.

Moving into this house and meeting Joan coincided with a lot of strangeness— that statue, intuitions, and those daffodils. Iris wasn't accustomed to events like these. She gazed at the image of Green Tara in the book, looking serene and filled with divine grace. Iris whispered a request: *Give me guidance and courage for what is coming.*

Iris closed the book, her fingers tracing the cover. The room was quiet, yet the air hummed with energy. A quiet peace settled over her.

Xena

Good gracious, great goddess. I watch in awe as Green Tara's presence fills the room and every corner of the house. There's a power here, something beyond what even I'm used to, and trust me, I've seen a lot! Every room is twinkling with light. Iris is blissfully unaware, but she just called in one of the great goddesses of the universe right into our tiny house. I think a part of her may sense the change, the shift in the air. Green Tara is the real deal, a force of nature, literally. Very impressive. I'm surprised the top doesn't blow off the house.

Tara is a friend of nature on this planet and of all nature in this diverse universe filled with life. To reiterate—she is a GODDESS OF THE UNIVERSE, not simply this little Earth. She is an upper-echelon goddess, people! Upper-echelon goddess in the house!

Green Tara sees me. She understands I have allied with Iris as a spirit helper, a baby bodhisattva. As a giant cloud of green in the room, she says, "I bless you, venerable feline."

Slowly, I blink, keeping my cool. "I accept your blessing." I realize this is more than just a visit; it signifies the beginning of something much bigger. Another level of assistance. The cavalry has been called.

CHAPTER 11

The last strong winds of spring swept through the Rio Grande Valley, whipping up clouds of dust that turned the sky a dull gray. The mountains, usually so clear and imposing, now appeared as mere shadowy outlines obscured by the swirling grit of the desert. It wouldn't be long before the true heat of summer took over.

As the winds settled in the early evening, Iris seized the opportunity to survey the yard. Tumbleweeds had piled up in the corner near the low wall separating her yard from her neighbor's. Hummingbirds buzzed low over her head to alert her to the empty feeder. *Okay, okay, I'm on it.*

She prepared the sugar-water solution according to Joan's instructions and filled the feeder. The hummingbirds hovered impatiently. Then, she began cleaning up tumbleweeds that had blown in, a spring ritual in this high-desert town.

The big, round tumbleweeds were lightweight and sharp with stickers—an ingenious strategy for propagation. Before moving here, she had only seen them in Warner Bros. cartoons. She gingerly lifted one, but despite her caution, a sharp thorn pricked her finger, drawing a drop of blood. Even more cautiously, she lifted another to toss into the garbage can by the curb.

She couldn't help but notice a car slow down as it passed her house. She couldn't see the driver through the heavily tinted windows. Her pulse quickened. When she thought to note the license plate number, it had already turned the corner. She didn't understand why she felt so nervous.

As she carried the tumbleweed to the curb, her eyes fell on the shed skin of a snake twisted into the latticework of the tumbleweed. She bent down to gently dislodge the skin, marveling at its delicate translucence—a perfect imprint of the creature it once housed. The symbol of transformation resonated. She brought the snake remnant inside and placed it on the fireplace mantel, along with Ella's photo, as a reminder of her changing and evolving self.

She remembered what Joan had written about the friendly Afghan pines in the corner of the yard. Walking back outside, she had to admit they radiated a welcoming feeling. Anything that grew in this climate was a gift, and these seemed to flourish. Their long green needles in large clusters reached toward the sky with exuberance. She thought she might try talking to them as Joan suggested. The idea didn't seem as strange as it once might have.

She was changing, and the door to a more mystical view of the world had opened a crack. Maybe it was the influence of Joan or Green Tara, or simply being free from the judgment of her ex-husband.

Lost in thought, Iris looked up at the sound of Joan's bicycle bell. Joan was steering toward the curb. *Funny, I was just thinking of her.* Iris decided she must be on Joan's regular route and walked over to greet her.

Seeing Joan was a reminder of her unsuccessful attempt at the forgiveness exercise from meditation class. She got stuck when trying to forgive her ex-husband. Whenever she thought of him, her feelings leaned toward a bitter mix of anger and victimization. Nothing resembling forgiveness felt ready to surface, even though she knew it was the right thing to do.

Joan said cheerfully, "How are you doing? Surviving the spring winds? I find they help in letting things go. Nature's way of blowing out the old and bringing in the new."

Iris thought this was a very positive spin on the relentless winds of spring. "Hmm, I guess I could use some blowing out the old and bringing in the new. I am working on the forgiveness exercise from class. Honestly, my heart still feels too broken from my divorce to forgive."

"Ah, yes." Joan's brown face crinkled into a smile, her white hair contrasting with her skin. "It's fine to start small with forgiveness. The easy lifts lay the foundation for the harder ones. Why don't you come by before the next meditation class, and we can have some tea and talk about it? Also, I have something I want to give you."

Plans were made, and Joan rode off. As Iris watched her pedal away, she wondered what Joan intended to give her. She had already loaned her the Goddess Tara book. *Was it another book?*

A couple walked by, arm in arm, and waved to her. She waved back, marveling at how friendly the people were in this neighborhood. In the evening, people strolled by while others sat on their front porches, waving to anyone passing. People would stop to chat, and everyone seemed to know each other.

She appreciated that it wasn't the kind of neighborhood where one would find a rude anonymous note taped to the door if the garbage can was left out an extra day. Living in California with her ex, that had actually happened. She shook her head.

Most of the neighbors here shared an interest in historic home preservation. Some could talk for hours about wood-hung windows and period-specific paint colors. Iris was learning new things and found this shared interest to be a comfortable way to socialize.

Being newly single, she thought she might feel lonely living in this large house. But no, there seemed to be plenty of interesting people and, of course, Xena. These additions to her life gradually filled the empty spaces inside and perhaps even healed a few cracks in her broken heart.

As Iris sat on her porch with Xena nestled beside her, the last light of the day faded into twilight. The neighborhood, the people, the trees—all of it was part of the new life she was slowly building. She closed her eyes, savoring a rare moment of perfect contentment. Quietly, she got up and went inside. Xena followed her in, and she clicked the door shut.

An explosion of glass shattering struck her like a physical blow. Her ears rang. In her disorientation, she looked toward the source of the sound and saw glittering shards carpeting the floor of her living room. A window was broken where a jagged rock, twice the size of her fist, had punched through. Affixed to the rock with a rubber band was a piece of paper. Her heart pounding, she picked up the rock and read the note. STAY AWAY FROM WHAT DOES NOT CONCERN YOU.

Still clutching the heavy rock, she dashed out the front door and scanned in all directions. The street was deserted, and darkness was closing in. She began to tremble, her fragile sense of safety shattered like the glass strewn across the floor. The threatening note was alarming enough, but it was the implication that truly terrified her: someone was watching her. Her intuition was correct—the man in the coffee shop, the car that drove past—she wasn't imagining it.

XENA

Just when everything was going so well, the yahoos had to show up. I sensed them circling these past few days, and now they've found us. The rock thrower is just a messenger. The real danger remains in the shadows.

I thought I had a little more time, but things are getting real, and I need to get busy dusting off the energetic protection around this house. I'm on it, and I'll enlist Ella and Green Tara for the cause. Then, I don't think we'll have any more problems here, but I can't protect Iris everywhere. She must continue sharpening her spidey senses to take care of herself. I'll help her with that, too, because I'm a full-service, professional spiritual helper. No job is too big or too small. Warrior princess to the rescue!

CHAPTER 12

Maria called from the kitchen, "Take Sparkpuff out for a walk, will you, dear?" Annabelle glanced at her dog, head tilted, one ear up, tail wagging at warp speed.

"Hey, Mom, have the crows shown up today?"

Maria looked up. "No, surprisingly quiet."

Annabelle scrunched her eyebrows as she did when trying to make sense of something. "That's unusual."

Her mom shrugged, "Who knows what they're up to?"

Annabelle and her mom were the unofficial Crow fan club in the neighborhood. Once, they nurtured a baby crow that had fallen from its nest until it could fly again, with help from the local wildlife rescue group. They were fairly certain that the crow still visited them from time to time. Admittedly, it was difficult to tell crows apart, so they couldn't know for sure.

Annabelle headed out the door with Sparkpuff, a mix of miniature poodle, terrier, and escape artist. They found him loitering on a median strip a few years ago and scooped him into their car, not realizing it was the beginning of a long-term relationship.

No one ever claimed him, so he claimed them. He found his

way deep into their hearts with his enthusiasm for all activities and his habit of making profound, deep eye contact that could convince anyone they were his one true love. Annabelle was completely under his spell.

The scent of damp spring soil, from the recent rain, enveloped Annabelle and Sparkpuff as they entered the forest. Sunlight filtered through the leaves, creating a mosaic of light and shadow on their path.

They turned onto an acequia trail, which was essentially a ditch trail, but the Spanish word sounded better to Annabelle. Sparkpuff led the way, tail high and nose twitching.

This acequia had provided irrigation from the Rio Grande River to family fields and farms for over a hundred years. In parts of New Mexico, there were acequias over four hundred years old. The winding, historic system of irrigation created the miracle of farming in the desert while also providing a green zone for animals and plants well beyond the river's edge.

Annabelle waved at the trail regulars: the tattooed couple with the friendly pit bull, the bald man with bright blue eyes who walked barefoot year-round, even in the cold, the woman with salt and pepper hair, and the giant white dog in the rainbow harness.

Sparkpuff barked at her like he was auditioning for a part in "Guardians of the Acequia." The bigger dog ignored him with elegant disdain.

Two crows circled above them, gazing down at the girl and dog as they had for many years. Annabelle felt completely rooted in this place, and her connections to the creatures living here ran deep.

Up ahead, a couple in shiny, new hiking gear paused. They were probably tourists visiting for the Cottonwood Hot Air Balloon Festival.

"Hey, do you by any chance know what kind of tree this is?"

the man asked, gesturing to the massive trunk of a cottonwood tree.

Annabelle smiled; they were definitely tourists. "That is a Rio Grande Cottonwood," she said, flipping into what her mother had called professor mode. "They're the capstone species of the Rio Grande bosque." The adults smiled, a bit indulgently. "They have a lifespan of about 80 years, like a human." This was a fact Annabelle found fascinating and assumed other people would as well.

She looked up at them, wondering if she should continue. Still seeming to have a captive audience, she decided to forge ahead. "But they're dying out because dams were built to stop this valley from flooding and, of course, climate change. Cottonwoods need flooding to continue to spread and grow. If you look around here, you'll only see old cottonwoods. They aren't reproducing, or at least not enough to maintain the forest after the old cottonwoods die."

"Well, how about that? You sure know a lot about trees. Did they teach you that in school?" the man in the REI tan lightweight vest asked.

Annabelle replied, "Some I learned from school, and some from volunteering with the Bosque Restoration Project. We plant native trees and pull out the invasive ones. It helps. A little."

"We need more kids like you." The woman in the wide-brimmed hat smiled.

Annabelle forced a smile. Inside, she thought: *We need more grown-ups like me.* They went their separate ways. Sparkpuff broke into a trot, happy to be moving again, his nose lifted and sniffing the breeze. However, the woman's innocuous comment triggered something in Annabelle. Her mood soured, and her frustration simmered as she walked.

It wasn't fair that she had to worry about saving the forest while the adults did nothing about it. *They should care more about global warming and less about money. They ought to be doing every-*

thing they can to save the forest. Someday, I'll be a grown-up. But that's a long way off. Annabelle's jaw was clenched as she looked down at the trail, walking faster.

She had always cared for what was vulnerable: small birds that fell from their nests, homeless people without warm clothing, and kids who were bullied at school, like her cousin Federico. Her mom called her a *protector*. She called it being a decent human. Sparkpuff stopped and sniffed a patch of grass.

The rant in Annabelle's mind continued. The Earth was warming, and it would cause all kinds of problems for people, animals, and plants, but it didn't need to happen! Her fuming thoughts provided momentum for a fast walk home.

MEANWHILE, in a less visible corner of the forest, Lola the Genii Loci faery of the area adjusted her leafy skirt and peeked from behind a cottonwood trunk.

She'd placed an ancient skeleton key on the dusty ground in a clearing among the trees. Her tiny wings buzzed excitedly, blending with the sound of the wind rustling through the leaves and the distant calls of birds. She was dressed in a skirt fashioned from layered, spring-green cottonwood leaves that flared outward like an upside-down tulip. Her tiara of braided tiny coyote willow branches, adorned with delicate blue flax and scarlet globemallow flowers, was slightly askew.

She waited behind a giant cottonwood trunk, keeping watch over the key. She knew that the key's sparkle would attract the crows. But it was meant for one particular crow. There were serious plans for the key, but there was no harm in having a bit of fun with it first. Mischievousness in direct proportion to seriousness was the law of Faery Land.

Lola didn't have to wait long. Marsilio, a bold and curious young crow, eyed the key with both suspicion and desire from the air. He swooped down for a closer look. As a young male crow, he held a rather high opinion of himself. He prided himself on always being ready for a challenge, and though the key was large—larger than anything he would usually attempt to pick up—it was somehow irresistible. He observed it on the ground, his head tilted.

He pecked at the key first, then tried to pick it up, but as soon as he secured it in his clawed feet, he couldn't fly. It felt as heavy as a small car. He let go and moved it with his beak; it was light, like a feather. The handsome young crow tilted his head. Again, he tried to lift the key, this time using his beak, and once more it became leaden, almost as if mocking him. Frustration began to rise within him. It didn't make sense, and the more he couldn't lift it, the more he wanted to.

Lola watched from behind the tree as Marsilio attempted to lift the key several times. "Not for you," she whispered, giggling behind her hand.

The crow pair, Roanoke and Delphinia, flew by overhead. They were also attracted to the faint sparkle of the key and circled back to investigate. Roanoke landed lightly on the ground with his wings outstretched, tucked them in, and politely greeted the young crow. Marsilio bowed his head and ceded his interest in the key to the older bird, flying up to a low branch to watch.

Roanoke picked up the key in his clawed feet, flapped his wings, and lifted into the sky. Marsilio's beak dropped open.

In the air, Roanoke felt in the flow of a larger plan. He knew exactly where the key belonged and flew straight to Annabelle's backyard. He landed on the stone birdbath while Delphinia waited on a high branch nearby. Roanoke carefully set the key at the water's edge, then flew up to join Delphinia to wait for Annabelle's return.

WHEN ANNABELLE GOT HOME, she took off Sparkpuff's harness and made sure he had water and food. Then she checked the backyard bird feeder and scattered some seed on the ground for the crows. While filling the birdbath with the hose, she noticed something unusual—something old and metal that hadn't been there before. She reached down to pick it up.

It was an old key with an ornate top. The top formed a circle that curled in on itself. The key had a thick stem with two projections at the bottom designed to fit into a lock. *An antique skeleton key?* She had seen pictures of them but had never encountered a real one.

She wondered where it might have come from. She surmised it must be another gift from the crows. But where had they found it? She looked at it closely, appreciating its weight. She felt a strange pull as she held the key, as if it wanted to guide her somewhere. She wondered what it might unlock. She recalled the recent afternoon visiting Tia Joan. *She mentioned a key and Ms. Barnes. And then, at home, I saw the Heirophant card from the tarot had two keys.* The memory made it feel like this key was part of a bigger, mysterious story unfolding.

As Annabelle examined the key, two crows watched from their perch above her, their black eyes gleaming with intelligence. This gift was more than just a symbol of their affection; it held faery magic and a commitment from another time. Moreover, it contained the possibility of a different future.

Looking at the key reminded Annabelle of the baby crow she had once cared for. She had found it on the ground, having fallen from its nest, its beak opening and closing to reveal its pink mouth. A kind man, William Hendricks from the animal rescue organization, taught her how to feed the hatchling and keep it safe until it was ready to return to the wild.

Annabelle wondered if that same crow might have brought her the key. Crows had been delivering gifts to her for years, likely because she had always fed them. One of her earliest memories was when she was two or three years old: a large black bird hopping behind her on the ground as she ran, laughing and looking back, dropping crumbs of bread for him. Annabelle smiled, recalling the pure delight of that moment. It felt as though they were playing a game.

Early on, her mother recognized that the crows were the source of the objects that arrived at the bird bath, so she began saving the trinkets in a designated box. As Annabelle grew older, the collection expanded to include small pieces of lost jewelry, pop tops, mirror shards, and colored glass fragments. Annabelle kept the box of crow gift treasures in her closet and continued to add to it regularly.

She recalled the time her mother lost an earring. A few days later, it appeared at the birdbath. She could never forget the shock on her mother's face as she said, "Did they know it was my earring, and did they return it to me?" Annabelle just shrugged her shoulders. *It was obvious, wasn't it?*

ANNABELLE WAS unaware that Lola was watching from nearby, congratulating herself on a well-executed plan. *Phase One: Complete. Phase Two: Well, that would be interesting.* However, the key had at least found its way into the right hands. The forest's future now relied on a young girl learning to talk to crows and a timid librarian with anxiety. *Ah, well, you work with what you have and hope for the best.*

CHAPTER 13

It was Saturday afternoon, and Ezra would arrive in about an hour to open the trunk in the attic. Iris decided to tackle the forgiveness exercise from meditation class. She stared at the blank page of her journal, as one would at an open wound. *Time to try the forgiveness exercise. Again. Third time's the charm.*

She followed Joan's advice, starting with the easiest things to forgive and gradually working up to the bigger issues. She'd decided to put the ex-husband forgiveness project, XHFP for short, on hold until after she talked with Joan in a few days.

The weight of past mistakes and regrets pressed heavily on her chest. A tight knot of resistance coiled in her heart, refusing to loosen. Memories surfaced unbidden—her mother's disappointed face, the sharp sting of a hurtful remark she had made to an old friend, and the time she turned away when someone needed her. The knot pulled tighter. But as she sat with her breath and Xena's warm presence on her lap, with the sound of purring filling the room like an incantation, the hard places inside began to soften. Each breath slowly unraveled a little more guilt and shame, weights she had carried for far too long.

Forgiving herself was the most challenging part. It always had been. But a quiet part of her understood it was the key to moving forward. She remained with it, allowing the flicker of forgiveness to grow, to take root, to radiate outward from her heart. A warmth surrounded her, the same presence she had felt in meditation class, but now she could swear it emanated from the fluffy cat on her lap.

Iris felt a ping of love flowing back and forth between her and Xena. A cloud of stillness and affection surrounded her. Iris opened her eyes and gently ran a hand over Xena's fur. *Are all cats this magical?* If so, everyone should have one, she decided.

A chime rang through the air—the doorbell. Iris blinked, breaking the spell of her meditation. She got up from the couch and opened the door to find Ezra wearing an Iron Man T-shirt and holding a small bag of tools.

"Hey, I'm here to open the treasure chest!"

Iris laughed. "Great! Thanks again for being willing to help me out with this."

"I'm hoping for a trunk of gold coins, but stacks of money from an old bank heist would be okay, too." Ezra smiled.

"Yeah, that would be sweet." Iris was momentarily distracted by the thought of what it would be like to suddenly be rich. She snapped out of her reverie and said, "I like Iron Man, by the way."

Ezra replied with the iconic Marvel comics line, "I still believe in heroes." This went over Iris's head.

"Mmmm," she murmured, thinking ahead to the dusty attic.

"I brought the essentials: flashlight, lock kit, screwdriver, and, because you never know, a protein bar."

"For emergencies?" Iris asked.

He nodded solemnly. "Like if we get stuck in the attic."

That made her laugh. "You joke, but the ladder to get up there is pretty rickety. If it broke, we could get stuck up there for who knows how long." She led Ezra to the hallway and pulled down the ladder. "Here it is. Watch your step. You only have one protein bar, and I'm right behind you."

The attic swallowed them in a breath of dry heat and silence thick with the smell of dust and forgotten things. Ezra had to crouch slightly to avoid hitting his head on the ceiling. His eyes adjusted to the dim light as he knelt in front of the trunk. Iris stood behind him in anticipation, watching and hoping he would succeed.

As Ezra worked on the lock, the silence was occasionally punctuated by the creak of the old house settling. He cycled through his tools. Nothing worked until he felt something give with a metallic click. But when he tried to lift the lid, the trunk still wouldn't open.

He frowned. "Hold on..." he ran his fingers along the back. "There's another lock." He swiveled the trunk around, creating a scraping sound on the attic floor.

"This trunk is harder to get into than my front door!"

Ezra half-smiled. "Yeah, most things are. This trunk is well-constructed. Okay, I got it. " He pried open the lid, lifting it off the trunk.

The trunk released a musty breath as if exhaling the past. Excited, they both leaned over to peer inside. Iris covered her mouth and sneezed twice, but she didn't want to look away.

It was hard to see in the dimly lit attic, but Iris could make out old paper files and stacks of black-and-white photos. With their shoulders touching, they carefully lifted the brittle, yellowed papers and curled photographs out of the trunk and stacked them on the floor. At the bottom of the trunk was a layer of white fluff, delicate and weightless. *Cottonwood seeds*. This spring, Iris had marveled at how the cottonwood seeds resembled snow floating on the breeze and scattering everywhere. Nestled among the cottonwood fluff at the bottom of the trunk were three black feathers and a beeswax candle with the letters F.I.S carved into the wax.

"Why would Ella have saved cottonwood seeds?" Iris murmured. She touched the candle lightly. Her fingers traced the initial F.I.S. Was it a name, a code? It felt important.

Ezra was quiet. Mystery hung in the air.

Iris shook off the trance of opening the trunk. "Well, it's clear this trunk was Ella's. Let's get these things downstairs to look at them where it's cooler and where there's more light." They carried everything downstairs and settled on the rug beside the coffee table.

"Whew!" Iris fanned her face from the heat of the attic. The air conditioning on the main floor of the house provided relief. Cottonwood was already nearing 90 degrees during the day.

She glanced at Ezra. "More mystery than answers so far."

He nodded, looking at the photos and papers piled around them. "I get the feeling that's going to be the theme."

Iris and Ezra began flipping through what appeared to be legal documents. The stack of papers and folders stood at least a foot high.

"This is going to take a while," Ezra said, flipping through a few pages.

"I was hoping to find something about the preserve," Iris admitted, "but that might have to wait." She set aside the papers and reached for the stack of photographs. "Let's look at these."

Ezra picked up the top photo, being careful to hold it by its edges. They both leaned in. The image showed Iris's front porch, nearly unchanged except for a dirt road out front. But what made her stomach flip was the cat.

There was a long-haired black cat sitting at the base of the front steps, and the resemblance to Xena was uncanny. This wasn't just a lookalike; it felt as though time had folded in on itself, allowing the past to reach out and touch the present. She stared at the photo, disoriented.

"Wow. That cat looks *exactly* like Xena," Ezra said. "See? The same notch in the right ear. That is one strange coincidence."

Iris scanned the room for Xena, who was usually ever-present, but she was nowhere to be seen. She looked at the photo again and would swear that the cat in the photo was the same cat who watched her make breakfast that morning.

They turned back to the stack of photos, and Ezra held up the next one. It was taken in the cottonwood forest near the Rio Grande River. Five women in dresses that brushed the earth, some wearing hats, surrounded a tree, clasping hands as they looked up into its branches.

Iris's eyes landed on one of the women. "She looks like Ella," she whispered. Ezra studied the image, squinting his eyes.

Iris flipped to the next photo. The same five women sat in a circle in the woods. A light illuminated the center of the circle, though the source of the light remained invisible.

Iris frowned. "That light in the middle- where is it coming from?"

Ezra squinted. "Probably some old photography effect." But then he hesitated. "Wait. Do you see that shape in there?"

"I see it." She got closer, searching for an explanation. She shook her head.

Her eyes widened at the next photo. In the heart of the circle, two winged figures hovered. Initially, they appeared to Iris to be large butterflies, but then she noticed they had faces. Human faces. Luminescent, impossible, real.

Ezra and Iris exchanged glances. Iris felt a cool sensation on the back of her neck as the hairs stood on end. Too shocked to speak for different reasons, they thumbed through the rest of the photos. The room hummed with energy.

All the photos were taken in the nearby woods, and many contained images of what appeared to be faeries. They were flying beings with wings and clothing made of woven leaves and flowers, featuring playful expressions on oval faces. The images looked impossibly real. The faeries had delicate wings and luminous auras that seemed to pulse even in the stillness of the old images. The photos looked far too old to be fakes, but too fantastical to be real. What else could they be, if not faeries?

Iris was the first to speak, her voice slow and disbelieving, "What… the…hell?" Her mind grappled with the possibilities. *Photoshop didn't exist back then. This couldn't be a hoax. Or could it? They looked legitimately old. Could someone have staged this?*

"Iris," Ezra said, his voice quiet, "I have to tell you something. I'm not sure you'll believe me."

Iris tensed. The weight in Ezra's voice sent a prickle of unease through her. "Okaaay."

Ezra took a breath, and Iris could see hesitation in his eyes. Then she noticed him sitting up taller. "I used to see them," he said. He pointed to one of the photos. "These faeries."

The words hung in the air between them— impossible and undeniable.

Iris blinked. A wash of goosebumps spread up her arms. "What?"

"Iris, I've never told anyone about this." His eyes were shadowed not with wonder or excitement but with sorrow.

Iris searched his face. Was this a joke? But his expression didn't have even a flicker of humor, just intensity. And pain.

"I thought I'd never see them again," he added softly, looking down.

Iris felt her brain lock up. This was absurd. This was not normal. Her rational mind flailed for footing. Was he hallucinating? Delusional? She didn't know him that well. What if he were unstable?

But then she looked back at the photos. They were too vivid, too strange, too real. If he were making it up, why did she feel like the room itself had shifted?

She swallowed hard. "This is… a lot. So, what— you're saying faeries are *real*?"

Ezra nodded. "Iris, when I was 11 years old, my best friend, Leo, died in a car accident. It was awful when he died. I went into the forest for comfort, to see my friends, the faeries, but they were gone. I never saw them again. My friend died, and the faeries disappeared on the same day. I've never felt so lonely. I still look for faeries in the woods, but I've never seen them again. I almost started to doubt they were real. Until today." Ezra searched Iris's face.

At that moment, Xena padded in, brushing against Ezra's leg. She lay down next to him. Ezra and Iris studied Xena closely before finding the old photo of the cat. They shifted their gazes from the photo to Xena and back again. Then, they looked at each other, but neither spoke.

Finally, Iris said, "I feel like I have to tell you something now. About the Bosque development and… Ella."

Ezra's eyes locked on hers, waiting.

She told him everything about the day she found out the bosque was for sale, how she didn't want to get involved, but then Annabelle's grief pushed her forward.

She shared what she discovered about Ella, the preserve, and the taxes. And how the lawyer, Eric Sutter, died suspiciously, and then his office burned down, destroying all his records. And then after she met with Blair, the widow, a rock had flown through her window with a note telling her to stay away.

Worry passed over Ezra's face.

Iris pointed to the photo of Ella on the mantel. "Somehow, I think she wants me to get involved. I know this sounds totally crazy." Ezra nodded in encouragement for her to continue. "I think Ella wants me to save the Cottonwood Preserve."

Saying it all out loud felt both terrifying and right.

Ezra turned to look at the picture on the mantel and studied Ella's face. "I think you're right. And I think the faeries are involved. Obviously, they knew Ella."

"This is all a lot to take in. Faeries…" Iris shook her head.

They were both quiet for a few moments.

Ezra's expression turned uneasy. "Iris, you need to tread carefully. You could be in danger. If someone actually killed for this development, and they know you're nosing around..." His voice trailed off.

The photos in Iris's hands felt heavier now, thick with a responsibility she hadn't asked for. *What had she gotten herself into?* Maybe she should have just let the trunk stay locked in the attic.

Iris was stubborn, not brave. Yet her stubbornness might have to be enough because something greater than herself— something invisible yet undeniable-was pushing her to get to the bottom of this mystery: faeries, developers, a murder, a young girl's grief, and a woman long dead reaching out from the past.

Iris lifted her chin resolutely. "Cottonwood is my home now," she said softly with steel in her spine. "For Annabelle and Ella and for the future of the Preserve, I *have* to try."

Ezra reluctantly nodded. "I get the feeling I can't stop you. But Iris, call me if you need me, and please be very careful."

Iris nodded. "I will." But inside, she believed this was her battle, and she needed to do this alone.

Xena

As we already know, faeries are as real as the breeze. Ezra remembers, and that kind of memory has a scent—grief, moss, old leaves, truth. I smelled it on him the moment he stepped through the door.

The world is harsh on the sensitive. Many children can see through the veil until the world trains them to look away. It's simply the current agreement regarding this world and the Otherworld: a forgetting baked into the contract of growing up. Most forget completely, while others, like Ezra, remember just enough for sadness to shadow them for a lifetime.

Iris is different. Her mind has been trained to doubt, but her heart? Her heart knows. The photos are a nudge to prepare her for what is to come. Ezra's story supports her fragile, tentative belief.

My role? I'm her compass when logic fails. Her whiskered whisperer between worlds. I am Iris's guide to seeing the world in its fullness and truth. The faeries have given the cosmic thumbs up to release these photos now. That makes it Iris's turn to step into her destiny. Trust me when I tell you she has an abundance of assistance, seen and unseen, cheering her on from both sides of the veil. She will never be alone in this battle, no matter what she thinks.

And was that me in that photo? Hmmm. As an agent of the ineffable, I cannot confirm or deny.

CHAPTER 14

It was a warm morning, and Iris sat on the couch, her knees folded to the side, sipping iced tea. She combed through the legal files she and Ezra had discovered in the trunk. Some of them were unreadable; the ink had faded with age, while others resembled business ledgers filled with columns of figures. There were notes from New Mexico Bar Association meetings, and reading them, Iris learned that Ella was the bar association's secretary, note-taker, and a stickler for ensuring members paid their dues. Iris smiled, pleased to have discovered something about Ella's personality.

But then she came across a faded paper written in calligraphy with dark brown ink. She could tell it had been created with a fountain pen due to the occasional ink blobs. Deciphering it wasn't easy, but it was a membership certificate. In very curlicue script, it read:

The Faery Investigative Society

Ella Ross: Member

In Good Standing 1919

The Faery Investigative Society? Huh? Iris decided to type this into her search window on her laptop just for kicks. Surprisingly, she discovered a very minimal website. It consisted of one page in plain text and had no images. It read:

For inquiries:

Please see Valerian Rose

513 1/4 Rio Grande Boulevard.

She had some time on her hands this weekend. She would pay a visit to the Faery Investigative Society. Xena walked across the living room rug, her tail held high like a flag, and jumped onto the coffee table in front of Iris.

"Well, what do you think, warrior princess? Is this a good idea?" Xena made her signature chirp, which seemed like an answer in the affirmative.

Iris wondered if she should mention this to Ezra. Maybe he would like to come with her, but she felt shy about calling him. Anyway, he had a girlfriend, and she didn't want to seem like she was chasing him. She would do this herself.

DRIVING DOWN RIO GRANDE BOULEVARD, Iris looked for the address 513 1/4. She didn't see it. She turned around and drove past again. Those numbers did not exist. The numbers went from 511 to 515. There was no 513, much less a 513 1/4. Hmmph. *Oh well, it's probably an internet prankster's idea of a joke.*

Just then, her phone rang. It was Ezra. She picked up. "Hey, you'll never guess what I'm doing."

"Hmm, if I'll never guess, you should probably tell me."

"Okay, I'm driving around trying to find the Faery Investigative Society."

"The what? Uh, no, I heard you."

"But I can't find it. I think it's a joke."

"What's the address?"

"513 1/4 Rio Grande Boulevard."

"Iris, I don't think that's a joke. Come pick me up, and we'll look together."

Iris pulled up to his Old Town apartment less than five minutes later. Ezra slid into the passenger seat, a spark of curiosity lighting up his face.

"I've been thinking," he said. "Remember the letters carved on that candle from the trunk?"

"F-I-S," Iris recalled. Then her eyes widened. "Faery Investigative Society?"

"Could be."

Focusing on the road, Iris said, "Ezra, I passed it three times. It goes from 511 to 515. There is no 513."

"Okay, but let's try again. I'll look. Sometimes, it helps if you're not driving." Iris couldn't argue with that. Driving back to the area, she stole a glance at Ezra. He seemed calm enough, but there was an energy about him. A charge humming beneath the surface.

An unspoken bond was developing between them. After discovering the photographs, they shared a secret that solidified their connection. She wondered if his girlfriend, Molly, was aware of the faeries.

Ezra pointed, "There it is!" And lo and behold, there was a narrow gravel road with a tiny white sign and an arrow pointing to 513 1/4. The address numbers shimmered a bit in the morning light.

"What? I feel like I'm losing it. This was absolutely not here a minute ago." In trying to make sense of this, Iris wondered again whether something was wrong with her vision.

Ezra's eyebrows raised, and he smiled. "Mmm."

As she turned down the inconspicuous gravel road, Iris felt the familiar flutter of anxiety stir in her chest, but she swatted it away and slipped into Nancy Drew mode instead, allowing her curiosity to overshadow her worry. She parked the car in front of a small adobe casita, the color of the muddy Rio Grande River. The air had a charged density, as if they were stepping across an invisible threshold. She was unexpectedly grateful Ezra had joined her, even though she hadn't planned on bringing him; his steady presence anchored her.

Walking under a large cottonwood tree, they approached the arched, wooden front door. They knocked, waited, and then knocked again. Some rustling could be heard inside. They looked at each other.

The door creaked open to reveal a tanned woman, roughly in her mid-sixties. Her striking silver-white hair was swept into a regal pile atop her head, held in place by antique hair combs shaped like crescent moons. She wore a flowing white dress embroidered with a gold agave bloom that shimmered as she moved. A heavy turquoise necklace lay against her chest like a protective talisman, its blue-green stones a striking contrast to her earth-toned complexion.

She peered over her round, metallic gold glasses with a knowing gleam in her eye. "Well now," she said, her voice like warm wind through dry leaves, "what have we here?"

Iris and Ezra stuck out their hands. "I'm Ezra."

"And I'm Iris."

Valerian Rose took each of their hands in turn. "And I am Valerian. Valerian Rose. I'm pleased to meet you. I haven't had visitors in a very long time, but I just baked some scones. Please come in, and I'll make a pot of tea." She turned and walked inside.

Iris and Ezra looked at each other, and Iris shrugged her shoulders as they entered the home. Iris noticed the slight, pleasing musical lilt in Valerian's voice as if she were half speaking and half singing. The smell of vanilla and warm butter mingled with the fragrance of the cottonwood tree outside as they entered.

Iris looked around and saw that the house appeared much bigger on the inside. The ceiling was higher than she had anticipated. In the middle of the room, a large table was covered with a white tablecloth and illuminated with candles. A centerpiece made of black feathers, red pomegranates, and green leafy branches caught her eye. It seemed like quite a presentation for someone not expecting visitors.

The room was decorated with heavy tapestries in gold and shades of green depicting cottonwood trees filled with birds and river scenes with cranes and coyotes. The flickering candlelight cast dancing shadows on the tapestries, making the scenes appear alive.

Valerian interrupted Iris's thoughts, "And are you members?" She looked over the top of her round glasses at them once more. "Because I haven't taken any new members, in well," she glanced up at the ceiling beams, "well, I guess that would have been 1963." Iris quickly calculated in her head and concluded that Valerian must be older than 65—perhaps 75 or even 80.

Iris and Ezra were directed to sit across from each other at the long table. Something very strange was happening, and Iris felt somehow outside the normal flow of time. Something was off, but she couldn't quite put her finger on what it was. She knew the house felt too large, the ceiling too high, and the tapestries too grand, but there was something else.

"Here we are." Valerian floated in carrying a willow basket filled with warm scones, butter, and prickly pear jam, along with small golden plates, forks, and knives. Then she took her seat at the head of the table between them. Ezra dug into his scone and, surprisingly, had nothing to say in this peculiar situation.

Iris remembered she had brought the Faery Investigative Society certificate from Ella's trunk, so she dug it out of her purse and placed it on the table. Valerian looked at it and made appreciative noises. Iris said, "We found this in an old trunk in the attic of my house. I just moved in a few months ago."

"Ah, yes, Ella. She was a lovely woman."

"You knew her?" Again, Iris found herself doing math in her head. *How old was this woman?* Could she be mistaken about knowing Ella, who died in 1955?

"Oh yes, dear. We were good friends. We went to school together. Law school, that is."

No longer able to stop herself, Iris said, "Pardon me, I don't mean to be rude, but how old are you? Because the Ella Ross we are talking about died in 1955."

"Was it that long ago? Well, what do you know? But she didn't die, dear. She went to live with them," she said with a twinkle in her eye.

Iris looked at Ezra but couldn't catch his gaze. He seemed only to have attention for a second scone. She felt like kicking him under the table, but instead she turned back to Valerian and, shaking her head, said, "You aren't saying she went to live with the faeries, are you?"

Valerian smiled at Iris sweetly. "What else would I mean?"

Valerian's words about Ella living with the faeries hung in the air. Iris wanted to dismiss it all as nonsense, but the photos, the house's sudden appearance, and the feeling of this place made it impossible. She was slipping into a world where reality seemed to bend and twist, and she was starting to think she didn't want any part of it.

Iris gave up and finally took a bite of a scone with butter and jam. It was heavenly. The crust was flaky and golden, and the prickly pear jam created a sweet burst on her tongue. Valerian smiled and nodded, indicating that she should eat more. Iris never thought of herself as a scone person. *But wow.*

Valerian sat back in her chair. "Ella was a dear friend. We were part of the Faery Investigation Society. FIS for short." Her eyes sparkled with nostalgia and pride. "I was the founder, actually." She smiled, warming to the subject. "It's a bit of a long story." Valerian shifted in her chair, lifted her scone from the golden plate, took a bite, and wiped her mouth delicately with her napkin.

"FIS was founded in the early 1900s and was dedicated to maintaining the delicate balance between our world and the

Otherworld. We documented faery interactions and worked to preserve the Cottonwood forest from encroaching threats. We also worshipped the trees.

"We would go to the forest, bringing offerings and prayers to the cottonwood trees. We weren't the first ones to do that. People had been doing that for years here, long before us. We simply joined in.

"The cottonwoods are wise trees, very deserving of our devotion. But then the faeries started showing up. They convinced us, Ella and I, that the forest needed saving. It needed to be *preserved*. So, being lawyers, we set something up, you know."

Iris wanted to blurt out that she couldn't have done that. That was over a hundred years ago! But she kept quiet. She continued to eat her scone, feeling transported with every bite.

Ezra looked up. "I have one question." Iris and Valerian looked at him, having almost forgotten he was there. "Do you still see them? The faeries?"

Valerian said, "Well, of course."

"Oh, because I used to see them." He looked at Valerian searchingly. "How do I see them again?"

Valerian paused, closing her eyes as if tuning in to something beyond the room. "You needn't see them, dear. Sometimes the unseen is asking for your trust. That's where the real magic begins."

When she opened her eyes, she said, "It's been lovely to have visitors again. Really, it's been *such* a long time. But I need to attend to some other matters now." Valerian looked at Iris. "And the key should be coming shortly, dear. Be ready."

Iris looked at her, confused. "The key to the trunk? Ezra opened it."

Valerian chuckled softly, as if amused. "Oh, no, dear, not that key. The key to the tree. You'll need to guard it well. It doesn't belong to you. It belongs to *them*."

Iris opened her mouth to ask more, but the moment had

already passed, and Valerian was gently ushering them to the door.

They stepped outside, and as they crossed the threshold, a sudden gust of wind rose, spinning into a tight spiral of light and sand. Iris shielded her eyes against the vortex and walked quickly to the car.

Inside, she turned to Ezra. He said nothing, but his smile was radiant and his eyes were alive with wonder, as though he'd just remembered something he'd always known but had long forgotten.

Iris, not ready to absorb the magic, clung to reason like a lifeline. "Ezra, she couldn't have done all those things with Ella that she claimed. She'd have to be 120 or 130 years old." She furrowed her brow. "But, I wonder if I should have mentioned the Preserve being for sale. Maybe she has some record of the trust or the preserve that would be helpful for us now." Iris felt a pang of regret at a missed opportunity. *Oh well, they could always return.*

Ezra, still smiling, said, "Iris, I don't think she has any records. And I don't believe that place will exist if we try to return there tomorrow."

"What? Of course, it will."

Ezra turned to look at her. "What time do you think we went into that house?"

Iris looked up. "Hmm, maybe 3:30."

"And how long were we there?"

"It seems like we were there for maybe 30 minutes at most." Iris looked at the clock on her dashboard. It was 6:35 p.m. *How could that be?* "We were there for over three hours! Where did all that time go? That doesn't make sense! NOTHING about that place made sense!" Iris said, her bewilderment finding expression in anger.

Ezra shrugged his shoulders. "Do you know what a glamour is?" Iris shook her head. "It's this power that faeries have to create beautiful spaces and experiences that warp time. I've experienced it before." Ezra looked toward the horizon.

Iris felt the need to put her foot down. "Ezra, Valerian Rose is not a faery. She is a sweet, slightly confused old lady who has very nice plates. I don't think it was anything more than that." Iris was making her last stand for normality.

"Uh-huh. Did you taste those scones?"

Iris nodded, closing her eyes. "Yeah, I think they serve those in heaven."

"Exactly. Heaven, the Otherworld, land of the dead, beyond the veil, whatever you want to call it. But they're not of this world."

IRIS DROVE down Rio Grande Boulevard the following day to prove to herself that the little house at 513 1/4 existed. She felt silly, but she needed to protect her sanity. Of course, it existed. She was there. She ate a scone, for goodness' sake.

Iris slowed down at 509 and slowed down more at 511. The cars behind her got closer, and the drivers became more agitated as she inched forward, not seeing 513. Now, this was getting ridiculous.

She turned and parked the car on a side street, got out, and walked the length of Rio Grande Boulevard from 519 back to 509. There was no little white sign. No gravel road. A large cottonwood tree stood where she remembered the house being, its leaves whispering secrets in the breeze she couldn't hear. But there was no house. It was gone. It had been there, and now it was gone.

Iris walked back and forth one more time, taking some deep breaths. She had a headache. She got out her phone and searched again for the Faery Investigative Society. She couldn't find the website. That's it. She was going crazy, and this was all too much.

Back in her car, she stared blankly at the fading daylight. She wondered if she should see a doctor.

AT HOME, she took some aspirin. *Maybe tomorrow, things will make more sense.* She entered her bedroom, closed the curtains, and went into a deep, dreamless sleep with Xena curled up at her feet.

XENA

Poor Iris. But it is better for this to happen sooner rather than later. The Otherworld is full of tricks, but it is completely real. There is a membrane, or some like to say, more poetically, a veil that separates you from it. Some can travel easily back and forth, like the Fae. But the veil is thinning, and the messages from the Otherworld are becoming harder to ignore for even very *normal* people.

In ancient times, the Fae lived exclusively in this world. However, with the arrival of humans and the Fae's discovery of the doorways to the Otherworld, they began to live in both worlds. They remain unwilling to give up their existence in either place. So they retain access to both.

There are many different groups with access to the Otherworld that I will not list here. However, I will mention the dead since Ella plays a large role in the story. The Otherworld is a misnomer, in a way. It is this world, set at a slightly different frequency on the dial. Like a cool jazz station, 95.5 FM, while you're stuck living in heavy metal 95.7 FM.

So when Valerian said that Ella went to live with the faeries, she was correct. And when Iris noted that Ella had died, well, she was also correct. Hopefully, you get the idea.

This is mind-bending for someone like Iris, who has lived her entire life as a solid materialist with a dash of intuition thrown in. This is an Olympic-level jump in worldview. Her path is only beginning, but things are happening fast, and she has upcoming obligations. The key is coming, and with it, all the responsibility that entails, so her development is being sped along. And yours truly is an integral part of that.

CHAPTER 15

Annabelle lay on the living room floor, her feet resting on the couch, one of her favorite ways to relax. The rug was soft, and she spent many hours here reading and thinking. Usually, Sparkpuff was by her side, but today, he was in her room, sleeping on her bed and taking advantage of the quiet. Her dad was at work, and her mom was running errands, so the house was unusually still.

Her thoughts lingered on the forest, as they often did lately. She closed her eyes, envisioning the rustling of the cottonwoods, the scent of earth after a monsoon, and the calls of the owls at night. The idea of bulldozers plowing through it all sent a sharp ache through her chest, as if the loss had already inflicted its wound in her heart.

She wondered if the adults, except for Tia Joan, truly understood the gravity of it all. She was frustrated by their lack of urgency and focus. She hoped they could manage to stop the development, but doubt gnawed at her. *What if they couldn't?* Hope felt like a luxury she couldn't afford. She had to do everything she could. She had already written letters to the mayor and the city council members, imploring them to reconsider the development. She persuaded her mom, dad, and Tia to write, too. She was determined to do *everything* she could.

A loud tap, tap, tap, tap, interrupted her thoughts. The sound echoed through the quiet house like a heartbeat, pulling Annabelle from her reverie. She blinked and looked toward the sliding glass door. There, staring back at her with black, intelligent eyes, was a crow. His head tilted slightly as if waiting for her to respond. Annabelle felt an instant connection to the crow, a sense of recognition. Memories of her recent afternoon with Tia Joan and the scrying bowl sprang to her mind. Intrigued, she got up and walked toward the door, mesmerized by the bird.

Meanwhile, Sparkpuff, awakened by the loud tapping, headed toward the kitchen, his thoughts on food and the possibility of crumbs on the floor. However, he was taken aback when he saw the large black crow at the glass door near Annabelle.

With the fierce determination of a knight protecting his castle, he charged to the glass. His bark echoed through the house with the intensity called for if the house were being robbed, on fire, and Annabelle was being taken hostage all at once. No big black bird was coming near his house like that. Sparkpuff only mildly tolerated the crows in the yard, but this was too much. It was an affront.

"Sparkpuff, no, no, no!" Annabelle yelled. But it was too late, the spell was shattered. Feathers flapped wildly as the crow took off, leaving behind only the nagging feeling that something important had just slipped through her fingers.

Sparkpuff wagged triumphantly, his tiny chest puffed up with pride. He looked at Annabelle, his eyes round with expectation. His delight at saving Annabelle from imminent danger was adorable and irresistible.

"Yes, yes, you're very brave," Annabelle said, unable to be mad at the sincere dog. She laughed and scooped him up. "Don't you know that crows are our friends? Hmmm?" She kissed the top of his head. Holding Sparkpuff close, she looked out the window, wondering what would have happened if Sparkpuff hadn't barked his head off like that.

IN HIS ENTHUSIASM TO make contact, Roanoke didn't factor in the dog's presence. Although this opportunity didn't pan out, crows are nothing if not persistent; he would wait for another chance. He shook out his feathers, trying to dispel the lingering adrenaline rush. Perched high in a cottonwood tree, Roanoke surveyed the city below. It stretched out like a patchwork quilt of streets and rooftops.

The crow elder, Serafina, gracefully landed next to him, causing the branch to sway slightly under her weight. She regarded Roanoke calmly as she listened to his retelling of the failed attempt at contact. Her voice was soothing. "Patience, Roanoke," she said, her feathers ruffling gently in the breeze. "The bond between our kind and the humans has been dormant for too long. Rekindling it will require time. We knew it would be difficult." Roanoke nodded in understanding.

As she looked toward the city, Serafina seemed to decide something. "I believe we should enlist the help of the Fae for the first contact."

"The Fae? Are you certain?"

Sarafina nodded slowly, her gaze unwavering. "Their connection to the Otherworld is strong. They excel at this sort of thing, and time is not a luxury we possess."

Bringing in the Fae felt to Roanoke like an admission of failure. He had never been fond of them. Serious and steadfast by nature, he had little patience for mischief, and even less for humor that came at someone else's expense. To him, the Fae were wild cards—unpredictable and often skirting the edge of cruelty. And yet, he couldn't deny that they were also a force of raw creation, born of ancient magic and, at their core, rooted in love.

He recalled a time he had accidentally wandered into Fae

territory and was tricked into believing there were pecans scattered on the ground. Every time he went to peck one open, it would roll away a few inches, and he would be pecking dirt. He left as soon as he realized where he was, but the lesson stayed with him.

"Alright, Sarafina. Whatever you think is best," he said, masking his reluctance.

"It will be Lola who will meet you in the forest." Inwardly, Roanoke groaned, but he feigned agreement on the surface. "I know she can be difficult, but she is strong and skilled. I believe her involvement will greatly facilitate contact." Roanoke nodded again. "You are doing well, Roanoke. The Elders and Grandmother Cottonwood appreciate your efforts. Time is running short. May you be successful."

"I will do my best," Roanoke replied, though he couldn't shake the uneasy feeling settling in his chest. The Fae were powerful but capricious, and he had never fully trusted them. Lola, in particular, was known for her sharp wit and even sharper tongue. He glanced toward the horizon, where dark clouds were gathering. He understood the stakes were too high to let his personal feelings interfere.

Roanoke flew back to Delphinia to their usual night roost. Perched side by side he recounted his conversation with the elder Sarafina. Delphinia thought for a moment and then said, "Roanoke, I have faith in your abilities and relationship with Annabelle. We know she is an extraordinary child. The two of you, together, will prevail with or without the Fae. But perhaps they can provide a bit of assistance. Trust in that." Roanoke nodded, comforted by Delphinia's words and conviction.

THE QUEENS

Meanwhile, the Fae queens convened, sitting tall on their thrones in a circle in the Cottonwood forest. The canopy of the

Cottonwood's heart-shaped leaves shaded the circle. Purple and blue orbs of light floated amongst them, pulsing gently with the rhythm of the forest.

Each Queen embodied a force of the natural world, their dominions spanning continents and oceans; their influence was interwoven into the fabric of the living earth. They had received Crow Elder Sarafina's request and had agreed that something was dangerously out of balance, and its ramifications impacted them all.

After a long-winded discussion with the usual debates and tangents, including whether humans still deserved mushrooms, the Fae Queen of the Mycological World, eager to move things along, cut to the chase in her usual fashion. "So, to summarize, we are helping the crows, to help the humans, to help the trees?" Her eyes glowed blue under her dark cloak.

"Yes, indeed." The Fae Queen of the Trees strummed her bark-entwined fingers on the moss-covered arms of her throne. "Interconnection is always the way nature works best."

The Fae Queen of the Flower Realm adjusted the golden blooms framing her radiant face. "And it is agreed to send Lola then? She is the faery genii loci of the Cottonwood Bosque. It is her territory." She pursed her lips. "But she is young, can be impulsive, and is prone to… a creative interpretation of orders."

Lola was just over 1,000 years old, barely an infant in faery years.

"Oh please," the Mycological Queen sighed, waving her hand dismissively. "Lola is smart and a firecracker, but so are we all. What is the point of eternity if not to stir the pot once in a while?"

The Fae Queen of Flowers sniffed, unimpressed. "Very well then. I will summon her."

Moments later, a gust of wind scattered petals and glowing spores as Lola materialized in the center of the circle.

When summoned by the Fae queens, one must not be slow to

respond. Lola flitted in a circle, gazing at each Fae Queen in turn. She was already aware of the plea Grandmother Cottonwood had made to the crows, and their plan to restore the crow-human bond. It was only right that she was called; it was her territory. She puffed up with importance and smiled her most winning smile. "Good day, queens." Following this, she executed an airy curtsey.

The Fae Queen of Trees leaned forward. "Lola, we have called you to request your assistance in the matter of restoring the communication bond between the Crow clan and the humans."

Lola dipped her head in acknowledgment, her wings vibrating to keep her hovering in the air. She already knew all this, of course. The crows were never quiet, and Grandmother Cottonwood's plea had sent ripples throughout the unseen world that could not be ignored.

"We would like you to facilitate their next attempt," the Fae Queen of the Mushrooms added, watching Lola closely. "And oversee the process."

Lola hovered in midair. "Yes, quite. I would be thrilled to do so. It is an honor!" She clasped her hands together in a display of exaggerated enthusiasm. Her true feelings were that the crows were annoying and the humans even more so. But it was her domain, and duty called.

The Flower Queen narrowed her eyes. "You will do it?"

Lola forced a dazzling smile. "Of course. I live to serve."

The Queens ignored her sarcasm. The decision had already been made.

The Tree Queen, feeling more directly connected to the plight of the Cottonwoods, said softly, "This is important, Lola. The forest depends on you."

Lola's wings stilled for a beat, and she bowed deeply.

The Queens nodded in approval. "Then off you go, Lola." The Queen of Flowers waved a delicate hand. Lola vanished in a swirl of light, and for a moment, silence settled over the circle.

The Fae Queen of Trees appeared worried. "I do hope she is up to the task." The light in the faery circle dimmed for a moment.

The Mycological Queen chuckled. "Oh, she'll do it, no doubt there. The real question is how much delightful chaos will she cause along the way?"

The orbs of light flickered. A single crow cawed three times in the distance, and the circle dispersed in a whoosh, leaving the forest silent.

CHAPTER 16

On the appointed day, Iris arrived on Joan's street and stepped out of her air-conditioned car. Warm air, laden with the scent of spring flowers, greeted her. She opened the wooden gate, and a crow perched on the adobe wall locked eyes with her.

Iris said, "Hello." The hello seemed to echo, not in the air but in her mind as the crow held her gaze, unmoving. Odd.

She saw Joan in a blue cotton dress, holding a metal watering can by her front door. The flagstone patio was adorned with a trellis of wisteria beginning to bloom, and the scene looked like something lifted from a dream.

Joan, noticing Iris, set her watering can down and ushered the younger woman inside the bright kitchen. "Sit down, sit down." Joan's warm smile and inviting gesture made Iris feel instantly at home. "I'll make tea."

Iris was surprised by the relief she felt upon entering Joan's house. After all the craziness of visiting Valerian Rose at the Faery Investigative Society, this place felt solid and real. She took a seat at the sturdy old wooden kitchen table pushed against the window. She noticed the spider plants cascading down from the fridge. More plants hung from macramé hangers, and although the boho look was back in style, Iris sensed that Joan had never left it behind. A crystal dangled from a string, gently twirling in the window and catching the eastern light.

The kettle whistled on the stove, and Joan poured steaming water into a blue ceramic teapot. "It's herb tea. Spearmint from the back garden," she offered as she delivered a ramekin of honey to the table along with one of those wooden spiral instruments used to deliver honey to a cup. Iris picked it up, inspecting it like a curious artifact.

"I heard you keep bees," Iris said, partly to postpone discussing what was on her mind.

"I do," Joan smiled and nodded. "The bees are good company. I had the hive at your place, and Ezra helped me move it here. They tell me they are happy, but who wouldn't be? Sticking their faces into flowers all day."

Iris laughed as Joan poured the tea into mismatched mugs. She brought the spearmint tea toward her nose, appreciating the minty steam. Breathing deeply, she felt her sinuses clear from the recent dusty winds. Iris decided to ask something she had been wondering about. "I'm just curious: Why did you sell the Silver Street house and move here?"

Joan wrapped her hands around the warm mug of tea. "Oh, my folks owned this house. My dad died a few years ago, and my mother just last year."

Iris looked up from her teacup and said, "Oh, I'm sorry, Joan. I didn't know that."

"Yes, and this was the house I grew up in." Joan waved her hand in a circular motion. "When it came down to it, I couldn't sell it. So I sold the Silver Street house and moved in here. I was ready for a change and to be closer to the river. And it's worked out great. I could live here until I die." She lifted the mug and took a sip of tea.

Iris thought Joan spoke unusually easily about death. But then her parents recently passed away. Iris's parents were alive, but like many families, they were never very close.

Iris would call them every month or two to hear about the discomfort of aching knees, how her father couldn't hear well anymore, or how another one of their friends had passed away. She always asked what they were reading. Her dad was inevitably into a historical fiction novel, typically set during the Civil War, which Iris found dreary. Her mother preferred self-improvement books or breezy women's fiction.

Sometimes, her mother would try to give her advice gleaned from the latest self-help craze. She should stand in a Wonder Woman pose for two minutes before asking for a raise, keep a gratitude journal, or create a vision board with cut-out magazine images. Iris felt tired yet slightly relieved when she hung up the phone, having fulfilled her obligation. They meant well. She envied people with close family ties; she just had never felt that way about her family.

"This tea is amazing, Joan." *Like a magical elixir.* It truly was delicious—better than any herbal tea she'd ever had. *Maybe it was the honey?*

I'll send you home with some. I harvest at the full moon, so it's potent." Joan paused and then said, "How is meditation going? And your forgiveness practice?"

Well, this was the crux of it. "I can't do it, Joan." Iris didn't want to disappoint Joan. She knew forgiveness was important. "I got divorced recently. My husband, uh, ex-husband, cheated on me. It's a wound that's not ready to heal, I guess. I still feel angry and disappointed. I don't want to forgive him. Frankly, I don't wish him well either. I know it's wrong, but I find myself hoping someone betrays him and that he experiences the pain I did."

"Ah, yes, that's honest." Joan peered into her teacup, then looked up. "Of course, you don't forgive for the other person's benefit. It's a gift you give yourself." Those words crystallized into a moment of stillness. Then they filtered through the air like magic dust, finding their way into Iris's chest and making a home there. The words were a potent spell. Iris felt a subtle shift and dismissed it, but forgiveness became more accessible after that day.

Joan watched her closely, then got up and went to the wall of books in the living room. She turned, calling back to the kitchen, "Iris, there's another reason I wanted you to come by before class. I have something for you. But first, I want to show you something."

She retrieved a folder from a high shelf and brought it to the kitchen table.

"You know, you are only the fourth owner of the Silver Street house. First, Ella Ross owned it, then Terry Goodfellow, then me, and now you."

Iris nodded. She recalled Joan's letter about the Silver Street house and the seen and unseen help. This was beginning to make more sense to her, but she had a feeling she had a journey ahead of her to truly understand it.

Joan gestured for Iris to open the folder. Inside, there was a letter typed on thick, old typing paper. Iris looked up at Joan, who waved for her to continue. Iris began to read.

July 22nd 1999

Welcome home!

My understanding is that you have been chosen to live here and to be the keeper of the key. I have kept it this long, but after 55 years, it is time for me to pass it on. I only know a few things.

The key is important. It is a secret, and only the person living in this house can keep it. But the problem is that I have no idea what the key is for! I have tried every door! Sometimes, I admit I get worked up about it. After I moved in, I contacted Ella and tried to ask her about it, but she was very mysterious, saying something about there being a time when it would be needed. I know it belongs here. And someday, it will be of use.

Anyway, this is an exceptional house. Good things happen here—they really do! I am sure you will enjoy it.

This house will be 100 years old in a few years. If you're still living here, please throw it a party!

Most sincerely,

Terry Goodfellow

IRIS SAID, "This is like the letter you left for me, a welcome home letter."

"Yes, exactly. Iris, I thought the key belonged with me. I've lived with this mystery for over twenty years since I moved into that house. I was sure I would be the one to solve the puzzle of the key. And I think with my mom passing away, it was something I wanted to hold onto. I wasn't thinking clearly. But after meeting you, I recognized the key belongs with you and the house."

Joan placed a box on the table and gestured for Iris to open it. The interior of the box was lined with faded red velvet, which was beginning to disintegrate in places. Iris's breath caught. Inside lay an antique skeleton key. Valerian Rose's words floated back to her: The key will be coming shortly. And here it was. Valerian said it was a key to a tree, which made no sense, just like most of what she said. But Iris couldn't deny that a key had found its way to her.

Iris examined the key closely. A light radiated outward, escaping the confines of the box. Perhaps it was a visual illusion created by the metal against the red velvet. Iris knew she perceived things differently when she was near Joan. Her awareness felt slightly altered as she held the key. The metal was cool against her skin. This was Ella's key, and now it belonged to her.

It was like looking through a vortex into another time, peering into a past with which she felt increasingly connected.

Iris struggled to organize her thoughts. "Joan, uhm, Ezra and I, we ended up going to well, we found some papers in a trunk in the attic of the house…"

A look of recognition passed through Joan's face. "Ah, yes, the trunk in the attic. I tried to open it and failed. I never thought of bringing in a locksmith. I guess I just forgot about that old trunk."

"We found some photos and papers in it. And uhm, we visited a woman in a house that disappeared…" Iris shook her head. Joan squinted her eyes and waited. "What I mean to say is someone who says she knew Ella… No, ahh, the house did disappear."

Joan looked at Iris and tilted her head. Iris could see that Joan was working hard to understand her. Iris tried one more time. "Ezra and I went to a little house on Rio Grande Boulevard. A woman lived there. Her name was Valerian Rose. Have you heard of her, by chance, or heard of something called the Faery Investigative Society? Because she told me a key would be coming to me. And," Iris looked down at the key and back up at Joan, "I think this could be the key she was referring to." Iris took a deep breath and felt relieved to have successfully communicated something that was still tough for her to wrap her head around.

Joan looked at Iris for a long time, as if she were contemplating what to say next. "I haven't heard of Valerian Rose or the Faery Investigative Society. But," Joan glanced sideways and continued, "I did have some experiences in that house that I believe were probably faery encounters. They were always around this box where I kept the key. So, I believe you. It makes sense that there is something about the key connected to them—the faeries, I mean. I believe that is true." Joan folded her hands on the table and looked down at them.

Iris nodded. "Yes, it seems so. I didn't believe in faeries last week, but now they seem to be everywhere."

Joan smiled. "Faeries, the little people, are part of many cultures all over the world. They may be getting more active now, since we humans seem to be in need of a little help."

"Huh." Iris paused. "So you believe they're real?"

Joan nodded. "Oh yes. They are real. They are conduits between this world and the Otherworld. I can't say I know much more, but I'm confident of that."

"Ezra says he saw faeries as a boy." After the words left her mouth, Iris wondered if she shouldn't have revealed his secret. But then she decided his secret was safe with Joan.

Joan nodded and didn't look surprised. "He's sensitive. That makes sense. Some people have the second sight." Iris looked at Joan quizzically. "It just means he can see through the veil a bit." Iris nodded as if this made sense, though it did not. But she was getting the idea that this new existence was a fake it 'til you make it sort of thing.

People began to filter through the front door for the meditation class, and Joan shut the box before handing it to Iris, who put it in her large purse. They exchanged glances, and Joan started greeting people while Iris headed to the living room.

Iris sat on a cushion on the floor, saving the chairs and couch for the older people. She looked up at the now familiar Green Tara statue on the mantel. Iris silently listed her qualities: protector of the forest, abolisher of fears, and goddess of the wind.

Joan began the meditation as usual, striking the gold Tibetan bowl. The sound swirled around the room several times before coming to a natural stop. Iris closed her eyes. The room became still and quiet. The orange tabby jumped off his perch on the couch and made his way to Iris's lap. Iris concluded that, for some unknown reason, she was suddenly attracting both faeries and cats.

Before Iris could start ruminating about the key and what it might unlock, a movie began playing on the screen of her closed eyelids. She found herself transported out of the room and deep into the green woods. She saw many beings made of light, air, and color moving through the forest. She inhaled the scent of wet leaves and mud. And looking up at the canopy of leaves, she heard the caw of crows and the twittering of small birds.

A woman in a long dress, with a large black bird perched on her shoulder, walked toward her. Her features were indistinct; it was as if Iris were seeing her through a veil. The woman playfully guided Iris through the forest to an ancient tree. A group of people encircled the tree. It was the exact image Iris had seen in the photos from the trunk, but now she saw it in vivid color. *The cottonwood worshippers.*

She watched as the women walked around the tree, offering rose petals and water to the base of the enormous trunk. Then, with their palms together at their hearts, they sat down and began chanting. The words of the chant were unfamiliar, but Iris sensed the emotion behind them, conveying appreciation and love for the tree and the forest.

When Joan rang the metal bowl to close the meditation, Iris felt as if she were emerging from a deep sleep. It took her a few minutes to bring her awareness out of the cottonwood forest and back into the room.

Sometimes, after shavasana in yoga class, an instructor would say something like, "Return to the room." But Iris had never felt that she had truly left a room until today. As the vision of the women in the forest faded, Iris felt a shift deep within her. A door was opening, and she wasn't sure what lay on the other side.

With her eyes open, Iris noticed people yawning, stretching, and shifting in their seats. They appeared happy, not like plastered-on fake happiness, but rather real contentment.

Iris tuned in to Joan's words: "We all have a voice in our heads. Often, it's a mean, contradictory voice that we would never normally be friends with." People smiled and nodded.

Everyone in the room had meditated enough to witness their thoughts. They grasped the inner voice's tendency to criticize and judge. Joan continued, "For the next month, I want you to practice putting down the knife." Joan looked around the room.

"The first cut of the knife comes from the outside. It may involve losing a job, a partner, someone disappointing you, or something unfair happening to you. Then there is a choice. Putting down the knife means the voice in your head doesn't administer the second, third, and fourth cuts with words like, you deserved it, or you will never be loved, or you brought this on yourself. Whatever words you tell yourself that are unkind. There will always be suffering, but then you have a choice. You can set down the knife."

Iris reflected on the inner voice she had been learning to interrupt since her divorce. It felt empowering to possess the awareness to make a choice. Speaking kindly to herself was another vital ingredient in becoming more comfortable in her own skin.

After class, people stood up and mingled while Joan prepared more tea. Iris no longer hurried out the door at the earliest opportunity; she felt comfortable enough now to sit and converse with people.

Ezra came to sit beside her and said casually, "Hey, cat lady, how are things going? Did you find anything else interesting in that trunk?"

Iris sensed the dissonance between his casual tone and his complex feelings about the trunk's contents. "I'm still going through all the papers we found. Mostly, they're ledgers and meeting notes. I haven't found anything connected to the Preserve in there, unfortunately. Oh, and I drove back down Rio Grande Boulevard. Guess what?"

"No 513 1/4 to be found?"

"How did you know it wouldn't be there?"

"I just had a feeling. It didn't quite," he paused and looked away, "feel real."

"But it was real! We both experienced the same thing. How could it not be real?"

"Yeah, it was real. I mean, just not the same *real* as this world. There are portals—doors to the Otherworld..." Ezra's voice trailed off.

Iris thought Ezra wasn't sure how much to share with her. He was holding back. She remembered the vision she had during the meditation. Was she becoming a twinkly-magic-portal-to-the-Otherworld type of person? She must have looked alarmed because Ezra smiled at her reassuringly and said, "I think you're changing."

"Well, I don't want to change. But weird things keep happening to me that defy logic." Iris said it sharply as if it were Ezra's fault. Inside, she was beginning to accept her intuition and the synchronicities occurring, but she wasn't ready to admit this to anyone yet.

He smiled and replied calmly, "Iris, you bought that house, and whether you accept it or not, there's a power associated with it- maybe it's the ghost of Ella, I don't know. I felt it when I came to unlock the door the first time I met you; I've felt it in the past when Joan lived there. You're part of something bigger. Maybe I am, too. Ella needs an ally in this world to help her. And she chose you."

Iris decided to come clean on this. "Yes, I actually feel that in my bones when you say it. It is true. I want to save that beautiful forest along the river. But I can't say that I know how. I want it to be clear, but I keep coming up with dead ends." She took a resigned breath.

Ezra responded with a reassuring tone. "Be patient. Our allies have a way of working behind the scenes. Ask for help in your meditations before you go to bed at night. Connect with Ella. The path will open up."

Iris nodded slowly, recognizing Ezra's faith. She contemplated the key Joan had given her. She didn't feel ready to show it to Ezra yet. She was still processing how what Valerian Rose had said had come true. She lifted her purse and sensed the weight of obligation inside. "Well, I guess we take it one step at a time and see where it all leads."

"Yeah, I have to get home to Molly. I'll see you later, cat lady."

The reminder that Ezra had a girlfriend settled over her like a sudden shadow across sunlight. She managed a faint smile. "Right, see you later."

XENA

Iris is dancing precariously on the bridge of belief and heartache. Personally, I prefer to take it seriously while holding it lightly. Holding fast to a belief has only ended poorly for humans. A healthy stance of not knowing or being quite flexible with beliefs will serve Iris better. No decision needs to be made. No stance needs to be taken. Sparkly magic or scientific fact: it all comes from the same place.

I open my awareness, slipping through the veils of time to check in on Ella.

The street is bustling with horses and carts, and dust swirls in the hot summer winds. Mayor Ringley is there. He is self-important yet quick to smile and shake hands. It is 1919, and Ella has worked patiently and persistently to bring her vision into reality.

She and the old mayor have struck a deal, rooted in their shared devotion to the cottonwoods, the river, and the future. They both understand that the forest must be protected. And they're not alone—the Fae are involved, of course. When it comes to matters of the forest, they're always involved.

Now I realize that Green Tara was part of the plan all along. It makes perfect sense. Nature needs her allies on this planet.

Ella and the mayor shake hands. The agreement is official.

The preserve is born. But fast-forward to this timeline, and it is all teetering on the edge. And Ella is not going to let it slip away without a fight.

CHAPTER 17

Federico arrived at the scheduled time to assist Ms. Barnes, the librarian. He stood in the parking lot near the field behind the school, hands shoved deep into his sweatshirt pocket, shoulders hunched. He appeared indifferent, but inside, he felt a flicker of something resembling pride. She had asked him. Not the popular kids. Not the robotics team. Him.

Ms. Barnes said warmly, "I'm so glad you could make it, Rico."

He nodded, not trusting his voice. Eye contact also felt risky. His veneer of not caring was too delicate.

A green forest service van pulled into the lot, engine rattling, as it parked. Federico straightened a bit without realizing it.

The man who stepped out was older, wiry, with sun-browned skin and thinning gray hair. He wore a forest green button-down, khaki slacks, and a brimmed ranger hat. On his shoulder was a patch with a pine tree and the words "U.S. Forest Service." It looked official and cool.

"I'm Iris Barnes," she said, reaching out her hand.

"George, George Miller. It's a pleasure."

George turned to Federico and offered his hand. "And who's this?"

Federico hesitated, then reached out. "Federico." He kept his eyes lowered, studying a crack in the asphalt.

"Good to meet you, Federico. Would you do the honors?" George handed him a large black case.

It looked heavy, but it wasn't. Federico gripped it tightly anyway, mindful of his responsibility. They crossed the field together, the sun warming the grass, while the air carried that late-spring scent of cut weeds and dust. The adults chatted—something about science, school outreach, tech job education, blah, blah, blah. Federico barely listened. He focused on the case in his hands, imagining flipping it open to reveal the sleek machinery inside, like something out of a spy movie.

When they reached the center of the field, George and Ms. Barnes started discussing the setup. Federico set the drone case down gently, then stepped back. A few kids were arriving in twos and threes. He kept his distance, eyes low, while his sneaker toe made a divot in the grass. Even now, he half expected someone to laugh at him.

George opened the case and pulled out the drone—a black quadcopter, professional-grade, not like the flimsy ones Federico had flown before. This one looked like it meant business, like it had flown actual missions.

"Let's get this started," George called out as more kids gathered in a loose circle. He gave a brief talk about the Forest Service and how drones were being used to monitor forest health, track wildfires, and map terrain. But then he smiled and said, "Let's be honest—you're here to see this baby fly." The kids laughed.

George looked at Federico. "Think you're up for the first flight?"

Federico froze. He looked around. Some of the kids were staring. He almost said no, but something inside nudged him.

He stepped forward. George handed him the controller and stood behind him. "It's pretty intuitive. I'll walk you through it."

The drone's propellers began to spin with a rising hum. Federico's hands trembled slightly on the controls.

"Good," George said gently. "Now ease it up. Slow and steady."

Federico pressed forward. The drone lifted, smooth and sure, rising above the field. A collective gasp came from the kids around him. He looked at the screen and saw the school, the field, and the town laid out below like a map.

Federico was focused on the controls but couldn't help hearing one boy whisper, "I didn't know we could see so much from up there." Another boy said excitedly, "It's like a video game, but real." Federico smiled just a little.

For the next few minutes, he guided the drone through the sky. The world looked small and manageable from 75 feet up. Bullies didn't matter, his crooked spine didn't matter either. Nothing did except the quiet precision of the machine, the air beneath it, and the strange new feeling expanding in his chest.

For the first time in a long while, Federico felt a spark of excitement, something more than the dull, heavy weight he usually carried. This elevated view offered a new perspective and a sense of freedom.

George told him, "Bring it down now."

Federico worked the controls to bring the drone down and softly land. He blinked at the screen, his heart racing.

Federico noticed Ms. Barnes and George Miller exchanging glances as they looked at him, but the smile wouldn't leave his face. He didn't care if it was obvious that he didn't want this feeling to end.

After the other kids had a chance to fly the drone, they all sat down together in the field. George led a brainstorming session: How could drones help the forest?

The kids shouted like popcorn popping: Count the trees, count the animals, track fires, find sick trees, spot birds' nesting.

Federico remained quiet, not ready to break the spell of the aerial view in his mind's eye.

George and Iris spoke after the demonstration, as the kids scattered to go home. "That was amazing, George. I've never seen the kids so engaged. It was great to see them excited."

George smiled, "Yeah, drones are cool. They make me feel like a kid again."

Iris was uncertain whether she should mention it, but she said, "George, are you aware of the development plans for the bosque near the river?"

George looked down, shaking his head. "So short-sighted and disappointing."

Iris nodded. "The community is fighting it."

"It's not public forest service land, so the federal government can't do anything about it. But my understanding is that it was a preserve under a trust."

Iris took a deep breath. "Yes." She didn't want to explain all that right now, but she said, "I wonder if the forest monitoring drones might be helpful in some way to the people working to save the forest." Iris was operating from an intuition—a slight folding of time in the direction of the future.

George thought about this. "Well, if you think of something, I will try to help as best I can. I live in this community and understand the damage this development will cause to the ecosystem. It's heartbreaking." His voice was thick with frustration. "We've worked so hard to protect these lands, only to see them sacrificed for a few dollars. The forests here are already under such stress from climate change. Every tree, every plant, the animals, the river—they're all interconnected. If this development goes through, it won't just be the loss of a few trees. It'll be the unraveling of an entire web of life. And once it's gone, we can't bring it back. We just can't let it go without a fight."

At that moment, Iris felt a kinship with George, a shared

understanding of what was at stake. "I agree," she said, her voice firm. "We have to find a way to stop this."

George nodded. "So, I'll be back in a few weeks, and you can let me know how many kids sign up for the summer class."

"Thanks, George. I'm excited about this and appreciate you volunteering your time."

"It's my pleasure. I had a lot of fun today."

As the other kids dispersed, Federico lingered, his mind still on the drone and the new view it had shown him. George clapped a hand on his shoulder, smiling. "You did great today, Federico. You've got a knack for this. If you're interested, you can learn more about programming drones in my summer class. I'd love to see you there."

Federico looked up. Not at the ground or the sky, but straight at George's face. "I'd like that." Something inside him believed this might be the start of something new.

CHAPTER 18

Annabelle rose from her bike seat and rode as fast as she could, kicking up dust on the dirt trails of the cottonwood forest. That morning, her mother informed her that the developers would soon begin cutting down trees. The words echoed in Annabelle's mind, igniting a fierce storm of emotions: fury at the injustice, sadness at the impending loss, and a deep powerlessness. Faster and faster, she pedaled, using exertion as a release valve for her anger.

But something shifted as she reached one of her favorite spots in the forest. Being among the trees began to calm her. Her breath steadied, and she slowed down. Then, quite unexpectedly, she noticed a new trail weaving through the underbrush. *That was impossible.* She knew this part of the forest as well as she knew her hand, didn't she? Curiosity slipped through the cracks of her anger like a cool breeze, urging her to investigate. She turned to follow the unfamiliar trail.

Pedaling slowly, she looked around, trying to orient herself. She was sure she had never been here, but how could that be? She stopped and leaned her bike against a tree, turning to survey the surroundings. The cottonwoods felt familiar, yet something was different; they appeared larger and brighter, and the usual plants had more vibrant colors. The very air sparkled, but there was an odd stillness.

She felt a sharp pinch on her ear and instinctively swatted at it.

A voice said, "Hey! You're not supposed to do that!" Annabelle's eyes widened in shock when she saw a tiny faery flitting near her face.

Wearing a lime green dress made of fresh cottonwood leaves and a tiara of yellow desert marigold petals, Lola flapped her tiny iridescent wings in frustration.

Internally, Lola reminded herself that she was a professional, empowered by the Fae queens to fulfill her duties. She regained her composure, still flapping, but now more slowly. She said with control, "I'm glad to make your acquaintance. I am Lola."

Lola watched as the human girl appeared frozen before she began to smile slightly. The faery, growing frustrated with the human's slowness and forgetting her commitment to composure, warned, "I'll pinch your ear again."

"No. Uh, I'm Annabelle."

"I know, dumdum. You've been chosen by the crows under the orders of Grandmother Cottonwood. *Everyone* knows who you are." Lola's patience was tested. Humans were impossibly dense and slow.

Lola called Roanoke down from the branches. "Roanoke is here, and he needs to speak with you, and you need to listen. It won't be easy. The bond was broken." She drew out the word "bond" and emphasized it. With her hand on her hip, she appeared bored, as if she facilitated crow-human meetings daily.

Annabelle felt like she was on a rollercoaster, from fury to shock, then amusement, and now completely confused. She looked at the large crow perched on the handlebars of her bike, still leaning against the tree. *Is this the crow that tapped on the glass door at the house?*

Roanoke began speaking into Annabelle's mind, and unlike the faery, he conveyed the profound importance of the conversation with a slow, patient tone. Annabelle sensed the emotion behind the words before she could fully comprehend them. In her brain, new synaptic connections began to form, and fresh ways of perceiving emerged.

The disgruntled faery continued to assist with the interaction, focusing her attention on strengthening the thread of awareness between the crow and human mind, connecting it to the current of life that pulses through root and feather, blood and breeze. In Faery territory, such alignments were easier to achieve because the veils between species and souls ran thin. The Crow People and Grandmother Cottonwood harbored hope that, once rekindled, the ancient bond between the two species would grow and flourish, enduring even beyond the boundaries of enchanted ground.

Roanoke continued softly, "We need you, Annabelle. We cannot do this alone." While the words echoed in Annabelle's mind, she couldn't initially comprehend them. She was attempting to understand this new form of communication.

"I don't get it." But as soon as those words left her mouth, she understood. In a jumble of images and feelings, she felt the truth. "You need me to help you? To save the forest? Your home? And an old tree?"

"Yes, that's good," the faery said, encouraging her to say more.

"And somehow, you want me to know that the crows—no, the Crow People and the Human People—have a bond. And this is the bond: this communication. We need each other."

Annabelle, with her entire body, mind, and spirit, grasped the significance and weight of this bond. In a single momentous thought download facilitated by Lola, Annabelle sensed the history behind the bond, the pain of losing it, and the urgency of rebuilding the connection. This marked the beginning of a new era for crows and humans and the last hope for saving this forest —and ultimately all forests.

She stared into Roanoke's dark, searching eyes. The crow was large, handsome, and appeared self-aware and composed. Suddenly, it felt like another door in her mind opened, allowing a flood of understanding to pour in.

Crows were not merely birds but beings like her, possessing thoughts, feelings, motivations, desires, and hopes. The false separation that classified animals in one category and humans in another fell away, outgrown and never to return.

She felt the deep entanglement of her life with the crows and the forest and sensed how they would work together in service to save the forest. She wasn't just a visitor in the forest; she was part of it, and it was part of her.

Annabelle's brain was rewiring rapidly, consuming resources at an alarming rate. Suddenly, she sank to the ground, unable to stand any longer, her energy drained. Her task, for the moment, was accomplished. The bond between the Crow People and the Human People, long forgotten, began to pulse with life again.

Lola flew around Annabelle's head, feeling both pleased and worried. She sprinkled faery dust to give Annabelle the energy boost she needed to get home. The last thing Lola wanted was to explain to the Fae queens why a human child was sleeping overnight in faery territory. While this had been somewhat common in the past, it hadn't happened in more than a century.

Lola watched as the girl pulled her bent legs to her chest and wrapped her arms around them, resting her forehead on her knees. "I think that is all for today," Lola said curtly, appearing perfectly in control. "Everyone can go home and get some rest."

Roanoke could scarcely fly. Almost all of his energy had been spent. Delphinia watched with great concern. She accompanied her mate to a nearby roost and, in an effort to revive him, brought seeds and bugs. He appeared unsteady on the branch. Delphinia was filled with doubt. Perhaps the task given to him by the Crow Elders was too much.

ALMOST AS IF IN A TRANCE, Annabelle, slightly rejuvenated by the faery dust, mounted her bike and rode slowly back the same way she had arrived. It felt like too much effort even to say goodbye. The faery guided her out of Fae territory and accompanied her to her driveway. Annabelle leaned her bike against the side of the house and entered. Lola watched her for a moment before flitting away.

Annabelle's first impression upon entering her house was that this world, her home, felt less than real. It lacked the vitality of faery territory.

Her mother heard Annabelle enter through the front door and called out, "Do you want some dinner?"

"No, I'm exhausted, Mom. I need to lie down." Annabelle noticed that speaking in words seemed awkward and inelegant after the telepathic communication she had just experienced.

Maria entered Annabelle's bedroom, where Annabelle lay with her eyes closed. She noticed a red mark on her daughter's ear and placed her hand on her forehead.

Already asleep and still under the faery spell, Annabelle was sent a dream. She saw the key, the faery, and the crow all high in a cottonwood tree, and she was trying to reach them, attempting to climb the tree, but she kept falling over and over again. A woman in a long black dress smiled at her kindly, placing her hand on Annabelle's forehead. "You shall prevail," she said.

THE NEXT MORNING, Annabelle felt groggy and knew it would take a few days to recover. She poured cereal and milk into a bowl while contemplating her next steps. Long summer days stretched out before her with few responsibilities, and she realized she needed a place to think and plan. She called to her mother down the hall, who was already in her office working, "I'm going to take Sparkpuff to the river, Mom."

"Alright, m'ija," Maria called back, already absorbed in the glow of her computer screen.

Sparkpuff stood by the door where his harness and leash hung on a hook. He danced from one foot to the other, thrilled as always at the prospect of a walk. Annabelle smiled at the dog's enthusiasm.

Annabelle and Sparkpuff walked toward the river through the cottonwood forest. On the shore, Annabelle unfastened Sparkpuff from his leash. He ran in circles, enjoying the warm sand beneath his paws. Annabelle settled close to the water, where clumps of lime-green coyote willows grew. The river ran high from the snowmelt, and small crests of waves broke the water's surface. A red-tailed hawk circled lazily above her.

Her thoughts drifted to everything that had happened. It was all so strange and new. Faeries were real and governed a magical part of the forest that had always been hidden from her. Crows could talk to people. When Annabelle thought of Roanoke, her heart swelled with unexpected warmth. He was serious and kind, standing in stark contrast to the wild and unpredictable Lola.

Annabelle wasn't sure what lay ahead, but she felt a deep commitment blossoming inside her. It was clear to her that she would play a role in restoring balance between crows and humans and, somehow, that would contribute to the effort to save the forest. She felt hope for the first time since hearing about the Bosque development. Perhaps, with the help of Roanoke and Lola, saving the forest was possible.

Sitting on the sandy shore of the river, her mind drifted aimlessly. Then, she became aware of a deep, flowing voice discussing many things. It was more than a voice and words. It was also pictures, feelings, smells, and tastes. Annabelle felt the difference between the flatness of when only words were used to communicate, and the richness of voiceless communication that happened when connecting with another mind. She was startled because she knew what she was picking up wasn't the thoughts in her own head, nor was it Roanoke's or even Lola's. No, this was something entirely different. It seemed to be coming from the river.

Was this the river speaking? She continued to listen. The Rio Grande, flowing right in front of her, gurgled, whooshed, and swirled like the current itself, not forming words but painting thoughts and images in her mind. In this way it spoke of sandhill cranes, blue herons, crows, cottonwoods, fish, people, coyotes, porcupines, beavers, the sky, and clouds—a whole world rushing past her in its flow.

Annabelle hesitated, unsure whether to interrupt. But eventually, she whispered, "Hello?"

The River, who easily communicated with trees, animals, and the earth itself, seemed surprised and taken aback by the sound of a Human addressing it. For many suns and moons, this had not happened.

"Hello?" River said, his voice rippling and flowing.

It is the river. "Are you... the river... speaking?" Annabelle asked, her voice small but filled with wonder.

"I am River, yes, and who might you be?"

Annabelle felt unsure of how to introduce herself to something so immense. "I'm a girl. My name is Annabelle," she began. Then she thought she needed to explain, "I learned yesterday that I can talk to crows—well, one particular crow, Roanoke." She held the picture of Roanoke in her mind. "And now, I guess I can talk to you, too."

"Ahhhh," River mused, his tone swelling with recognition. "Yes, you are the one Grandmother Cottonwood has spoken of." This was the second time Annabelle had heard Grandmother

Cottonwood mentioned, but she still didn't fully understand who or what she was.

Unsure of what to say to River, Annabelle spoke plainly, her heart guiding her words and feelings. "I'm happy to know you. I love that you flow through here, near my home. You make the forest come alive, and so many creatures depend on you. I appreciate you."

River's voice deepened into a gentle, whooshing rumble. "I thank you, dear Annabelle. You make me happy to be River. I wish you every success, and I hope that we may speak again."

"Yes, me too." Annabelle began to feel tired from the newness of this interaction, and Sparkpuff was pawing at her leg, eager to be on the move again. "Goodbye, River. I'll see you again soon," Annabelle said, getting up and brushing the sand off her hands.

As Annabelle clipped Sparkpuff's leash and began walking home, the world around her shimmered. Everything—every tree, every stone, every creature—was alive, animated by a pulsing spirit and nourished by water. The river was the sustenance of the forest, and now it was a part of her.

The realization settled inside her. She wasn't separate from this world; she was woven into its fabric. She contained it all and was contained by it all. This knowledge was too vast to grasp fully, but she let it wash over and through her as she made her way home.

CHAPTER 19

Federico picked at his fingernails in the backseat of the car. They were driving to a doctor's appointment to discuss his back. His parents were unusually quiet. Federico looked out of the open window as they passed the Dog House hot dog stand, where he had recently visited with his new friends.

He wondered if he could call them friends. Federico wasn't sure why Joey had taken him under his wing. He felt like he was walking a razor's edge between camaraderie and danger with those boys.

His mind wandered back to flying the drone. That memory held no confusion, only joy. He smiled without meaning to. He wanted to take the summer coding class George Miller had mentioned, and he also wanted his own drone. The idea of asking his parents knotted his stomach. What if they said no?

At Carrie Ringley Children's Hospital, Federico and his parents were ushered into a small, windowless exam room. The old tile floors gleamed under the buzzing fluorescent lights, which seemed hell-bent on giving him a headache. The room smelled like every other doctor's office: disinfectant, plastic, and fear. The air conditioning felt arctic. His T-shirt clung to his back, damp from the walk in.

Dr. Onate swept into the room like a man who had three other appointments waiting, X-rays in hand and lab coat flapping. He wore blue scrubs under a long white lab coat, which had various doctor's tools in the pockets. He placed the X-rays on a lit panel and said, "Federico has a spinal condition known as Scheuermann's disease, also known as Scheuermann's kyphosis."

Federico's mom inhaled sharply at the word "disease," her hand flying to her mouth. Federico didn't move. He stared at the floor tiles, hoping they would swallow him.

The doctor was unfazed by the tension in the room and seemed oblivious to their distress. "What that means is that the back part of his vertebrae in this section of his spine," he pointed to the x-ray, "has grown a little faster than the front part of the vertebrae, making his upper spine more rounded than usual. Federico has about a 62-degree curve in his upper back." Doctor Onate's voice was clinical and efficient.

Federico's father asked, "Is that bad? What can be done about it?"

"For now, bracing and physical therapy. A brace worn 22 hours a day will help keep the curve from worsening, but without it, there's a risk that the curve could become more severe, leading to chronic pain, breathing difficulties, and even surgery down the road. Physical therapy will help Federico strengthen the muscles that keep him sitting straighter."

"We're always telling him to sit up straight," his mother murmured, half to herself. "Why does he have this problem?"

"We don't know exactly, but it can run in families." He looked at them expectantly.

"My mother-in-law told me once her uncle and father had backs that looked similar to Federico's."

"Not uncommon," Dr. Onate said crisply. He stood up to leave. "I'll prescribe a brace fitting and physical therapy. After the brace is made, we'll do another set of X-rays and talk again." He walked out of the room. At the door, he looked back at Federico. "Do you experience any pain?"

Federico's heart thudded. "A little, sometimes."

"Physical therapy should help with that. The nurse will be in momentarily to give you your paperwork." He left the room, and the door whooshed shut.

His mother stared at him. "Federico, you never told me you have pain."

Federico mumbled, "It's not that bad." He didn't mention how the pain he was feeling now came more from the word "brace" than anything else. As the implications sank in, a cold panic spread through his chest.

A brace. Every day. At school. *I might as well wear a sign that says "Bully Me."*

On the ride home, he folded his arms and stared out the window. From the back seat, he said, "I'm not wearing a brace to school. I'm not."

His father didn't reply at first. His mother sighed. "Oh, Rico. I know. It's not what we want. But if it will help your back stay straighter… You have to think about your future. It's a… it's a health matter," she added, in a voice that tried to sound calm but didn't quite succeed.

His father finally spoke. "We can't make you do anything, Rico. The choice is yours. But it's a sign of maturity to make choices based on your best interest and not on fears about what other people think. I know it's tough at your age, and kids can be mean." His father paused as if looking for the right words. "Anyway, give the brace a try for the summer. Get used to it, and then we can revisit this conversation in the fall when school starts."

Federico said nothing. He clenched his jaw and bit the inside of his cheek. *A brace. Just perfect. It sounds like a torture device.*

When they got home, Federico didn't stop to talk. He went straight to his room and powered up his gaming computer. The screen's glow illuminated his face as his fingers moved over the keys. In this world, his back didn't matter. No braces. No stares. Just pixels, rules he understood, and a safe haven.

The memory of the drone flight returned to him, evoking a feeling of soaring above it all. That world had rules, too, but it also had sky and hope. He needed more of both.

CHAPTER 20

Iris sat at her favorite coffee shop, the warm sunlight spilling through the windows, a promise of long summer days ahead. A sense of freedom and possibility hung in the air. Summer break was one of the best things about working at a school. Although she did run a few special short summer school programs, they were nothing like the scheduled grind of the regular school year. She enjoyed the luxury of spending as long as she liked sipping a latte in a real mug instead of rushing out the door with a to-go cup.

She opened her laptop. Her thoughts circled back to Eric Sutter's death, a dark undercurrent that pulled at her in quiet moments. The more she uncovered, the more it felt like she was wading into dangerous waters, yet she couldn't resist. In one police report, a tire mark from another vehicle was referenced, but in the final report, that detail was missing. *It might be nothing, but what if evidence was being suppressed?*

From reading old newspaper articles, she discovered that the mayor, along with the police and fire departments, tended to resemble a good old boys' club. Stories circulated in Cottonwood about police misconduct and backroom deals. Furthermore, there were rumors that the mayor and his inner circle accepted bribes from local business owners in exchange for overlooking zoning violations and expediting permits.

After finishing her latte and coming up with no new leads, Iris packed up her laptop. It was time for meditation class. A man scrolled absently through his phone in the corner, but every so often, he glanced up from his screen in Iris's direction, following her movements. Iris shook off her feelings of uneasiness about the man.

IRIS SETTLED into her cushion on the floor in Joan's familiar living room, sinking into stillness as Joan rang the Tibetan bowl. The note continued for a long time, gradually losing volume and eventually resting in silence. Iris followed the breath coming in and out of her nose. But her mind did not want to let go of the topic of Eric Sutter's murder. How could she uncover the proof she needed that the developers, or investors, or the mayor, or perhaps all of them, were connected to the murder?

She returned to the breath, feeling the cool inhale and the warmer exhale in her nostrils but clouds of thoughts floated through the screen of her mind's eye: reading the newspaper headline about the forest being for sale, Joan giving her the key, speaking with Eric Sutter's widow, the upcoming protest.

Sooner than she anticipated, Joan rang the bell again. She opened her eyes. Her mind had been more active than usual during the meditation. She felt on the verge of figuring something out, and her thoughts wouldn't let it go.

Joan began to speak, but to Iris, it almost felt as if she were speaking from far away. The statue on the mantel seemed to turn its head to look at Iris, slightly changing its expression.

"There is an animating spirit in everything. And we live in a world where abundant help is available from the seen and unseen." Joan continued talking, but Iris's mind was elsewhere.

. . .

AFTER CLASS ENDED and the group began forming smaller side conversations, Joan approached Iris and said, "There's someone I want you to meet. This is Victor Montes. He lives in your neighborhood, also in a historic home."

Iris reached out to shake Victor's hand. She had noticed that he was a new addition to the group today. Appearing to be in his mid-50s, the corners of his eyes crinkled as he smiled, but his face had a hard-living pallor to it.

Joan said, "Victor and I served on the neighborhood association together back in the day. He ended up returning to law school, and now he has been a trial attorney for many years."

"I've had some stressful cases lately. I recognized I needed to get back on the meditation cushion, so here I am." Victor shrugged.

Iris became very focused. "An attorney?" She wondered if Victor was someone she could trust. Joan knew him, which seemed like a good sign.

Victor smiled again, a calculated warmth in his eyes. "Yeah, criminal law has been my bread and butter, but these days, I'm more drawn to environmental cases."

Hmm, what about a case that involved both? "Victor, do you have time to talk? And Joan, would it be okay if we used your kitchen to talk privately?" Joan and Victor both looked at Iris with surprise. Iris was taking charge in a way that was unusual for her, but she thought Victor might be the help she needed.

Iris, Joan, and Victor sat at the kitchen table. Ezra stood in the doorway with his arms crossed. The air in the room felt heavy. Iris, looking at Victor, asked, "Are you aware of the city's recent decision to build shops and restaurants in what is now the cottonwood forest?"

Victor shook his head. "It's a terrible shame. The mayor and council are looking for profit when they should be conserving the unique environment we have here." He echoed the cynical but accurate assessment that many had already expressed.

Ezra cleared his throat as if to interrupt, but then exhaled, shifting his weight against the doorway with his arms still crossed.

Iris nodded in Victor's direction, her lips pressed together. She proceeded to share everything she knew about the preserve Ella had established, the suspicious death of Eric Sutter, the fire in his office, and the uncanny timing of the developers' arrival after the legal preserve was voided due to the tax issue.

Ezra shifted uncomfortably, his eyes darting from Joan to Iris to Victor.

Victor's eyes flickered with interest, then a fleeting, unreadable expression crossed his face. Curiosity? Calculation? Then it was gone, replaced by a practiced look of concern. "If what you're saying is true, this could be a game-changer. I'll need to reach out to the attorney general and maybe stir the pot a bit. We'll need to tread carefully, though. People don't usually appreciate having their dirty laundry aired in public."

Victor and Iris exchanged contact information, and Victor said, "I'll be in touch." His parting smile lingered just a moment too long, but Iris didn't notice.

Ezra, leaning casually against the kitchen doorframe, watched as Victor left. Joan's eyes squinted, clouded with worry. "I have a feeling something that could be dangerous has been set into motion." Joan reached for the chain around her neck, pulled it over her head, and handed it to Iris.

Iris gazed at the piece of jewelry. "A Green Tara pendant?"

Joan's voice dropped. "I want you to wear this, Iris. All the time. Tara can help those who are... in over their heads." Joan locked eyes with Iris. "I'm not saying you are, but something doesn't feel right."

Iris pulled out her chain to show Joan that she was wearing the skeleton key around her neck. She took the Tara pendant off

Joan's necklace and placed it onto her own chain, allowing the key and Green Tara to rest together at her chest, creating a gentle warmth that pulsed near her heart. "Thank you, Joan," Iris said, looking into Joan's blue eyes. "I will be careful."

As Iris walked out, Ezra fell into step with her. He hesitated, running a hand over the back of his neck. "Iris, uhm, I don't get a good feeling from that Victor guy."

Iris looked up sharply at him. With some defensiveness, she said, "What? Really? I think he could help." *Could Ezra be jealous? But he has a girlfriend. Maybe they broke up?* She needed a breakthrough and some help. But then doubt crept in. *Could he be right?*

CHAPTER 21

Afew days after his doctor's appointment, Federico had recovered enough to start making his case for getting a drone. At the dinner table, he leaned forward, eyes wide with excitement. "Did you know drones can plant trees? I mean, like, thousands of them in a day. And they can put out wildfires! Actual drones that fly in and spray water like little robot fire-fighters!" He waved his fork through the air, mimicking a drone's path.

His mom, Emma, stirred her mashed potatoes and glanced at Marco. "You've mentioned that," she said, smiling, "once or twice."

Federico barely noticed. He was already scrolling on his phone. "Look, here's the summer coding class I told you about. It's all about programming drones to do stuff."

Emma leaned closer to study the screen. "A coding class, huh?"

Federico nodded eagerly. "It starts in a few weeks. I'm serious, Mom. This is what I want to do."

Marco raised an eyebrow at Emma. Emma turned to Federico, "We'll sign you up, honey. I think that would be great."

The house echoed with drone videos and Federico's breathless commentary for the next few days. He filled every conversation with new facts—thermal imaging, crop monitoring, drone swarms. He had gone from interested to obsessed.

The next day, Marco was in the garage sharpening tools when he was interrupted by more drone facts. Federico, his tone carefully casual. "So, I was thinking. What if we got a drone? You know, for practice. It doesn't have to be a fancy one, just something I could mess around with before the class starts."

Marco looked up from the chainsaw blade with a half-smile. "I'll tell you what, Rico. You come to work with me for the next few weeks before summer school starts, and you can earn enough money to buy your drone."

Federico's face lit up. "Seriously?"

Marco had an expression like he had just won a poker round. "But it's a two-part bargain. I want you to wear that brace every day, for the summer and the school year."

Federico grasped that his dad was a step ahead of him. He thought to argue, but then bit his tongue. "Yeah, okay."

FEDERICO GOT FITTED for his brace and was able to choose the color and design on the plastic. He chose black with stars and galaxies. Plain white felt too clinical. Space, at least, felt like freedom. It was awkward at first, but with some adjustments, he started wearing it more. The kids in the coding class were all nerds anyway, with braces, glasses, and social weirdness. He figured he'd blend in.

He was avoiding Joey and his gang for now, telling himself he didn't want to socialize because of the brace, but he also felt some relief about this choice.

His mom bought him some baggy T-shirts to wear over the brace. His family kept telling him that the brace was hardly noticeable. He knew better. Still, thinking about getting a drone was enough of a distraction that he didn't get too down about it.

ON HIS FIRST day of work with his dad, Federico struggled with getting into the truck while wearing his brace. The brace didn't allow his back to bend, so he had to learn to hinge at his hips. Every movement was awkward, but he was learning.

The scent of fresh-cut lumber and the sound of saws greeted Marco and Federico as they walked the perimeter of the home Marco's crew was framing. The tight-knit group of men, with their sun-weathered faces and easy banter, looked up as Marco introduced his son.

Over the next few weeks, Federico learned to fetch tools and nails, switch out batteries, and hammer a nail straight. He appreciated how the men included him in their good-natured teasing.

"Hey, Rico," one of the men said, laughing, "I could get used to having a tool runner."

"Don't get too used to it. I've got drones to program."

"Yeah," another man said, "Federico is going to fly over this job site on his drone! And he's going to drop the tools from the sky." Everyone laughed, including Federico.

The days on the job site were tiring. By 8 p.m., he was in bed, sleeping through the night, even while wearing the brace.

TWO WEEKS LATER, Federico stepped into the cool, air-conditioned classroom of his summer drone class. The contrast was stark, like stepping from one world into another. He missed joking around at the job site, but here, surrounded by the quiet hum of computers and the focused attention of his classmates, Federico discovered a new kind of satisfaction. Each line of code was a puzzle, and each solution was a small victory.

As he programmed a drone to navigate through a virtual

forest, avoiding obstacles and mapping terrain, he realized that the focus and patience he had learned from his summer job helped him in the classroom. For the first time, he found that he enjoyed problem-solving and detail-oriented work. When he looked up to check the time, he was surprised at how quickly the hours passed. He clicked with coding.

Looking over Federico's work, George Miller said, "Excellent, as always."

Federico smiled with satisfaction. He turned off his computer and gathered his things to leave.

His mom was waiting outside the school. When he got into the car, she said, "Federico, something came for you today."

His eyes wide, he asked, "The drone?"

Emma smiled, "I don't know. I think so."

When they got home, Federico burst through the front door and into the kitchen, where a large box sat on the kitchen table. He assembled the drone, glanced briefly at the directions, and then dashed outside with it.

As the drone soared into the sky, Federico felt a rush of exhilaration that made his heart pound. Watching the world from above, with the trees shrinking into a green sea beneath him, he experienced that same shift inside that he had felt during the school drone demonstration. The freedom of the sky made the brace and the teasing at school seem far away and small.

CHAPTER 22

"We're getting ready to leeeeave!" Maria called out with cheerful urgency toward Annabelle's room.

Annabelle glanced at Tia Joan, who was helping her tape the last edge of her protest sign. Joan's eyes sparkled.

"Coming, Mother," Annabelle called.

The house buzzed with purpose. Water bottles were filled, snacks were packed, and cardboard signs were leaning against the wall like waiting soldiers. Today was the day: the *Save the Forest* protest.

"We're picking up your cousin, Federico, on the way. We need to hurry."

NATE PULLED INTO A DRIVEWAY, and Federico ran out of the house and piled into the crowded car. Maria asked, "Hey Federico, how's it going?" Concern tinged her voice.

"Oh, living the dream," Federico smiled in a way that did not reach his eyes. He understood the subtext of his aunt's question but chose not to address his doctor's visit or the new brace. He felt the familiar constriction of the brace tightening around his

151

torso as he adjusted his position in the car. He had decided to bring the drone along to the protest and placed the black case near his feet in the car.

THE DOWNTOWN PARK overflowed with people waving signs. Annabelle and Federico had never attended a protest before, so they wandered into the park, excited to be part of a large crowd. They joined in the chant, "Save our forest, save our bosque."

The park sprawled like a natural amphitheater, its grassy slopes curving gently around a central speaker platform. The air buzzed with the sound of defiance, the enthusiastic cawing of crows, and the rustle of cottonwood leaves around the park. The fresh scent of cut grass mingled with the faint aroma of grilled meats from the nearby food trucks.

Some teens dressed mainly in black were vaping under some trees. Police patrolled the perimeter, their two-way radios blending static sounds with reports of lost children and suspicious individuals. A grandmother held a photo of her childhood treehouse. A boy with red curly hair offered handmade seed packets to the crowd.

The grown-ups, Nate, Maria, and Joan, tried to inch their way to the front of the crowd to hear the speakers. Nina Rivera, founder of the Bosque Restoration Project, spoke on the platform. Maria and Annabelle volunteered for the project, doing quarterly bosque clean-ups, rooting out invasive species, and planting yerba mansa, cottonwoods, and other native forest species. They loved soaking up Nina's wisdom about everything related to the bosque, and they always learned something new.

Nina spoke into a microphone over the crowd, "We have the privilege of living near this very fragile, beautiful, and unique ecosystem that has supported human life and animal life for so many generations. Will we lose this precious resource for a brew pub or some shops?"

The crowd screamed, "NO!" and waved their signs.

"Are we willing to tell our children and our grandchildren that we were the ones who allowed this irreplaceable forest to be cut down?"

Maria and Nate exchanged glances. They yelled with the crowd, "NO!"

Nina spoke directly to the children. Her passion was teaching them about the bosque. "Kids, this fight is not over. We will do everything we can to *stop* this development and *keep* our forest, and we invite you to help. You are not powerless; just by showing up here today, you are doing something that makes a difference. That matters."

Annabelle and Federico found a spot to sit at the top of the grassy slope. Nina's words echoed in Annabelle's ears, providing her with some comfort.

Federico was soaking in the party atmosphere of the protest. Food trucks were stationed along the streets surrounding the park. The aroma of grilled taco meat filled the air. Face painting stations were turning out children adorned with tree and butterfly designs.

He spotted Joey's blue Chevy Impala parked at the edge of the field and felt relieved to be there with Annabelle, appreciating the ease of being with someone he had known his entire life.

"I had to go see a doctor about my back, and he says I have to wear this brace and go to physical therapy," Federico said, his upper lip lifting as if he had tasted something sour.

Annabelle had overheard her parents talking about this. She watched him with quiet sympathy and thought for a moment. "You know," she began softly, "it reminds me of when I was nine and had to get braces for my teeth. I hated them. I thought everyone would stare at me and I'd be known as 'metal mouth' forever."

She paused, recalling the anxiety that had gripped her back then, how it felt like the end of the world. "But after a while, no one cared. They didn't even notice." She looked at Federico, her expression sincere. "Maybe the same thing will happen to you. They'll notice it at first, but after that, it's no big deal."

Federico nodded. He knew Annabelle had recently gotten her braces off. Annabelle continued, "I guess like braces helped my teeth get straighter, your brace will help your back get straighter."

Federico chewed on this briefly. "But I have to wear it *22 hours* a day. I have to wear it to school. The kids already tease me, and now it will get worse."

"I'm sorry, Rico. Maybe it won't be so bad." Annabelle was empathetic.

Joey walked by, holding hands with a girl wearing a snug shirt with a bit of lacy bra showing, "Rrrico," he said in a low voice and continued walking.

Annabelle looked at Federico, wrinkling her nose, "You know him?"

Federico shrugged, unprepared to respond when such different parts of his world collided. Changing the subject, he said, "Belles, do you want to see my drone? I think we can make it lift off over there." He pointed to a vacant, relatively flat area across the street.

The cousins walked to the spot and Federico put the drone on the dusty ground. He guided it upward, his face tilted toward the sky.

"Wow, that is amazing," Annabelle said, genuinely impressed as she watched the video footage showing the entire park from above. Other people turned to look up at the drone, but then their attention shifted back to the speaker on the platform.

Iris, exiting her car at the park, felt a surge of hope upon seeing the passionate faces in the crowd. The collective energy lifted her spirits, easing the tight grip of her recent anxiety. She scanned the crowd for Ezra. Although she didn't see him, she recognized some of the kids from school and their parents. She briefly wondered if Ezra would be there with his girlfriend.

She noticed that Nina Rivera was just finishing speaking. Iris collaborated with Nina to organize field trips into the bosque so that kids could learn about the plants and animals in the forest. It was wonderful to see such a large turnout. When there was a break in the speakers, she joined the crowd in chanting, "Save our forest, save our bosque."

Iris continued scanning for Ezra. Finally, she spotted him near some trees on the other side of the park. He was alone, so she walked toward him through the dense crowd.

"Hi, stranger," Iris said with a smile.

He turned, grinning. "Iris! Good to see you. Wild turnout, huh?"

"It is. Kind of restores your faith in people."

"You got a minute?" he asked, glancing around. "Let's walk. Too many ears here." They fell into step as the crowd noise thinned while they moved toward the Old Town Plaza. Chants still echoed behind them like a heartbeat.

"I've been thinking about Sutter's murder," Ezra said. "I keep circling back to the mayor. Regulus always struck me as a spotlight-chaser, not a public servant. If this development goes through, it lines his pockets and boosts his image for reelection."

Iris nodded slowly. "Yeah. He probably didn't expect this much pushback." The crowd's energy still hummed in her chest. She hoped it would help sustain Ella's legacy. She wondered if she should bring up Victor, but hesitated. Ezra had had such a negative reaction to him at Joan's. Instead, she pivoted. "I've been looking into Ella Ross more. I thought there might be something to that name."

"What did you find?"

"Turns out, she was a distant cousin of Betsy Ross."

"The flag lady?" Ezra raised a bushy eyebrow. "That's wild. How'd she end up out here?"

"Get this. Her grandfather got rich in the timber industry on the East Coast. But then he got TB, and they moved west. New Mexico was known for its warm, dry healing air back then."

Ezra nodded. "So the family made their fortune cutting down forests, and Ella used some of that money to protect one. Poetic justice."

"Exactly."

He gave a half-laugh, then lowered his voice. "I know this might sound paranoid, but… I don't trust Victor. Something about him feels off. Like he showed up, saying all the right things. Did you check into him online?"

Iris didn't reply. She was watching the sky. A soft hum floated over the crowd. Across the park, she spotted Federico holding the drone controls, face upturned in concentration. She smiled, remembering how lit up he had been during the drone demo at school.

Then she saw Annabelle approaching. "Annabelle! It's great to see you. That sign's amazing. Did you make it?"

"With my mom." She proudly pointed across the grass where Maria and Joan talked with Nate.

Joan came over and hugged Iris. "Have you met Annabelle's parents?"

After introductions, they all engaged in warm small talk, appreciating the protest's turnout, lamenting the threat to the forest, and expressing hope that the development could be halted.

"Did you know Annabelle's dad researches the forest?" Joan added.

Iris perked up. "I'm always looking for speakers for the kids. Especially anything that makes math and science more alive for them."

Nate smiled. "Happy to help. I'm working on how specific

mycelium strains might make the cottonwoods more resilient to climate change."

"Perfect. I'm teaching a fall unit on the Rio Grande Bosque. I'll follow up with you."

The light shifted, and the park's energy began to ebb. People drifted toward their cars. Nate glanced across the park. "I'd better round up Federico so we can go."

Iris and Ezra began walking out of the park toward their cars. Ezra said at the park's edge, "I'll see you later, cat lady. Be careful. If you need anything, call me."

"Yeah, so I have a question. Am I a 'cat lady' like an old lady with a bunch of cats, or like Catwoman, the superhero?"

Ezra laughed. "Maybe a combination of both?"

Iris laughed too. Watching Ezra walk away, she felt a surprising hollowness in her chest. She had grown accustomed to solitude, but moments like this reminded her that she was alone. She wondered if he thought she was flirting. It was enjoyable to banter with him; that was all she told herself.

The small crowd that remained was getting louder and rowdier. Some teens were climbing light poles. Others huddled together, passing cans and bottles. It was time to get going, she thought. She was reaching for her car keys when—

CRACK. A single gunshot cut through the air like a lightning strike.

For a brief, terrifying moment, the crowd seemed frozen in disbelief before the panic hit. Screams rose like a wave. People scattered, signs dropped, water bottles tumbled, and feet pounded across the grass and pavement. Iris spun around, searching for Ezra, but he was already running back toward her.

"Down!" he shouted, grabbing her hand and pulling her toward the cover of the bushes.

Iris's heart hammered so loudly that she could barely hear the shouts and sirens. Across the field, police flooded in with weapons drawn. Chaos rippled outward in every direction.

. . .

IN THE MAYHEM, Nate quickly got his family out of the park and into the car but realized he was still missing Federico. A teenager ran through the park yelling, "A boy got shot! A boy got shot!"

Annabelle's hand flew to her mouth. "Dad, Federico was flying his drone on the other side of the park!" Nate said determinedly, "Everyone stays here. Keep the car locked and stay down. I'll find Federico." Sirens blared as more squad cars surrounded the park. Annabelle, her mother, and Aunt Joan all slumped in the backseat, holding hands for comfort.

ON THE OTHER side of the park, just minutes earlier, Federico had watched from the drone's bird's eye view as Joey approached an older man near the park's edge. Initially, the exchange seemed casual, merely two people talking. However, Federico's chest tightened as Joey handed the man a small bag, and the man, glancing around furtively, slipped him an envelope in return. They parted.

Something about the interaction felt off. He zoomed in, watching Joey open the envelope and pull out a stack of cash. Joey counted the money and then took off running back toward the man.

Frederico's heart pounded as the drone captured every movement. Joey running. The man pulling out a gun. He aimed. Frederico continued to watch through the drone camera's eye. He heard the crack of a gunshot, and then he saw Joey collapse, clutching his leg.

Panic gripped Federico as he followed the gunman's hurried retreat, his trembling fingers flying over the controls to capture every detail: the man's face and the license plate of the car. The man sped off in his car toward the freeway. As Federico brought the drone down, his hands shaking, the police were already at Joey's side, administering first aid and calling for help.

STILL HUNKERED down in the backseat, holding hands, Annabelle felt the current of Joan's strength flowing into her, then through her and into her mother. She became the conduit. The three of them breathed in and out, slowly syncing.

Joan closed her eyes. *Green Tara, swift protector, come now.*

"Our ancestors are with us, protecting us, holding us close," Joan said softly. "The Castillo line is strong."

Something shifted. Maria relaxed her shoulders. Annabelle sat up taller.

Joan continued, "Will you join me in a prayer for the boy who was hurt, for the person who was so hurt he used a gun, for all who experienced fear?" Maria and Annabelle nodded and closed their eyes.

"Dios mio, may all beings be free from suffering and the causes of suffering. May all beings rejoice in the well-being of others. May all beings live in peace, free from greed and hatred. May all beings know the beauty of their true nature."

Annabelle whispered, "Say it again, Tia."

Joan did, and a cloud of peace and well-being descended over them.

EZRA AND IRIS peered over the bushes. They spotted the cops across the park. Most people had fled, but a crowd had gathered around the two officers who reached Joey first.

"I think it's safe. I think we can get out of here," Ezra said.

Embarrassed, Iris self-consciously let go of Ezra's hand. "Okay, let's go."

They stood up and walked quickly toward their cars, with

Ezra's hand resting on Iris's back. Everything had happened so fast. Iris's heart was still pounding.

FEDERICO WAS TREMBLING as he put away his drone, knowing he had to cross the park again. Nate caught up with him. He blurted out, "Uncle Nate, I saw the guy who shot Joey. We need to go talk to the police."

"You saw the whole thing?"

"Yes, with the drone, and I saved the video." He glanced toward the police officers who had fanned out across the park.

Nate and Federico walked towards them. Nate said, "Excuse me, my nephew, here, was flying a drone and caught some video footage of what happened."

The officer raised an eyebrow, unimpressed by the kid with the gadget. However, when Federico whipped out his phone and showed the video, the officer's expression changed. Before pocketing their phone numbers, he scribbled down the license plate number and the suspect's description from the video.

Softly, Federico asked, "Is he going to be okay?"

The officer gave him a weary smile. "Looks like it was his lucky day. The shooter was a lousy shot. Just caught him in the leg."

Uncle Nate placed a hand on Federico's shoulder and steered him back toward the car. "Let's not make this a habit, please."

They approached the car, where Annabelle, Maria, and Joan were waiting and talking quietly. The moment she saw them, Annabelle leaned out the window. "What happened?" Her eyes darted between them.

With a grim smile, Federico said, "I caught footage of the shooting with the drone."

In the back seat, Annabelle felt immensely relieved that Federico was okay. She whispered, "That was the guy who walked past us. The guy you knew."

"I know," he whispered back, not wanting to say more in front of the adults.

Nate said, "Probably a drug deal that went south."

Maria said, "He looked so young."

"I think he's going to be okay."

Federico looked out the window, watching the downtown streets pass by. Annabelle watched Federico. She wondered how Federico was involved with the boy who was shot. But that conversation would have to wait for another time.

CHAPTER 23

$\mathcal{A}$ crowd of reporters pointed their recording devices at Mayor Regulus as he purposefully walked toward the entrance of City Hall. They hurled questions at him.

"What do you say about the violence at the protest?"

"Are the Rio Grande Bosque developers a local group?"

"Can you comment on the protesters who are saying they aren't going to allow this to be built?"

"When did the forest stop being a preserve?"

Ronald Regulus, with his blonde hair slicked back, dressed in a dark blue suit and tie, turned to face the crowd of reporters, the tall city hall building reaching toward the sky behind him. He smiled, his perfect white teeth gleaming. "Look, violence will not be tolerated at public gatherings. We are calling for a moratorium on protests until we can fully investigate what happened. Regarding the Rio Grande Bosque development project, it's good for the bosque and good for Cottonwood. This development will be done sensitively and sensibly, and I think when it's finished, it will be a crown jewel for New Mexico, for locals and tourists alike. It will be better than the San Antonio Riverwalk area. I assure you, construction will conform to conservation laws. Ultimately, it will increase tax revenue for the city and allow us to build more parks."

Regulus turned and entered the imposing twelve-story building, with reporters still shouting questions behind him. Holding his head high, he strode directly to the elevators for a meeting on the seventh floor with the project developers and investors.

The phones at City Hall had been ringing constantly since the protest, and people were angry. He entered the meeting room and glanced around at the faces of the men sitting at the long table. "Gentlemen," he began, his voice low, "the development is in trouble."

Ivan Storic leaned back in his chair, unbothered. "Listen, Ronny, you're not going to let a few tree huggers and kids derail a project worth millions to the city. We knew there'd be some pushback. We just push back harder."

A few men exchanged glances. They understood that sacrifices had been made, including the unfortunate Sutter incident. However, he shouldn't have been so stubborn. They had made him a generous offer, but, regrettably, he refused. What could be done? The stakes were too high.

Regulus wasn't in it for the money. He was more interested in money's twin: power. He viewed power as a ladder; this project could be his step up to senator or governor, even. His legacy as mayor would hinge on the success of the riverfront, as would his political future.

He paced the room. "We need to get ahead of this. Get it in front of the city council before people get more organized or informed. We need to make this a done deal fast. The quicker this happens, the better for all of us."

He stopped and placed his hands on the back of an empty chair. "In a way, the drug deal shooting at the protest worked to our advantage. We can stop the protests for now, but not for long."

The men at the long table agreed. "Get it to the council," Storic said, locking eyes with Regulus. "Fast."

Regulus nodded. The council leaned pro-business, but it was essential to secure their vote before public pressure increased. Storic and Regulus understood political types. The more constituents they heard from, the softer their stances became.

MEANWHILE, the first surveyors were already in the forest, measuring and parceling the land for development. However, as they attempted to work, they faced persistent harassment from birds. Crows swooped close, flapping their black wings and dropping objects on the head of the men. Tools went missing, and the relentless cawing was like nothing they had ever experienced. By the end of the day, the entire team had quit.

"There's something wrong with the birds in that forest," they said.

The next day, they were replaced by more men, only to be met with more crows determined to get in the way.

BACK IN HIS OFFICE, Regulus plotted, already envisioning the tourist ads running in California and Arizona magazines. He pictured Cottonwood residents sitting outside a brewpub beside the river, watching sandhill cranes fish, and kayakers waving as they paddled by. The development would become a tourist magnet, bringing more dollars to Cottonwood. It was beneficial for the city in so many ways.

There was only a flicker of doubt in his mind. He sighed. A memory surfaced of lying on his back in the forest as a child, looking up at the leaf canopy, and feeling a rare sense of peace and safety. But he was no longer a child, and consequential decisions needed to be made. He could not waver. He dialed the president of the city council.

. . .

A FEW DAYS LATER, the city council convened to hear the riverfront development proposal and vote on releasing city funds to assist with infrastructure. A large, full moon hung over the meeting room outside. An owl swooped low in a nearby field to catch a mouse. A skunk waddled slowly across the parking lot. Coyotes sang in the distance. Nature was on full display outside, but remained invisible to the participants inside the packed, windowless room.

Nate and Annabelle stood with dozens of others in the overflowing council chamber. Community members approached the podium one by one to share their thoughts. A two-minute timer counted down on the wall for each speaker.

Nate spoke into the microphone. "Cutting down the Cottowoods removes more than the trees. The mycelium networks— the forest's communication system will be damaged. This is a fragile ecology already under stress from climate change. We can't afford to break what's barely holding on."

Soon after, Annabelle approached the microphone. A man adjusted it to her height. She scanned the room, meeting the eyes of each council member before looking down at the floor. Then, with a deep breath, she looked up, steely-eyed, and said, "My name is Annabelle Castillo. I'm 11 years old. I live near the part of the forest that will be clear-cut for development. I've played, walked, and biked through that forest, probably since before I could talk. I want you to know that if you vote yes for the development, we will all lose a special place."

She took a breath, and her gaze hardened even more. "You think we need more buildings, stores, breweries, and maybe more money. But once those old cottonwoods are cut down, we can't bring them back. They are irreplaceable." She looked down to regain her composure.

"Don't forget the animals that live there. If you tear down the forest, where will they go? Where will the birds, coyotes, porcupines, skunks, and even the insects go? Where will kids play? Where will we go to learn about nature?

"I recommend you visit the bosque. Go there tomorrow and smell the yerba mansa blooms. Breathe in the scent of the wet leaves on the forest floor. Taste a wolfberry. Watch the water of the acequia flow by. Listen to the river and the birds singing. And then tell me it should be destroyed. I don't think you would be able to say that." She looked down and then quietly said, "Thank you for listening. Thank you for reconsidering."

She stepped back. Silence filled the room, followed by murmurs of support. Several people wiped tears from their eyes.

It was not enough. The council voted four to three in favor of proceeding with the development. For many years, development along the river had been discussed, and there had always been a sense that Cottonwood was underutilizing its prime location next to the Rio Grande. The barrier was the forest's preservation status and finding an investor. Now that these issues were resolved, the development would go forward. The gavel came down, and the room erupted in noise, with cheers from one side and cries of outrage from the other.

ANNABELLE BURST into tears when they announced the vote... Iris was furious and resolved to fight this until the end... Nate shifted the focus of his research to other parts of the forest, north and south of the city, where the development pressure wasn't as intense, and the forest could be helped... Maria felt she had somehow failed Annabelle... Ezra knew the situation was still in flux and that the ending had not been written... Federico, still shaken after seeing Joey shot, was lying low and reevaluating his choices... Joan didn't follow the news and was unaware of what had happened at the meeting, but she felt a shift in the field of things, a change she couldn't quite grasp, but comprehended it had something to do with the key she had given Iris…Roanoke and Delphinia were uninformed of the ways of human people and their meetings and decisions; nevertheless, they already knew the forest was in great danger and that the plan to save it needed to move forward. They needed to speed up their process of communicating with Annabelle.

CHAPTER 24

*S*ummer had officially arrived, and Annabelle was inconsolable about the city council vote. It was wrong in every respect. She tracked news of the bosque development by eavesdropping on her parents' hushed conversations in the kitchen, their voices low currents of unease.

She often escaped to the tire swing that hung over the cool, glimmering acequia, where she sailed back and forth for hours, toes skimming the air.

She walked the acequia trail and visited the river often. River had become a trusted friend, his low voice soothing, sometimes rippling with laughter, and at other times whispering the secrets of the forest. Annabelle had grown adept at slipping into that quiet, expansive state required to communicate with nature by slowing her breath, relaxing her body, and quieting her mind. With each conversation, she felt more rooted and more awake. River's wisdom was seeping into the dry soil of her thoughts, making her fertile ground for something bigger.

Most afternoons, she would lose herself in a book, traveling to other times and worlds. When she grew tired of reading, she sketched the plants and birds she saw in the woods, her pencil capturing the intricate lines of a leaf or the curious tilt of a sparrow's head. Her mind always drifted back to the forest, to Roanoke and the unanswered question of what she could do to protect it all.

The council's vote still stung. But she held tight to the seed of hope planted by Roanoke. He had promised he would return, and she was waiting, impatient, but ready.

ROANOKE, perched in a nearby tree, observed Annabelle. He felt nervousness flutter through his breast. It was time to approach Annabelle and try out the bond again. *What if it didn't work? What if he wasn't the right crow for the job?* He ruffled his feathers, shaking off his doubts, and swooped down to Annabelle's level.

Annabelle was filling the bird feeders when she noticed that the forest seemed different today; it was quieter, as if waiting. Just then, Roanoke landed awkwardly on a low branch at eye level with her. He overestimated the branch's ability to hold him and swayed to regain his balance. Then he decided to fly to the ground. That didn't feel right, so he returned to a sturdier branch. He looked down at Annabelle, who was looking up at him.

"Greetings," Roanoke spoke into her mind. He felt a bit ruffled but noticed that the connection was easier and smoother.

"Oh, hi! I was wondering when you would return," she said aloud, beaming. She switched to their mind-to-mind communication and quickly relayed to him her primary concern: "The council has voted for the development project. It looks like it is happening, but there's still something we can do, right?"

"Ah, I don't know a lot about the governance of the Human People." Roanoke had flown to the ground and walked, alternating between looking up at Annabelle and pecking at the earth as if searching for seeds or bugs. His words prompted Annabelle to wonder for the first time if there was some governance among the crows. It was another brand-new thought.

"Annabelle, there are two things you need to work on."

Annabelle said without reservation, "I will do anything."

"I don't know exactly how to say this to you, but we, the Crow People, would like you to strengthen your wings."

Annabelle quizzically looked at the large black bird. "But Ro, I don't have wings."

"No, no, you have what you have," Roanoke was flustered, "Your... your claws?"

Lola, nearby, slapped her hand against her forehead.

"Wait, do you mean my arms?"

"Yes, yes, yes, that's it!" Roanoke said excitedly, thrilled to have successfully conveyed the message.

"So you're saying you want me to strengthen my arms? Why? I don't understand."

"Yes, well, we need you to be able to climb high up in a huge and ancient tree. Unfortunately, humans lack wings, so you can't fly. Having wings would make it ever so much easier. Therefore, we need you to be very strong in your arms. We need you to be able to climb the Grandmother Cottonwood tree, even in inclement circumstances. Of course, this will all be delicately timed."

Roanoke paused, uncertain whether his communication was effective. This was still so new. They weren't in faery territory, but a bond had been established. He reminded himself they needed to continue working patiently at it, and it would keep strengthening.

"So, if I understand you correctly, you want me to climb a big cottonwood, and to do that, I will need strong arms?"

"Yes, yes!"

"It's been a long time since I've climbed a tree. And I've grown a lot lately. So I think you are right. I need to strengthen my wings," she smiled.

Roanoke believed she had just made a joke, but wasn't entirely sure. Crows were adept at jokes, but he didn't realize that humans made them. "Yes, little one. And also one more thing. You must practice remaining calm, especially when things get strange or dangerous. Calm will be your greatest power."

Annabelle nodded solemnly. "That's fair. I do get emotional sometimes." She inhaled slowly. "Okay. I'll practice. Strong and calm."

Roanoke's black eyes gleamed. "Very good, then. I am always nearby, and you can always call me in your mind if you need me. Work on these tasks, and when you are ready, I will return." With a flick of his wings, he lifted into the sky, joining another crow at the top of a nearby tree.

Annabelle watched him soar, feeling both excitement and worry swirling in her chest. The idea of climbing the Grandmother Cottonwood filled her with awe and a bit of fear. What if she wasn't strong enough? What if she failed the Crow People? *I can do this. I can do this.* And never one to let a to-do list linger, Annabelle started to plan how to accomplish her assigned tasks. The forest needed her, and she wouldn't let it down.

CHAPTER 25

"*I*ris, I found something." Blair Sutter's voice on the phone sliced through lazy afternoon air like a knife. Iris froze, mid-breath.

"Blair, what is it?"

"I came across some of Eric's day planners. He kept it old school and didn't keep a digital calendar." There was a brief, suspenseful silence. "You're not going to believe what I found."

Iris felt a chill and gripped the phone tightly. "I'll be right over."

In less than an hour, Iris found herself standing in front of Blair's two-story house, her heart pounding. The home, nestled in the Cottonwood country club neighborhood, starkly contrasted with Iris's. Ivy draped elegantly over the brick walls, and the expansive, impossibly green lawn whispered of wealth in a town where maintaining grass required a small fortune. Cottonwood's water bills for a lawn like this could rival a mortgage payment. Most yards in town were bare dirt, with a few hardy weeds.

Iris knocked, and the door swung open. Blair, dressed in

black leggings and an oversized maroon T-shirt, had her blonde hair styled into a loose bun.

"Iris, come in," Blair said, her voice quiet. She bit her lip.

They sat together on the blue velvet couch, the day planner open on the glass coffee table. "Let me show you. Here." Blair's long red nail contrasted with the white paper. "This was two weeks before he died. It says 3 pm, City Hall, Victor. And Victor was added to his contacts just a week before his death.

"And then, get this. There were two calls from him, three and five days after the initial meeting." Blair looked up. "I mean, it could be anything, I guess, but I looked up the phone number. The guy is a lawyer for Ivan Storic."

Iris's eyes widened. "Storic? The Storic? The main investor in the Bosque project?" Blair nodded grimly.

"Uhm, what's Victor's last name?"

Blair scrolled, "Montes. Victor Montes."

Something inside Iris caved in. *Victor Montes.* The man who'd sat across from her in meditation class, serene and attentive. The man who seemed to drop down from the sky like a gift from the synchronicity gods.

"Dammit," Iris muttered. She got up and walked on the thick carpet to the window. She carefully looked through the sheer curtain. A white Ford Escape was parked across the street with two men in the front seat. One was eating, glancing upward toward Blair's house, and the other appeared to be looking at his phone. She unconsciously touched the Tara pendant and key, still hanging around her neck.

"Iris, what is it?"

"Blair, I think I was followed here." It was all starting to make sense. She'd had a feeling she was being watched. The coffee shop. The rock thrower. And she was right.

"You were *what?*"

"Victor showed up at my meditation class. He was a lawyer and said all the right things. I thought... he was on our side." She took a breath. "I told him everything about my suspicions about your husband being murdered and someone from the development being involved."

"Oh no," Blair whispered.

A cold wave of regret washed over Iris. The realization hit hard. She'd put her faith in the wrong person. Again. After the mess of her marriage, she'd been trying to rebuild trust in herself, in her instincts.

How could I have misjudged Victor completely? But no, she caught herself. *Wishful thinking is what got me off track.* Her intuition had been right all along. She had felt like she was being watched. That meant she could trust herself. She would trust herself. This was a lesson not to give her trust away to a charming liar. Trust and verify with an emphasis on the *verify*, she thought.

She had to admit Ezra was right about Victor. She thought that Ezra was jealous, but that was yet more wishful thinking, making it difficult for her to hear the truth from him. *I'm evolving. I don't have to be perfect.*

"Okay." Iris inhaled. "Blair, I want you to stay alert and be careful. I think the Ford Escape parked across the street will try to follow me when I leave. Get the license plate number if you can."

"I have an excellent alarm system for the house. I don't think anyone could get in here," Blair said nervously, lines of worry etching her face.

Iris, divorced, knew that Blair was widowed, and she felt the bond of their single status. Neither woman was interested in feeling dependent on a man, but Iris knew she wasn't looking forward to sleeping alone and hearing noises at night. It was fortunate that Blair had the money for an alarm system. However, Iris couldn't add another bill to her list.

"Should we call the police, do you think?" Blair said.

Iris wished this could be resolved by alerting the authorities, but recognized that the authorities could no longer be trusted.

"No, I know we can't do that, sorry," Blair said quickly, reading Iris's face.

"Blair, when you go out, try to stay in places where there are lots of people around."

"I will. You too, okay?"

Iris left through the front door, got in her car, and drove away. Looking in the rearview mirror, she saw the Ford Escape slowly pull in behind her, a short distance away, trailing her like a shadow. She took a sharp breath. She was right. It would be hard to forgive herself for this if anything happened to Blair.

Driving home, Iris gripped the wheel, trying to piece everything together. What did she *actually* know? Smooth-talking Victor was Ivan Storic's attorney! He was the middleman, doing the dirty work for powerful and corrupt men like Ivan Storic. There was a high probability that he offered Eric Sutter a bribe, and that payoff would clear the path for development and obscene profits for his boss. But Eric had a spine and refused and then was murdered. And she had naively wandered onto Victor's radar, dragging Blair with her.

Victor attempted to mislead her by pointing fingers at the mayor, the police, and the fire chief. Maybe one or two of them were complicit. Maybe the fire chief accepted a bribe. Maybe the mayor knew more than he let on. But the trail had to start with Ivan Storic.

She cursed herself for being so open with Victor. He had the upper hand now. But she wasn't going to stay off balance for long. *It was time to follow the money.* She shook her head. *It always came down to that, didn't it?*

Iris pulled up to her house and killed the engine. The Ford Escape rolled past, slow and smooth, before settling like a predator a few houses down. Luckily, she lived on a street with a lot of activity. She entered her home, quickly locked the front door, and checked all the other doors and windows.

The familiar knot in her stomach returned with renewed

intensity. Ever since the rock incident, she had not felt completely safe in her home. What if the two men in the Ford Escape weren't just watching her or attempting to intimidate her? What if they were waiting for the perfect moment to silence her for good? She felt overwhelmed.

The adrenaline made her antsy, as if she needed to do something. Should she call Ezra? She didn't want to run to him every time she faced a problem. *He probably wouldn't mind. And he'd feel vindicated that he was right about Victor.* She couldn't handle that right now. And anyhow, she was single, he had a girlfriend, and leaning on him too much wasn't the answer. She needed to work this out on her own.

She went to her closet and rummaged through one of her moving boxes, which she still hadn't emptied. After searching for a few minutes, she found what she was looking for—her birding binoculars. She peeked through the curtain again. *Yep. Captain Creepmobile was still parked outside. I'm on to you, and I'm not scared of you.* At the window, she adjusted the binoculars to read the license plate. She wrote down the numbers, then went to her computer to access a free plate number lookup site.

The screen glowed with the final word: Rental. She shut the curtain, left the binoculars on the table, and told herself she'd sleep. But her bravado was an act. Every creak and thump of the old house jolted her awake with another surge of adrenaline until dawn finally broke.

XENA

The dark forces have arrived. Cue the ominous soundtrack. And Iris? Let's just say she's not exactly a Jedi Master of inner calm and intuitive clarity. Her mind is racing a mile a minute, and her heart is hiding behind a locked door.

She will figure it out and learn to trust, connect, and lean on her people, but not today. Possibly not tomorrow either. Luckily, she has me. Bodhisattva, guardian, universal furball of love and light. I've wrapped this house in so much spiritual protection that it's basically an invisible force field of cosmic duct tape. Ella helped too, reaching across time to slap a protection spell on the whole neighborhood like a cosmic grandmother securing the perimeter.

Now the real challenge is breaking through Iris's fortress of anxiety and her tragic overcommitment to *doing it herself.* Because this place is no solo gig. Trust me.

CHAPTER 26

The following day, Iris looked down at her phone and saw a text from Ezra. It read, "Want to go geocaching tonight? It might be good to get out in the forest." The text was followed by a winking emoji at the end.

Iris responded, "Actually, that would be great. What time?"

Ezra responded, "Pick you up at 7."

Iris typed into her phone, "You should know something before you come. I talked to Blair Sutter yesterday. Eric Sutter's death was no accident. And I think I'm being followed." She would leave the Victor revelation for an in-person discussion.

Ezra responded with an open-mouthed, surprise emoji, "Let's talk when I pick you up."

IT WAS EARLY EVENING, and Iris waited on the porch swing, eyeing the Captain Creepmobile parked a few houses away. Ezra stepped out of his van, all superhero T-shirt and an easy grin.

"Hey," Iris said.

"Cat lady! Ready for another treasure hunt?" He smiled, his eyes crinkling.

"Only if I don't end up buried under it." Iris tugged on her boots and shook her head. *Again with the cat lady?* She wore a white T-shirt and jeans, her shoulder-length dark hair tucked behind her ears. She wasn't much for makeup, but she applied a bit of lip gloss and subtle eyeliner for the occasion, although she hadn't considered Ezra as a romantic possibility since she found out about Molly. She gave Xena a final pat and walked down the front steps into Ezra's van.

"Iris, meet Molly." Ezra gestured toward the backseat. The small Australian shepherd mix looked at her with interested brown eyes. Iris felt everything mentally rearrange. She reached back to scratch the dog's ears, trying to hide her expression of shock. Iris found herself suddenly glad for the lip gloss and eyeliner as Molly gave a quick lick to her hand.

Iris surveyed the chaos of the van, filled with old to-go coffee cups, stir sticks, receipts, and crumpled fast food bags. She wondered what his apartment looked like and resisted the urge to tidy up.

Trying to focus, Iris relayed everything she had learned from her recent conversation with Blair to Ezra. She ended with, "So you were right. Victor is a bad guy. He tried to bribe Eric Sutter to turn over the preserve, and when Eric Sutter turned him down, he was killed. It looked like an accident, but I'm sure it wasn't. I can't believe I was so off on my judgment of him." She shook her head. "I told Victor everything."

"Don't feel bad, Iris. Who expects a corrupt lawyer-murderer to show up at a meditation class, anyway? We'll figure this out."

"Yeah, but maybe I shouldn't have rushed to see him as a perfect answer to my prayers either. I feel duped, but I'm trying not to be too hard on myself. I've done enough of that these past few years."

Ezra looked in his rearview mirror and said, "So the white Ford Escape? That's the car that's been following you?"

"Yep, that's the one."

"Let's see if we can't lose them." A few alley detours and one dramatic U-turn later and the Ford was gone. Ezra parked near the trailhead. "Come on. You'll like this."

Iris looked in her side mirror and said, "Do you think this is a good idea? Walking in the woods? What if they see the van parked near the trail?" Iris felt safer with Ezra, but wondered if it was a smart move to go strolling through the woods by themselves.

"I don't see them. I think we're fine. They're just trying to scare you."

"Well, it's working," she muttered. She wanted to lose herself in easy banter with Ezra, to pretend this was just a casual evening out, but she couldn't shake her hyper-vigilance. Fear had been awakened in her.

She noticed the weight of the key around her neck felt heavier. She touched the green Tara pendant, also on the chain. Although she didn't believe in luck or protection from inanimate objects, she thought that if green Tara could help her, she would accept. *Desperate times call for desperate measures.*

Ezra didn't bother to leash Molly, and she trotted next to him as they started down the dusty trail. He opened an app and began navigating to the cache site. Iris followed behind on the narrow path, marveling at how calm he seemed.

There were impressively large cottonwood trees with giant trunks flanking the trail, and the water was flowing through the acequia irrigation ditch. Looking down the path, they could see for a long distance. Muddy river water siphoned from the Rio Grande flowed gently toward them, with green cottonwood leaves framing the path and providing shade. The tranquility and beauty were a welcome solace. Being near water in the desert was magical and almost enough to bring Iris some peace.

She knew she had been spending too much time on her computer screen lately, and perhaps too much time alone. It felt good to move. When the trees occasionally gave way to alfalfa fields, she felt her eyes stretch to see the Sandia Mountain range in the distance. Breathing air with some moisture in it was a delight. Some of the dark clouds that had been surrounding her began to dissipate.

There was something comforting about being with Ezra; he seemed to take everything in stride. But she also had a small voice in her mind nagging her. *Am I relying on him too much?*

"Hey, I think we're getting close to the cache site. Let's see. We're looking for something the size of a shoebox somewhere around here." He checked his app. "The clue is: Where faeries dance, there is treasure." They both looked at each other and couldn't help but laugh. Iris shook her head. They looked around, and Molly did her part by sniffing the ground.

"I think I see something!" Iris exclaimed. She pointed and looked up, excitement flooding her. There was a hole in the tree about six feet up. She couldn't reach it, but Ezra's long arm stretched upward, pulling a box out of the hole. The box lid had a picture of a faery glued onto it. Ezra lifted the lid, and inside was a logbook to sign and a tarot card—the Magician. He gave the card to Iris. Then he reached into his pocket and put a crystal into the box in exchange for the card.

She looked curiously at the card. "A tarot card?"

"Yeah, it's the Magician card," he said nonchalantly.

"Oh, I don't know anything about the tarot." Iris was solidly situated in the mundane world of facts until recently. Divination was not in her wheelhouse. However, she remembered the idea of archetypes from her academic training. She studied the works of Carl Jung and Joseph Campbell in school. She felt an academic curiosity about what the Magician tarot card might mean symbolically.

"The Magician is about manifestation and will. It's about having the resources you need to accomplish your goals, even if you don't realize it." Ezra paused, thinking, looking toward the sky to bring the words in as he often did. "It's about taking something out of the field of potential and bringing it into being." He smiled in a satisfied way. "Hey, would you be willing to humor me?"

"Sure," Iris said, and then wondered if she had agreed too fast.

"Let's sit with this tree for a few minutes, and if you don't mind, I'd like to talk to the tree."

Iris could not have anticipated that her life would bring her to this moment, but she decided to go with the flow. Since starting what she referred to as her *new life*, she had met people who stretched the boundaries of what she considered normal. And she was surprised to feel herself becoming more and more open to what she would have closed herself off to in the past.

Ezra, Molly, and Iris sat on the ground under the tree. Molly was panting lightly. Ezra and Iris took a breath at the same time. Ezra began to speak, "Beautiful Cottonwood, we come here to wish you well, to wish you a long life, to tell you how much we enjoy your beauty, your bark, your leaves, your shade in the summer, and your profile against the sky in the winter. We appreciate all you do here. We ask that you bless us with your spirit, share your wisdom, and keep us oriented toward nature and protecting the natural world. Know that we are your allies."

Iris had anticipated this might be a silent prayer kind of thing.

Ezra smiled without shame. "I thought we could revive the Cottonwood worship society."

They sat a few minutes longer, taking in the forest's sounds and smells. Iris felt the air on her skin and the cool ground she was sitting on. She closed her eyes. She wondered if Ezra was hoping for faeries to appear.

With her eyes closed, Iris saw the woman again, more clearly this time, on the screen of her mind. Dark hair pinned back, boots laced tight, her dress catching faint starlight. The forest around her pulsed with hidden life. The basket she carried glowed faintly from within. The woman looked back at Iris, her gaze not so much meeting Iris's as seeing through her. She gestured at the entire forest with her hand. It was a message, but the vision faded. A message? A warning? She said nothing to Ezra. Maybe later.

Iris and Ezra got up silently and began walking back toward the car. After a quiet pause, Iris said, "So, another thing I haven't told you, something interesting happened before meditation class. I met with Joan, and she let me read a letter from Terry Goodfellow, the owner of my house, before Joan." She looked at Ezra, who indicated to continue by raising his eyebrows.

"He left her a letter when she moved in. It was all about a mysterious key." Iris noticed this caught the locksmith's attention. "Ella gave him a skeleton key in a fancy box when he moved in. She told him it belonged with the house, but he tried the key in every door, and it didn't fit any of them. When he moved out, he passed the key to Joan, telling her it would be useful someday."

"And now," Iris said as she looked up at Ezra, "Joan says the key belongs to me." She pulled the key on the chain around her neck out of her shirt and showed it to Ezra.

Ezra said, "Valerian Rose said a key was coming to you, didn't she?" Iris nodded. Ezra came close to examine it. "That's old, at least a hundred years, maybe more. Looking at that, I have a feeling I remember from childhood. It's an odd sensation. It's hard to explain. It's like something is not lining up. I felt it when we were with Valerian Rose, too. And now it feels like the key is here but not here." He shook his head. "I know it doesn't make sense."

Iris nodded, though she didn't exactly follow.

They walked slowly toward the car, catching the pink glow of the Sandias at sunset. After a thoughtful silence, Iris spoke up. "So, in some super weird way, I feel like the sale of the Preserve and this key have something to do with each other. They both tie back to Ella. I have no idea what this means, but I think I'm supposed to do something with this key." Saying it aloud gave the idea a solidity that made it clear and true in her mind.

Ezra nodded, "I think you're right."

"You know it's a strange coincidence about that Magician card. When I first met Joan, she said you were a magician. Then she said, maybe you're more of a wizard. Hey," she teased, "I think I have a nickname for you! You call me a cat lady. I think I'll call you Wizard. No, Wiz!"

Ezra smiled playfully. "I practice a little magic here and there."

Iris glanced at him, trying to read his expression. "You don't think all this is just a coincidence, do you? The key, the card, the trunk, everything that's been happening?"

Ezra's smile faded, replaced by a more serious look. "No, I don't. And I don't think you do either."

In the van, she noticed a religious charm with a blue tassel hanging from the rearview mirror. She recognized it as a saint but didn't know which one. Finding herself nervous again, she scrambled for conversation and said, "Hey, who is this?"

"Oh, that's Anthony of Padua. He's the saint of lost and stolen articles. He was a Franciscan. Pretty cool, as far as I know." Iris smiled at this. Her knowledge of saints was limited to St. Francis of Assisi and St. Michael. However, saints were visible everywhere in New Mexico: on candles at the local grocery store, in murals downtown, and in shrines in people's yards.

"He rides with me because I am one of his workers. What do people lose the most often?" Ezra asked rhetorically. "Keys. I help the people who lose keys, and maybe Anthony here helps a little too." Iris categorized this as yet another one of Ezra's strange quirks, like wearing superhero T-shirts.

"So how'd you become a locksmith?"

"Family business. My dad taught me. I took over when he retired."

"You like it?"

"I do. Especially the forensics work. Break-ins, safes, and figuring out how someone got in. I get to play detective sometimes."

"Like a spy."

"Exactly. A spy with pliers and a lock kit."

"Huh." Iris decided to ask something else she had been curious about. "You said you were traveling. Where did you travel?"

"Mostly Southeast Asia. I spent some time in Thailand at a Buddhist monastery for about nine months, then traveled around Vietnam, Cambodia, and Bali. I was gone for over a year, and then I was ready to come home."

"That sounds like an adventure. What was it like living in a monastery?"

"Hmm, it was lots of things, boring, interesting, hard. It did help me make a shift, though. And that was valuable." They were quiet for a few moments. "And what about you?" he asked.

"Oh, nothing so interesting. I've lived here for about four months. I came here for the librarian job at the middle school. I grew up in California and attended San Jose State University. Got married, then divorced seven years later. Then I moved here. I was ready to experience something different, someplace smaller. The skies here are amazing. I moved into the Silver Street house just a few months ago." Iris wondered if she should have mentioned her divorce.

"How do you like being a librarian in a middle school?"

"Oh, I love it. I love the kids. You know, middle school is difficult. They're figuring a lot out, changing, differentiating from their parents. I still feel like an awkward middle schooler myself, so I relate to them." Iris laughed.

"Ah, the awkward middle schooler," he teased.

Ezra pulled up to the curb next to Iris's house and then walked Iris to her door.

"Do you want to come in and sit on the porch swing for a bit?"

"Oh, hey, I don't think Xena would appreciate Molly waltzing onto your porch," he said, pointing to the cat on the porch swing.

"She loves the swing. I don't know why." Iris suddenly

remembered the white Ford Escape. She looked out the screened porch and scanned the street of her block, and there it was, parked two houses away. She felt the weight of stress and worry quickly return after the short respite of the walk in the woods. Ezra saw the car and felt the change in Iris.

"It's just intimidation. Don't let it get to you. I'll see you later. Be careful. Lock your doors. Keep your phone with you. You'll be fine."

"Okay, see you later. Thanks for inviting me. Getting into the forest was good."

Iris unlocked the front door and followed Xena into the living room, and then immediately locked the front door. Thoughts about fearing for her safety competed with thoughts about whether she was just on a date. She was unconvinced that this was a date, but she liked Ezra and was thankful for his friendship. He helped her calm down and gave her things to think about, both qualities she appreciated.

Iris glanced at the picture of Ella on the mantel. She looked at the snakeskin. There was no doubt in her mind that she was shedding one identity and building another. Or maybe she was becoming more herself, she thought.

XENA

Good move on the dog, Wiz. Speaking of good and evil, there are cats and then there are dogs. Just kidding.

An impenetrable wall of safety surrounds the house so Iris cannot be harmed here. I can't control what happens out there, though. But she does carry the key. The key, dormant no longer, is increasing in power. It hums now, faint but rising.

As the carrier of the key, Iris's power grows every day as she draws closer to Ella. Being a carrier of the key is an enormous responsibility. Annabelle, the other key carrier, has her helpers. Iris is my responsibility.

I see Ella in the before-times, in the forest, entering into an agreement with the Fae. She and one of the tall Queens exchange paper for iron—a valuable piece of paper for the key. They foresaw the future. And that future is now. Coiling like smoke, their futures intermingle: Annabelle, Iris, and Ella, the Fae, and their keys.

CHAPTER 27

Federico panicked, pressing all the drone control buttons at once, but it wouldn't budge. *Uh oh, ground control, we have a problem.* He had challenged himself to fly his drone higher and closer to the treetops, and today, a sudden downdraft sent it straight into the tree's branches. Although Federico wasn't too worried, he estimated it would be dark in about half an hour.

The camera displayed only a blue sky, indicating that the drone was upside down. He could see it cradled in the gnarled fork of a cottonwood tree. A pair of crows gazed down at him from their perches.

Barely thinking, and with no time to waste, Federico removed his shoes, stuffed the controls into his pants pocket, dug his fingers and toes into the crevices of the bark, and started to make his way up the tree.

Climbing slowly, he approached the drone. He glanced down. He was twenty feet above the ground. His stomach dropped, in the way that happened when he gazed over the edge of a cliff while hiking with his family in the Sandia Mountains. *I can do this, I can do this. I have to do this.* The drone was so much more than a toy to him. He continued up the tree, his arms and legs beginning to shake with the effort.

He was close but needed to climb onto a horizontal branch to reach the drone. He approached the branch and lay on his stomach. When he looked down, a swimming sensation filled his head. For a moment, he considered turning back. He was thirty feet from the ground. His fingers ached from gripping so tightly, but the drone was the one thing that made him feel powerful and free, and losing it was not an option. But nothing eased the feeling of fear at this height. The superpower he felt while flying the drone evaporated. He was a fragile human, too far from the ground.

Desperation to recover the drone overcame his fear, prompting him to crawl on his belly while grasping the branch with his arms and legs. The brace made sliding easier and protected his front from the bark. As he got closer to the drone, the branch became thinner. He forced himself to focus on the drone, now just a few feet away, pushing his fear aside.

He snapped a slender branch off the main limb to extend his reach. With the branch, he could almost touch the drone. However, leaning threw him off balance, causing him to fall toward his outstretched arm. He dropped the stick and grabbed the main branch with both hands, but now he was hanging upside down, his legs and arms wrapped around the tree's limb.

A cold wave of dread washed over him. His heart raced, and his hands grew increasingly slippery with sweat. Instead of resting his body weight on the branch, he was suspended, the muscles of his arms and legs keeping him from falling. He felt his grip loosen, and he hung momentarily from just his legs before they also gave way, leading to his long fall.

Time slowed as the sky receded and the drone got further and further away. He struck branches as he fell, the world blurring into shadow and pain. Until finally, silence. Then the shape of reality shifted. He stood impossibly upright, the forest around him altered, darker and colder.

Then he watched as a beautiful, tall woman with large black eyes stepped out of a tree as if through an invisible door. She wore a blue cloak lined with white fur, secured with a round metal clasp at her shoulder. Saying nothing, she looked sadly at Federico.

Then her face seemed to melt, transforming her from a lovely woman into the black stump of a tree. Federico was frightened but found he couldn't run; he couldn't move at all. He saw a dark world filled with the skeletons of trees. There were no green leaves, only bare and broken branches. What had once been fertile earth was now just sand. The river and birdsong were silenced. Federico, unable to move, could only gaze at this forest of death and despair.

Joan picked up her phone to hear Emma's panicked voice. "Is Federico there? He hasn't come home." Joan looked at the clock. It was 8:30 and dark outside. Emma continued, "He was out with that drone again. He's not answering his phone."

Joan replied, "I'll be right there." She grabbed a coat and flashlight and drove to Emma and Marco's house to help search for Federico.

Marco called his sister Maria: "Federico's missing. Could you guys come over and help us look for him? We think he's in the forest. His bike is here. He's been flying that drone every day."

"Oh, Marco, of course, we'll be right there." Maria called out to Nate to grab flashlights and water bottles for everyone. Annabelle and her parents piled into the car to drive to Federico's house.

. . .

ANNABELLE HEARD HER PARENTS' measured voices as they tried to mask their worry during the short drive to Federico's house. She sat in the backseat, looking out the window, her eyes already searching for her cousin in the dark.

Before reaching the house, they saw flashlight beams nearby. It was Aunt Joan and Emma. Joan wore a long coat and a scarf, and Emma had on a puffy fleece. Cottonwood was at an elevation of 5,000 feet, making it warm during the day but still chilly at night. As they approached the house, they could hear people calling Federico's name. In addition to the family, some neighbors had joined the search.

Annabelle closed her eyes and reached out to Roanoke in her mind. Unsure if this would work, she silently said, "Please help me find Federico." She felt a jolt of affirmation and then jumped out of the car with her flashlight.

She heard Roanoke's voice in her mind. "Annabelle, now is a time to practice staying calm. Keep breathing, making your exhales longer than your inhales."

Annabelle knew exactly where to go. The forest itself seemed to guide her. Nate took off after his daughter. "Where are you going? We should coordinate with the others."

"I know the forest better than anyone here. Follow me." Confidence and power infused her voice. Nate fell in line behind her. The forest was dense and dark. Nate shone his flashlight in front of Annabelle to light the way. Annabelle got off the path and walked through the brush. Bats circled above them.

Annabelle continued to slow her breathing. She wasn't thinking anymore; she was just breathing in rhythm with her walking and moving in the direction she knew she needed to go. She had no fear, only resolve. It was as if the forest walked with her.

Owl wings whooshed above. Something rustled in the brush,

probably a porcupine or skunk. She walked without stopping, with a single focus, gradually leaving the other flashlight beams and the shouts of Federico's name behind. Back on the trail, they came to a fork. Annabelle paused, went to the right, and walked another three hundred yards through the dense woods. She stopped.

"He's here!" At the same time, both Annabelle and her dad saw Federico lying on his back at the base of a large tree, with his drone beside him.

They ran to him. Federico's eyes were closed. While shaking Federico's shoulder, Nate loudly called out his name.

There was no response.

Nate checked his nephew's breathing and pulse. Both were faint. He took off his coat and covered the boy. Turning to Annabelle, he said, "You need to go back and tell the others we found him. I'll stay here with him." Nate checked Federico's breathing and pulse again. He pulled out his cell phone and tapped 911. Annabelle hesitated; she wanted to stay with Federico.

"Hurry," Nate said. She turned and ran back through the forest, knowing this was what she had to do. The forest was cold and filled with shadows. Annabelle felt no fear of the forest or the night, only worry for Federico. She connected to the forest's intelligence with her mind and heart as she ran.

In response, a faint glow on the forest floor led her to where she needed to go. Annabelle quickly found her aunts, Emma and Joan, and led them back through the woods to Federico and her father, following the same faint glow.

Seeing her son lying on the ground, Emma brought her hand to her mouth and stifled a sob.

"He's breathing, he has a pulse, paramedics are on the way. It's going to be okay, Emma," Nate reassured her.

Annabelle observed the adults. Emma knelt beside Federico, her hands trembling as she brushed his hair away from his closed eyes. Joan and Nate stood just behind Emma, exchanging glances.

Annabelle stood back a bit. She silently contacted Roanoke and included the Fae for good measure. "Please help him," she whispered, her voice tight with worry.

They all looked up when they heard the sirens. Knowing what she needed to do, Annabelle quickly glanced at her dad and ran through the woods again, not even bothering to turn on her flashlight. Emma looked at Nate, questioning. Nate shrugged his shoulders.

Annabelle reached the paramedics and said, "Follow me!" She then led the two of them, weighed down by the stretcher and their equipment, quickly back deep into the forest.

The paramedics exchanged glances as they began walking through the dark forest. "Are you sure you know where you're going?"

She didn't stop. "Yes, follow me, this is the way."

After they reached Federico, time seemed to speed up. Vitals were taken, Federico's neck stabilized, he was hoisted onto a stretcher, and his brace was noted.

Federico's mother, Emma, walked alongside one paramedic, answering all the questions she could: how long had he been out there, how long had he been unconscious, what was his medical history?

As Annabelle led the group back to the house, she silently thanked Roanoke for his help. The small group walked over a mile back to the road, where the paramedics lifted the stretcher with Federico on it, still unconscious, into the small, light-filled space at the back of the ambulance. The paramedics started an IV. Emma climbed into the back of the ambulance with them as they shut the doors. The ambulance lights flashed red on the road as it pulled away from the house. Federico's dad followed behind in the car.

Left standing in front of the house, Annabelle, her parents, and Aunt Joan watched as the ambulance sped away, listening to the siren until it faded from earshot. Maria had her arm around Joan, while Nate wrapped his arm around both Maria and Annabelle. Maria and Joan discussed it and decided to head to the hospital to wait with Marco and Emma.

Maria looked at Annabelle, who was shivering, and exchanged a glance with Nate. Nate said, "Come on, Annabelle, let's go home."

WHILE WAITING at home for news about Federico, Annabelle fell asleep on the couch. Nate carried her to bed, marveling at what his daughter was capable of that night. He recognized he often became caught up in the ideas and details of his work. Somehow, Annabelle had grown strong and independent, and what is it that her mother has always called her? Fierce. This all happened right under Nate's nose. There was so much he hadn't noticed until tonight.

Nate couldn't imagine what Emma and Marco were experiencing at the hospital. He hoped Federico would recover fully and return to being the goofy kid he remembered from family get-togethers. Still, he thought, it was all so fragile, hanging by a thread: the forest, the kids, the future.

Nate was a solutions guy, a problem solver. He wasn't a philosopher and didn't think much about the meaning of life. He did his part to keep the place running. But on a night like tonight, he couldn't help but think about the mystery and fragility and beauty of it all. Some things required faith, a belief in something bigger than himself. Annabelle had shown him that tonight. She had led him through the darkness, guided by something he couldn't see or understand.

His cell phone vibrated. "Maria, what's happening?" he asked when he saw her name on the phone screen.

"It looks like he's going to be ok," she said through tears.

"You should come home," Nate said, knowing she wouldn't but wishing she were here with him now.

"I'm going to stay, Nate. They need me."

"Yeah, I know, you stay. We'll see you in the morning. Love you."

"Love you."

CHAPTER 28

*I*ris learned about Federico's fall when she bumped into a woman from her meditation class at the grocery store. The woman explained how Annabelle had discovered him, and the news left Iris feeling anxious. First, the shooting at the protest, and now this. Annabelle had faced a lot recently. *I guess we all have.*

She wondered if Federico's fall was somehow her fault. He had been so excited about flying the drone with George Miller. But had she led him straight into danger? She shook her head, reflecting on how invincible young boys could feel and how easily that feeling could lead to tragedy. Iris decided to pay Federico a visit at the hospital.

Hospitals always made her uneasy, but she eventually found her way to the children's floor. Federico's room was completely white: white sheets, curtains, walls, and tile floor, broken only by a few Mylar get-well-soon balloons and a bouquet of carnations. Federico looked small in the bed. His arms and face were bruised; the blue and white hospital gown covered his thin frame, and an IV trailed from his arm. The woman from the store said that the head injury wasn't too serious and that the brace had likely saved him from worse.

"Ms. Barnes!" Federico's face lit up.

Iris joked, "What were you trying to do, Federico? Fly up to join the birds?"

"Ms. Barnes, we have to save the forest, and I have an idea, but I might need your help."

Iris, not expecting this, but skilled in listening when a child took the lead, leaned closer. "Tell me."

Federico worked the switch on the side of the hospital bed and shifted under the white sheets to sit up taller. "Okay, so here's what I'm thinking. Like the Forest Service, we map all the trees in the bosque. We'll use a drone, of course. Maybe Mr. Miller's. Once we map them, we'll tag each one with a metal number." He gestured excitedly.

As he talked, the image of the woman in the blue cloak returned. She hadn't been just a dream. He felt her presence close to him, almost guiding him.

"Then we'll set up a website where people can adopt a tree. Each tree has a QR code. People can post why they adopted the tree and add pictures, poems, or anything. It's like their own social media page for their tree, and everyone can visit other people's pages, too."

He paused to take a breath and then continued. "You know the way people pay money to be able to name a star? This is like that, but better. They can visit the tree, bring friends, watch it change with the seasons."

He paused. "We'll need some money to set up the website and the server. I want to give the rest of the money we raise with tree adoptions to the Bosque Preservation Project to keep the forest healthy."

Iris beamed. "Federico, I love this idea! Tell me what spurred this."

"When I fell," his voice uncertain, "I saw, I don't know, a vision? A woman came out of a tree. She kinda looked like you. Then she melted, and the forest turned to black stumps. It was awful."

Iris nodded. "Go on."

"It felt like she was asking for help. I think we need to do this. I believe we can stop the development. I just…feel it."

Iris smiled. "I hope so, Federico. I really do."

Federico thought that if his grandmother Lucy were alive, she would say: *From your lips to God's ears.* That line always made him smile.

After the librarian left, Federico's energy surged. He decided to get out of bed and stretch his legs. He'd walked with the physical therapist before and knew he could unplug his IV pole and walk with it for a short time. As he stood up, the dizziness came in waves, but it was getting better, and he leaned on the pole for stability.

At the nurse's station, he asked, "Excuse me. Do you know what room Joey is in? He had a gunshot wound to his leg."

"Yes, is he a friend of yours?" She raised her eyebrows.

"Kind of," Federico said self-consciously.

"He's in room 411 down the hall and to the right."

Federico hesitated at the door, his hand on the knob. It felt like he needed to make something right, and the feeling wouldn't let go until he spoke with Joey. Taking a deep breath, he turned the handle and entered Joey's room.

The room looked much like his own, white everywhere, and it had the same sterile smell. But one thing caught his attention immediately. Joey had a teddy bear on the bed. It was old, fur worn thin, a button eye replaced, arms slack. Federico blinked. The bear didn't fit his image of Joey as a cool, tough guy.

Joey, propped up in the bed, was drawing on a sketch pad

when Federico entered the room. "Rrrrico! Hey, what happened to you, man?"

"My drone got stuck in a tree, and I tried to climb up and get it. But I fell. And I hit my head." Federico tapped his temple.

"Well, lucky you didn't hit that pretty face." They laughed a little too loudly.

Joey saw Federico glance at the bear again. "My mom brought it. I've had it since I was a kid. She thought, you know, it'd make me feel better."

There was an unspoken admission in Joey's voice, a crack in the armor he usually wore. Federico felt the weight of it. For a moment, he wasn't Joey the cool kid. He was a boy who needed comfort.

"Yeah, I get it," Federico said softly.

Joey shrugged as if to dismiss what he'd just revealed. "Anyway, what's up with you?"

Federico, not experienced in small talk, gathered himself and took a breath. "I saw you get shot. I was flying my drone at the protest. I saw the whole thing."

"You were the one who gave the cops the license plate number?"

"Yeah." Federico nodded and looked down.

"I thought so." He paused, thinking. "You know I'm in a little bit of trouble." Joey looked away. "For selling." He crossed his arms over his chest. "I was mad for a while. Ratting isn't cool. It's against the code. But...I've had some time to think. What you did... it was for the best."

Federico nodded, feeling reassured. "Do you have to go to jail?" he asked quietly.

"Me? No, I won't go to jail. But I'll have to do some community service. Picking up trash, that kind of thing. When my leg heals." Joey smiled with a bit of bravado that didn't stand up to scrutiny, with a stuffed bear lying beside him.

Relieved that Joey wasn't going to prison, Federico shared,

"I'm building a website. I'm going to; that is when I get out of here. It's to save the forest. Maybe you could help me. For your community service or something."

"I don't know anything about building websites, man. But look at this." Joey handed Federico the sketch pad he had been holding.

Federico flipped through it. Life-like animals jumped off the pages—birds, a porcupine, coyotes, and fish. The drawings pulsed with life. He turned to look at Joey. "You drew these?"

"Yeah. I used to draw when I was younger, but then I got away from it. But being in here," he looked around the hospital room, "there's not much to do."

"Yeah, I know." Federico paused, their shared experience making the conversation easier. "You know, you're really good. Maybe I could put some of these drawings on my website, you know, giving you credit, and people would see your artwork."

Joey's smile faltered slightly. "Yeah, maybe." He glanced away, his fingers absentmindedly tracing the edges of the sketchpad. "I don't know about all that. Drawing pictures doesn't change how people see you."

"People *can* change," Federico said slowly. He felt a thought taking shape. "Flying drones changed me. And then when I fell… that changed me too. You getting shot, that's bound to change you."

Joey snorted. "Yeah, it gave me a limp." But his eyes softened.

They sat in silence for a moment, the bear sitting between them as a witness to their conversation. Federico wanted to say more, to tell Joey that he didn't have to go back to the same friends who'd gotten him into trouble in the first place. But he didn't want to sound like a know-it-all. Instead, he leaned forward slightly, lowering his voice as if what he was about to say was a secret. "When we get out of here, we could meet up at the city library. That's where I'm going to work on the website."

Joey nodded, but his eyes had turned distant. "Yeah, sure. I'll think about it."

"Okay, well," Federico paused, unsure. "Keep drawing. You're really good. I'm going home tomorrow, but I'll see you around. At the library?"

"Yeah, thanks for coming by, Rrrico. Yeah, maybe I'll see you at the library."

As Federico walked back in his non-skid socks, gown flapping, doubt walked with him. *Could Joey really change?* He didn't know. But he hoped.

CHAPTER 29

$\mathcal{A}$nnabelle joined her parents at the outdoor dining table in the backyard. The aroma of hamburgers on the grill enticed her outside. She took a patty on a bun and began squeezing ketchup onto it, then twirled a sweet potato fry between her fingers.

"So, how do I strengthen my arms?" she asked casually.

Nate looked up, a little surprised. "Well, I can tell you, your legs are strong! You ran like a track star that night in the forest with Federico."

"It was adrenaline, Dad," she said, rolling her eyes a bit. This was a new habit.

"Honey, I'm sure your arms are perfectly strong," Maria added.

"Actually, I tried to climb a tree recently, and my arms weren't strong enough to lift me."

Maria shot Nate a look. "Well, considering what just happened to Federico, I don't think we want you climbing up any trees."

Annabelle started to regret bringing the topic up and was resigning herself to figuring out the problem on her own. But then her dad said, "What do you say we go to the climbing gym together this weekend?"

Annabelle perked up. "Thanks, Dad." *Climbing a rock wall seems different than climbing a tree, but it might work.* Turning to her mom, she asked, "Can you take me to visit Federico later tonight?"

"Sure, I'd be happy to." The cousins were close. Since Annabelle was an only child, Federico was almost like a brother to her.

Annabelle went to her room and drew a get-well card for Federico, featuring a drone flying over the forest and two crows in a tree. She folded the paper and wrote "Get Well Soon" on the inside and "Love, Cousin Belles."

Maria packed some cookies and, at the last moment, remembered to grab the cottonwood bud salve Joan had made for Federico. Joan had said, "It heals and soothes with its warmth." Maria opened the jar near Annabelle's nose, and Annabelle closed her eyes, smiling at the scent of resinous cottonwood buds.

"Aunt Joan's salves are the best."

"Mmm hmm."

At the hospital, Annabelle sat in the big chair next to Federico's bed. Federico was sitting upright. His tray table held a cup of ice water and a drone manual. The room's white walls and tile floor gave the space a clinical chill. Federico looked like himself, but was marked with bruises on his arms and a fading bump on his forehead.

Maria moved around the room, turning off the television, closing the drapes, and picking up tissues and food wrappers while making cheerful small talk with the kids about summer plans.

"We brought cookies." She smiled and placed them on Federico's tray table. She lingered for a few more minutes, then excused herself to the lobby, where the wi-fi was better for doing work.

Annabelle had been quiet, but as soon as they were alone, she leaned toward him. "Tell me what happened."

Frederico became animated, telling her every detail of his vision of the dead forest and the woman in the blue cape. Then, brimming with excitement, he shared his idea of creating a website to save the forest. "But I need to get out of here and start building it. The logging could start any day now. We don't have a lot of time."

Annabelle's heart sank at the word *logging*. She shared his urgency but had no clear plan. When would Roanoke contact her again? Would she be able to help the forest?

"Rico, this is going to be hard to believe, okay?" Federico looked at her intently with all his attention. "I've been talking to a crow and a faery." Federico blinked, unsure if he should laugh. But his cousin appeared serious, so he stayed quiet to hear what she had to say.

Annabelle glanced out the window toward the forest before looking back at Federico. Quietly, she shared everything about her conversations with Roanoke, River, and Lola, expressing her determination to save the forest, even though she didn't know how yet.

She also told Federico how she was guided to find him in the forest. "I was so afraid for you that night," she said, her eyes shimmering.

"I'm lucky you were there," Federico said, considering everything Annabelle told him. It was a lot to think about. "I think we're both supposed to help save the forest in different ways. You know how Aunt Joan always says things happen for a reason?"

"Yeah, I've been thinking about that too."

"I think I fell from the tree to meet the woman in the blue cloak and get this idea about the website. And you've always been friends with the crows."

Annabelle nodded. It felt good to have a purpose, even if hers still felt a little blurry. She was jealous of Federico's clarity.

She glanced at her cousin, heart thudding, as she voiced her biggest fear. "Rico, do you really think two kids can save the forest?" Her voice was barely a whisper.

Federico looked out the window. Outside, the wind stirred the leaves of the cottonwoods. "I don't know, but Aunt Joan says we need to have faith, even when things seem impossible. And maybe..." He looked up toward the ceiling, "Maybe it's not just us. Maybe others are doing their part. I don't know." He turned his palms up to the ceiling and shrugged. "So I'm going to have faith and do my part."

Annabelle nodded slowly. *Have faith and do your part. That sounded like Aunt Joan.* She wasn't sure how they'd pull it off, or even if they could. But they had to try.

Roanoke and Sarafina perched on the top wire of a fence overlooking a quiet pasture. Baby sheep cavorted, and horses grazed. The pecan trees nearby were a favorite of the crows.

"I am getting the hang of the connection. It was hard at first. I think the Fae helped a lot, but Lola..." Roanoke shook his head.

Sarafina knew the faery and could sympathize, "Yes, the Fae are not always easy to work with, but they do have abilities I respect."

"I was so tired initially, and Delphinia was very worried. But it's easier now. It's gotten easier every time. I think we are ready."

"Excellent work, Roanoke; we will let you know when."

Roanoke swelled with the praise.

"One more thing," she added. "The time is coming when our partnership with the Humans will be more important than ever. They will need our messages, even if they don't realize it." Roanoke nodded, trying to imagine this new world.

Serafina continued, "We will start with the young ones, strengthening the bond, and then maybe with some of the elders, too, if they're able." Serafina turned away from the grassy field to look directly at Roanoke. "You will help the Crow People learn to grow this bond. Know that you have already done well, my friend."

Sarafina took to the air from the wire fence without saying goodbye. Roanoke, suddenly uneasy, watched her fly for a few moments and then took off to join Delphinia.

CHAPTER 30

$\mathcal{I}$t was early in the morning when Iris peeked out of her front window to look down the street to see if the white Ford was still there. It was. She had had a restless night, waking up frequently and feeling nervous with every creaky noise she heard in the old house. Maybe it was the lack of sleep, but by the time she got out of bed, fear had boiled over to anger.

It was a Saturday. She debated whether to text Ezra.

Her phone buzzed. It was Ezra. *Of course.*

"Hey, Iris, how are you this morning?" Her anger melted, and she bit her lip to hold back a rush of emotion.

"I'm okay. To be honest, I didn't sleep much."

"Are you up for a walk?"

"Yes. Actually, that would be great. But," she paused, an idea forming. "Can you give me an hour?" Iris dressed quickly and ran a brush through her hair. She looked in the mirror. *You can do this.*

She glanced at Ella's photo and the snakeskin in the living room on the way out the door. She turned to Xena. "I'll be right back," and marched out, letting the door slam behind her. She

207

flew down the front steps and crossed the street toward the white Ford Escape. The tinted windows were up, but she could see the two men inside through the front window. She tapped firmly on the passenger-side glass, and after a few seconds, it rolled down an inch.

"What are you doing following me? Who sent you? Was it Victor?"

The man in the passenger seat, bald with bad skin, wrinkled his nose. "You're crazy, lady." The stale stench of old food and sweat wafted out of the car.

"Maybe. But don't pretend you haven't been following me for days. It stops now. I'm calling the police. And if I have to, I'll call my congressman. I'll call the governor! I won't stop." The sharp, commanding tone she used on defiant teenagers in the classroom was called up for duty. "This is OVER, do you hear me?"

The driver stared ahead. The bald man shook his head. The car pulled slowly away. Iris didn't know how long the reprieve would last, but triumph coursed through her as she watched them drive away.

EZRA ARRIVED in the white van at the agreed time. Iris had showered and changed since the confrontation. Climbing into the familiar jumble of coffee cups and crumpled receipts, she felt strangely powerful. Molly wagged her tail in greeting from the backseat, and Iris reached back to scratch her head.

"You seem lighter," Ezra said as he pulled onto the road. "Happier."

"Yeah. I don't think I'm being followed today, so that's a win."

Ezra gave her a long, sideways look. She sensed his suspicion but allowed the silence to linger.

When Iris didn't say anything for a few minutes, he spoke. "Okay, so what's the next step? You have proof from Blair that her husband was in contact with Victor, and Victor works for Ivan Storic, so…"

"Yeah. Good question. I'm not sure we can go to the police."

"Then maybe we take it to the public."

"Hmm." Her brows knitted together. "How do you suggest we do that?" She had been thinking along similar lines, but the evidence Blair provided seemed too thin for a news story.

At the trailhead, they walked single-file down the dirt path, with the river to their left and the forest to their right. A flock of terns circled above the swollen river, still running strong from the upstream dam release. Lime-green coyote willows swayed gently, obscuring the view. As they walked, nature slowly worked her magic. Iris felt her breath deepen, and her body settle.

Ezra took a deep breath, his eyes distant for a moment. He spoke quietly. "I think I know someone who can help. A friend—he's in cybersecurity. He's… unconventional, but he's good."

Iris's eyes flashed hope. "Really? You think he could find more evidence?"

Ezra thought back to the cybersecurity conference when he first met Zero, a charismatic hacker with a Robin Hood streak. Their paths had crossed when Zero's safe was broken into, leading Ezra to use his locksmithing skills to track down the culprit. Since then, they'd exchanged favors, though Ezra had never learned his real name.

"Depending on what my friend finds, I also know a reporter who would be interested in this kind of information. He protects his sources so you would stay anonymous. I have the feeling this information needs to be shared with as many people as possible. And the faster, the better. For your safety."

Iris considered. "I want to go with you to see your friend."

Ezra shook his head. "Not a good idea. He's a cybersecurity guy. In other words, he's paranoid. He knows me. It's better if I go alone."

Iris squinted her eyes. "Do *you* think we might be able to save the forest from development?"

"Depends on what he finds, but I think if there was criminal activity involved in this land deal, it would need to be reexamined." They both stopped and stood to look at the river as it flowed toward them. "But we need to act fast. I'll try to make contact tonight. He works out of a place downtown. It's been a while since I've seen him. If he's not still there... I don't know. The chances of finding him are slim." Iris quietly nodded.

The river sparkled under the sunshine, insects buzzed, and the breeze rustled the leaves on the trees. Life pulsed all around them, and they let it lift them.

After their walk, Ezra took Iris home. As she opened the van door to leave, Ezra leaned toward her. "Be careful, but have faith. I think we can do this."

Iris smiled and nodded. "Okay, good luck with your friend. Text me."

Back inside the house, with the magic of the forest fading, hope and worry danced uneasily. Would the SUV return? Would Ezra's hacker friend help? She had no answers. But she believed something was shifting.

Xena curled up in her lap as she sat by the window. Iris scratched around the cat's ears and gazed out at the light filtering through the trees. Sleep tugged at her, and she allowed herself to drift.

Xena

Humans. Always complicating things, but so cute anyway.

Iris's second body—the subtle field that surrounds the physical form—is frayed today, tangled with threads of worry. That's why I stay near. Soothing the field is one of the primary duties of cats. Dogs try, bless them, but they lack finesse.

Once the subtle body is calm, the physical form can draw strength from it. When the field is balanced, it can receive messages from the Otherworld. This is sacred work—my work.

Her fingers find my ears. Perfect. It is a fair exchange, though treats later would be appreciated.

CHAPTER 31

*A*fter talking to Iris, Ezra was ready to act. He just hoped he could track down his elusive friend, Zero. The guy didn't rise before mid-afternoon and didn't start working until midnight.

At 1 a.m., Ezra drove through the sleeping city and parked on Broadway. Downtown was mostly empty. High-rise office buildings loomed like silent sentries. He circled the block, scanning his surroundings. No sign of anyone following, but that didn't mean he wasn't being watched. They followed Iris, so they knew about him, too. The bars hadn't closed yet, but the streets were dark and still.

He approached the alley, each step echoing. A streetlight was out, likely on purpose if he knew Zero. The alley reeked of urine, and garbage spilled from bins against the wall. A broken shopping cart with a dirty red blanket slumped beside a graffiti-covered dumpster.

Some people found charm in the seedier side of Cottonwood. Ezra wasn't one of them. He preferred staying closer to the forest and the river.

He descended a narrow flight of concrete stairs, dropping

below street level. At the bottom stood a heavy, black, handleless door, featuring just a keypad. Ezra punched in a code he'd memorized years ago. Overhead, a small camera swiveled with a soft mechanical whir. Ezra waited, alert, his heartbeat quickening, hoping Zero was still here.

After waiting a few minutes, he was almost ready to leave when the door creaked open. A hulking silhouette filled the doorway.

"Ezra!" boomed a voice. A large arm wrapped around Ezra's shoulder. "Haven't seen you in forever, man."

Zero appeared as though he had just stepped out of a biker bar in the dead of night. Dressed in a leather jacket with stringy brown hair and a stubbled jaw, he had a presence that commanded attention. He could have been intimidating, if not for the warmth in his eyes. Rather than riding motorcycles, Zero navigated data streams and was likely one of the best hackers alive.

They stepped into a dimly lit room, lit only by the gentle glow of five large monitors. A huge screen hung from the ceiling, showcasing a blinking, digitized world map.

Zero grinned. "What brings you to the Batcave, man?"

Ezra returned the smile. "I've got a favor to ask you."

"Course you do. They always come for favors," Zero said with a gravelly laugh.

Ezra filled him in on the forest preserve, the development plans, Victor Montes, and Eric Sutter's death.

Zero nodded, fingers already twitching. "Anything for nature, man. That's what it's all about." He smiled an ironic smile. It would be hard to say when Zero last visited nature. His skin was preternaturally white. Ezra doubted he'd seen sunlight in years.

Zero popped an energy drink, draining it in three gulps, then cracked his knuckles and got to work. His fingers flew across the keyboard, muttering all the while. "C'mon.. Yeah, no… oh, you've got to be kidding me… there we go."

Ezra surveyed the room while Zero worked. It hadn't changed in years. Measuring about 25 by 50 feet, the walls were made of gray cinder blocks, and the floor was concrete with a shine. There were no windows, but the ceiling was surprisingly high. A few large couches and upholstered chairs formed a circle in one corner, and mismatched throw pillows were scattered across the furniture. Empty takeout boxes and coffee cups dotted the tables. Bookshelves overflowed with programming manuals. A large book titled "Cryptanalysis" rested beneath a monitor on a motorized height-adjustable desk.

Ezra began to differentiate between the various beeps coming from different screens. Warning banners flickered across the large ceiling screen.

Zero scoffed. "They think a basic firewall is going to keep me out? Amateurs." Lines of code raced across the screen. "Found him. You're right about Montes. That guy's a snake. He has a side hustle with the Cottonwood police department, bribing cops for business and then getting DUI offenders off by having the cops not show up to the hearings. You can bet the Chronicle would be all over that. Also, he seems to have a hard time walking away from the blackjack tables. Sky high gambling debt." Zero shook his head.

"Wow, so he needed the bribe money for gambling debt." Ezra felt even more vindicated about his initial impression of Victor.

"That's not all." Zero kept typing, his face hardening. "Phone records show Blair Sutter and Victor Montes were in contact a week before her husband died."

Ezra felt the air leave his lungs. "Blair?"

"Yep. She deposited a suspicious 500k after her husband's death, then another 500k in life insurance money. She's all set up. Looks like she took down her husband for the cash. Your instincts were right, but you needed a wider net."

Ezra's mind reeled. He had to call Iris. And call his friend at the Cottonwood Chronicle. This was way bigger than he thought.

Zero leaned back, cracking his neck. "The money trail leads to Ivan Storic, the Bosque project mastermind, like you figured."

Ezra shook his head. "I thought he might be involved, but I still can't believe Blair's a part of this."

Zero stood and stretched. "She's more than involved. She's an accomplice to murdering her husband."

Ezra got up off the couch. "I owe you one, man."

"Yeah, you do, man." Grinning, he walked Ezra out the door and back into the alley. "Hey, there's not a girl for you involved in this, is there?"

"Well, maybe," Ezra tried to stifle a smile.

Zero laughed loudly while slapping Ezra's back, saying, "I knew it."

Ezra made his exit quickly, looking in all directions. *There's no hiding anything from Zero. And he sees through people like he sees through code.* He shook his head. With his hands in his pockets, he returned to his van. Just to be safe, he checked the back. When he pulled out, he checked the side mirrors for any unwanted taga-longs. But it was all quiet.

CHAPTER 32

First thing in the morning, Ezra texted Iris. "Meet me at Trifecta?"

Ezra kept opening his phone and checking for a response. *Why isn't she answering?* He texted two more times. An hour passed. Worried, he decided to drive to Iris's house.

Ezra's grip tightened on the steering wheel as his mind raced with worst-case scenarios. *What if Victor had already gotten to her? What if Blair had sent someone? Or lured her into danger?* As he drove, his mind entertained various scenarios of Iris being kidnapped or killed. He was increasingly convinced she was in grave danger. Driving too fast, he hit the high curb in front of Iris's house, scraping his bumper.

He leaped out of the van and bounded up the steps two at a time to her front door. He quickly scanned the door, and a scratch on the lock mechanism confirmed his fears—it had been tampered with. He knocked. No answer.

He tried peering through the windows, but the curtains were drawn. Every second felt like it could mean the difference between life and death.

Running back to his van, he rummaged through his bag to find the tool to unlock her front door. Hurrying up the steps, his fingers shook as he managed to turn the old metal knob with his lock pick. He swung open the door, and with all his senses heightened, he entered Iris's living room. Then he froze.

"Ezra, what are you doing here? Did you just break into my house?" Iris stood in the living room, freshly dressed in jeans and a plain yellow T-shirt, toweling off her wet hair.

He exhaled, hand to chest, and the words tumbled out. "You weren't answering my texts. I got really worried. I thought you might be in danger. There's a scratch on your lock. I thought someone broke in."

Iris continued to dry her hair with the towel. "Well, I'm not sure if I should be mad or flattered." Her smile diffused the situation.

Ezra stepped further into the room, still keyed up. He took a deep breath, trying to calm the adrenaline spike. "Sorry. I know this looks bad. But after what I found out last night, I couldn't just sit around."

Iris raised an eyebrow. "What did you find out?"

"I saw my friend, Zero. You won't believe this."

Iris nodded toward the couch, and they moved to the living room. She sank into the leather cushions, towel still draped around her shoulders. Ezra took the oversized Stickley chair and leaned forward, elbows on his knees. Xena strolled by, circling once before curling up on the sunlit rug.

"Tell me," she said.

Ezra launched into what he'd learned—the data trail, the depth of Victor's criminal life, the bombshell of Blair being an accomplice to the murder of her husband, the money involved, and its origin. As he spoke, the tension in his body eased.

When he finished, Iris sat frozen. She pressed her forehead into her hand, her stomach twisting. "So, I fell for Victor's story and then got duped by Blair, too? I actually felt some girl-power solidarity with her. Ugh." She groaned. "People are the worst." She looked at Xena, who blinked serenely, then closed her eyes as if unfazed by the world's darkness.

"Don't beat yourself up. These people are experts at manipulation." Ezra shook his head. "I sent the scoop to my journalist friend. When it goes public, I think the authorities will have to act."

Iris's eyes narrowed. "One thing doesn't make sense. Why would Blair, if Blair and Victor are accomplices, try to steer me toward him as the murderer?"

"I thought about that, too. I guess criminals don't have much loyalty. It could be that she saw the walls closing in and tried to get ahead of the fallout. My guess is Victor arranged the murder, and Blair burned the office, but whatever. They're both criminals. The important thing is that the public will not view the Bosque development favorably, knowing it was based on a bribe that resulted in a murder. It's already turning into a headache for the mayor. The poll numbers are bad."

"Yeah, that will be hard to move on from. We have to make sure the information isn't suppressed. When powerful people are involved..." Iris's voice trailed off, and she looked down at the rug.

"Agreed. And speaking of that, I don't think you're safe until this information is out. Both Victor and Blair tried to throw you off the trail. You're a threat to both of them. Iris, I hate to say this, but you're not safe here."

She nodded slowly. "Yeah, I've been thinking that too."

"And you need an alarm system. This neighborhood is not the best, and these old locks are easy to break into," Ezra said firmly.

"Yes, you've mentioned that." Iris glanced down toward the floor.

"I want you to stay at my place just until this plays out." He looked expectantly at her as if anticipating an argument.

Iris remembered her multiple sleepless nights since this all started. It would be a relief to feel safe. At the same time, she felt a little unclear about their relationship potential. Were they friends or friends on the verge of becoming something more? Her lips pressed together. "Hmmm, I hate to impose on you. Maybe I should get a motel room."

"No way, pack a bag, and let's go. You're staying with me."

Ezra's resolve convinced Iris. With that settled, Iris packed a bag and called a neighbor to feed Xena. Although Iris felt terrible leaving the cat alone, it wouldn't be for long. *Hopefully, this will get sorted out in a few days.*

IRIS HESITATED at the door to Ezra's apartment, her overnight bag slung over one shoulder. He opened the double locks and stepped aside to let her in.

"Welcome to Casa Ezra," he said with a mock bow.

Molly greeted them with jumps, twirls, and sniffs. Finding everything acceptable, she curled up small on the couch, her tail covering her face, looking more like a fox than a dog.

Iris took in the small one-bedroom apartment and immediately wondered about the sleeping arrangements. "I'll take the couch," Ezra said, reading Iris's mind.

With that clarified, Iris scanned the place with interest. It was minimalist and surprisingly tidy, considering what she knew of the interior of his van. He had leather furniture, a Persian rug over Saltillo tile, a small altar in one corner with a zafu cushion, a white candle, incense, the Magician tarot card, and a small elephant statue.

Ezra's eyes followed Iris's. "That's Ganesha, he's a Hindu god, a slayer of obstacles."

She also noticed a small jar on the altar that looked like it contained sugar. "What's this for? Is this sugar?"

"Ahh, that's a little something I'm working on." Iris sensed she would not get more out of him on this topic and dropped the subject.

"Huh," Iris replied, eyeing his bookshelf—*The I Ching*, a few books of poetry, *The Tibetan Book of the Dead*, Aiden Wachter's *Six Ways: Approaches and Entries to Practical Magic*. She picked up a book by Richard Rohr, *Radical Grace Daily Meditations*. She remembered that in one of their first conversations, Ezra had spoken about allowing grace to infuse her burdens. That felt like a long time ago.

"Rohr is a Franciscan. He has a center in the South Valley; they do excellent work," he offered.

"I don't see any fiction," she said, trying to sound casual.

Ezra smiled. "I check fiction out from the library."

"Oh," Iris said, chastened. Extra-good human confirmed.

They migrated to the kitchen where Ezra began preparations for a simple dinner of chicken, vegetables and rice. While he chopped peppers, Iris shared her conversation with Federico at the hospital and his idea for an adopt-a-tree website.

Ezra brightened. "I do web design. I can help him."

Iris's eyes shone. "Really? That'd mean a lot to him."

"You know, I could see that catching on- adopting a tree. I want to adopt one for my niece and nephew. Heck, and for myself. If I can get in on the ground floor, I can get one of those huge cottonwoods." He grinned, holding the knife mid-air.

Iris laughed. Molly looked up and tilted her head, smiling in response. But then Iris became serious. "Federico told me he had a vision... of a dead forest and a woman in a blue cloak. This vision inspired him to develop this plan to save the forest." Iris paused. Federico fell from a tree, which could explain a hallucination. Yet she was having strange visions about the forest as well. *Were other people having these experiences?* She hadn't told Ezra about her experiences during meditation class or during their geocache adventure. In her mind, she attributed the visions to Ella, but maybe the forest itself was exerting its influence on the community. *That was a strange thought, but could it be true?*

THEY SETTLED INTO A RHYTHM. Ezra got up early and would meditate and then make breakfast. Iris prepared dinner. In the evening, they rewatched old Star Wars movies. Ezra silently mouthed all the lines, sometimes jumping off the couch to act them out. This made Iris laugh and shake her head. "You're such a nerd."

"Thank you," Ezra replied, hand to heart with mock earnestness.

Each morning, Iris would pretend to sleep while Ezra said a prayer aloud at his altar. "Benevolent allies and ancestors, Fae people, spirits of the land and trees, please keep everyone in this home safe, happy, and healthy. Accept this offering and draw strength and sustenance from it." He would then place a small cup of coffee on the altar.

On the second morning, Iris took a bite of toast and thoughtfully chewed. "Hey, you know I teased you before about Joan calling you a wizard, but I was wondering," she paused, trying to formulate words, "What does magic mean to you?"

"Mmmm. Well, fundamentally, magic, to me, is working with the unseen forces, the world on the other side of the veil, to impact this world in various ways. I think of it as a relationship. Something that needs tending and attention."

"Oh, I've been wondering about the prayer and offering you do every morning."

Ezra smiled and looked down into his coffee cup for a moment, and then met her eyes. "I've found that honoring my ancestors is one of the most powerful things I can do to impact my life. Lots of cultures do it. I have other allies, but my ancestors are probably the most helpful to me, personally. It's a lot easier to get their attention."

"Hmmm," Iris said, unsure how to continue.

Ezra warmed up to the topic. "It's like we are the point of the spear, but the spear is long and composed of everyone who went before us. All those ancestors care about the trajectory of that spear." He paused, watching Iris.

"Hmmm." Iris nodded tentatively. She appeared lost in thought.

Ezra continued. "I believe there is a constant flow of energy, inspiration, and help that goes in both directions between us and the Otherworld. The messages we receive from them are often symbolic or subtle."

This was a touchstone Iris was starting to understand. "Like the tarot and dreams and synchronicities?"

"Exactly."

Iris crossed her arms, leaning back in her chair. "But what if all of this," she waved her hands, "magic, ancestors, and the Otherworld, what if it's just a way for people to make sense of things they can't control? What if we're just here alone, without any help?" Even as she said it, she knew she no longer believed this to be true.

Ezra smiled, unfazed by her skepticism. "Yeah, maybe." He shrugged. "I find my life works better if I approach it with the idea that everything is alive and connected across space and time. The past isn't gone, and the future's already reaching back to us. We have allies we can't see, and magic is the deep intelligence moving through all things, connecting them. And at the heart of it all, what holds it together is love. That's what works best for me. For my life." He shrugged again but watched Iris carefully.

"So belief is practical, even if uncertain," Iris mused.

"Yeah, you could say it that way. You know, the Greeks had two types of knowledge: Logos and mythos. Logic and story. Modern life leans hard on logos. But without myth, we lose heart and meaning."

Iris nodded, thoughtful. Ezra's openness stirred something in her. She still held magic at arm's length, yet part of her wanted to draw it closer. She had crossed the bridge of belief that Ella really was exerting some sort of force from the Otherworld. And if that were true, then maybe the world was more alive and filled with allies than she had allowed herself to believe.

CHAPTER 33

Blair Sutter dialed Victor's number. Iris nosing around was making her nervous, and something needed to be done. She couldn't risk losing everything.

She recalled the first time she called Victor. Her husband, Eric, came home one night, pale and troubled, and told her he had been offered a million dollars to turn the Bosque preserve over to the city. Blair's heart jumped. A million dollars. It could pay off their loans, get them out of their old rental, and into a new house in the country club area.

"Do it, honey, we deserve it."

Eric shook his head. "It's not right. Somebody trusted my dad to set up the preserve. I would be betraying my dad's word if I took that money."

"But they're all dead. We're alive, and that money would help us." They argued the same points back and forth. Blair pleaded with him to take the bribe, but Eric stood firm.

"I'm going to tell him no." He shook his head. "I shouldn't have brought it up."

That night, Blair stared at the ceiling, watching the slow rotation of the fan. She felt the crash of disappointment as the dream of comfort and wealth slipped through her fingers. It wasn't just the money. It was years of being overlooked. It was Eric's dedication to his work and his father's legacy, while she spent evenings alone. Their marriage felt stale. She saw a chance to break free and live the life she'd always imagined. Without him.

She began to fantasize about spending the money. She could take the acting lessons she had always wanted, upgrade her wardrobe, buy a new house and car, and get involved in theater. She realized there was one way to turn this into a reality, and it didn't take her long to decide.

"Hello, Victor, this is Blair. Eric Sutter's wife," her voice shook despite her best efforts. "I have a proposition for you. One that'll make us both very rich."

Victor's instinct was to shut down the call immediately. Blair's plan was reckless; it wasn't straightforward, like a bribe. Victor had the game of bribery down pat. Everyone was greedy, and it was easy. He paid the city DUI unit cops to refer their DUI citations to him and then not show up for arraignments, so all charges were dropped. He charged these DUI clients exorbitant fees for his guarantee to get them off the hook. Everyone was happy: the cops, the clients, and his bank account.

But as she kept talking, the wheels in his mind started turning. She was greedy, but maybe he could steer this. Blair offered to split the bribe money from Ivan Storic, and she'd also receive the stiff's life insurance money. It wouldn't be easy, but the payoff was tempting. Gambling debt weighed heavily on his mind, and this deal had the potential to clear it all. In the end, greed won out and Ivan Storic grudgingly signed off on the plan.

Eric's car careened off the edge of a mountain road on the way to his weekly golf game after swerving to avoid another car. Victor was driving that car. Days later, Blair set fire to Eric's office, making it appear as though it was an accident. The flames conveniently consumed all records of the Preserve.

It had gone perfectly—until Iris Barnes showed up. A friend at the city records department alerted Victor when Iris began looking at the Preserve tax records. Victor put a tail on her right away. Then, Blair told him Iris was suspicious about Eric Sutter's death. Once he discovered Iris attended Joan's meditation class, he decided to see if he could throw her off the trail. Joan was an old neighbor, so it was the perfect cover.

He tossed her some red herrings: the mayor, the police chief—anything to muddy the waters regarding his involvement. It worked better than he had imagined. Iris actually trusted him to get involved.

Now, Blair was calling again, and he was furious. She had gotten scared and implicated him in Eric's murder to Iris. Blair was forcing his hand. This whole situation was turning into a giant headache. Blair wanted him to do damage control and find a way to get Iris out of the picture, which he would probably have to do somehow.

But he also couldn't trust Blair. This whole thing was unraveling too fast. Blair had pushed him into a corner, and Iris was getting too close. If he didn't clean up this mess soon, then everything- his reputation, career, and freedom- could all go up in flames.

Iris Barnes' amateur sleuthing was putting the whole project at risk. He had to think. Things were bad, but they might be about to get a lot worse, and he needed Ivan's protection against any accusations coming his way. He needed a plan.

VICTOR CALLED in a favor to one of the cadre of police officers involved in his DUI bribery scheme. The officers were all reliably corrupt, but he called Officer Griegos, the one who owed him the biggest favor. Victor had gotten Griego's brother out of jail after a hit-and-run a year ago that left a teenager in a wheelchair.

Gruffly, he said into the phone, "Griegos, I need something handled today."

"Yeah, what kind of something?" The officer's voice was cautious.

"That librarian. Iris Barnes. She's causing problems." Victor clenched his jaw.

"The one digging into the river development? What do you need?"

"Scare her. A lot. Make her understand she's in over her head."

There was a pause. "Yeah, I can do that, but it'll cost you."

Annoyed at having his own tactics used against him, Victor gripped the phone tightly and snarled, "How much?"

"I'll do it for $3,000."

"Fine." Victor hung up the phone, cursing under his breath.

CHAPTER 34

The whine of chainsaws woke Annabelle from a restless sleep. She glanced at the clock: 7:30 am. *So, this was the day.* She threw on jeans and a T-shirt, then moved quietly toward the front door. Since her talk with Federico at the hospital, she had made her own plan to help the forest.

"Where are you going, Annabelle?" her mother called from the kitchen. "Are you taking Sparkpuff out? You haven't had breakfast yet."

"I know, Mom, I want to get outside for a little bit, uh, before breakfast."

"Stay away from the development. It's not safe there this morning- they're cutting trees."

Annabelle rushed out the door and broke into a run straight toward the development. The scent of gasoline and sawdust hit her first, followed by the sight of cottonwood trees ringed with yellow caution tape, large branches already on the ground.

Two massive trucks loomed like mechanical beasts, out of place in this natural setting. Men in bucket lifts raised roaring chainsaws high into the trees. Seeing this made fury rise in Annabelle's chest.

"Arrrrgh!" she screamed, racing toward the tree and the men who were cutting it down. A branch cracked and fell with a heavy thud a few feet from her, rattling the ground.

A worker caught a glimpse of her from the corner of his eye. He frantically drew his hand across his throat, signaling his team to turn off the chainsaws.

The roar died. Ear protection came off, and heads turned. There she stood at the base of a cottonwood tree. A wisp of a girl, barely eleven, trembling but unyielding, arms crossed.

"No! No! No!" she shouted to the men.

The foreman on the ground stepped forward, trying to make sense of the situation. "Honey, it's not safe here. You could get hurt. You don't belong here."

The indignant rage building inside her since she learned of the Bosque development project found its target. "Oh yeah? How many years have *you* spent in this forest? Do you know where the porcupines sleep? Where the crows nest? Where the coyote den is? No? Then *you* don't belong here!"

The men exchanged stunned glances, bewildered at finding themselves scolded by a young girl. The foreman nodded to the other men, signaling that he would handle the situation. He approached the girl and stood at a respectful distance, as if acknowledging her authority in the forest.

"My name is Glen."

Annabelle looked at him warily, anticipating a trick and prepared to lash out if necessary. She said nothing, her fists clenched at her sides.

"You know, I grew up around here, too. I fished in the river. I climbed trees as a kid. Still do, technically." He smiled.

Annabelle didn't budge, and her eyes remained steely.

"To tell the truth, I don't think this development is a good idea either. But it's work. And I've got a crew with families to feed."

She said nothing, yet something about his words caused her anger to dissipate slightly. Her eyes grew softer.

"I love trees," he added. "Most days, I'm trimming trees to keep them healthy. Cutting down a healthy tree always breaks my heart a little. What's your name?"

"Annabelle."

"Well, Annabelle, you just did a very brave thing. Kind of a stupid thing, too, but in my experience, brave acts often require a little stupidity."

Annabelle could see the truth in this. She didn't know where this was going, but as he kept talking, her grip on her rage was becoming harder to maintain, and she was getting dangerously close to tears. She desperately did not want to cry.

She wasn't ready to give up. She pleaded, "Please don't cut down these trees."

Glen stared at her for a long moment. While doing so, she did something she had done only once before. She reached out in her mind to Roanoke and the Fae. *Help.*

"Let me talk to my guys." Glen turned and walked back toward his crew. They spoke in muffled voices.

Annabelle stood frozen while the men huddled in discussion. She did not know what would happen next, but at least she knew she had done everything she could.

After what felt like hours to Annabelle, Glen returned.

"Okay. We think you might be right. We don't belong here. We're canceling our contract with the city and packing up."

Annabelle's eyes widened, stunned.

"You should know they will probably have another company out here within a few days, maybe a week. I want you to promise me you're not going to risk your life again. The next time, you might not be so lucky."

She hadn't actually thought through the possibility that she might be successful, and so she wasn't sure what to do next. Eventually, she said, "Thank you." Then she turned and walked toward home, a little shaky and not knowing whether she should laugh or cry. Behind her, the chainsaws stayed quiet. And the trees stood. For now.

GLEN CALLED the city and explained about the young girl in the forest, that he had reconsidered the job, and that he was voiding his contract. The man on the phone, who managed the city works department, asked who the girl was. Glen told him, "Annabelle."

Word got around the city offices that a young girl named Annabelle had managed to stop the clearing of the bosque land. A reporter overheard the story and called Glen for an interview.

Glen appeared on the six o'clock news and told the story of his encounter with the girl in the woods and how she had caused him to reconsider cutting down the trees.

The reporter asked, "What do you think of the Bosque development project?"

Glenn shook his head. "Honestly? I think it's a damn shame."

The next day, Glen's phone rang continuously. He filled the company calendar with enough work for the next six months, and people were thanking him for standing up for the forest. He thought he was making the worst business decision ever, but it turned out that listening to his conscience and to a young girl was actually the best business decision he ever made.

Meanwhile, Annabelle became a legend. Reporters tried to find the mysterious young girl who had single-handedly stopped a crew of loggers. Her folk hero status grew in the community as the story circulated through the coffee houses and grocery store checkout lines. Reporters chased down rumors and whispers about the girl. But they never found her.

Eventually, years later, one of those same reporters wrote a book about her titled *The Legend of Annabelle and the Loggers*. There were embellishments, but he knew the essence of the story was true.

Maria and Nate, Annabelle's parents, didn't watch the TV news. In fact, they didn't own a TV. However, Joan happened to watch the news that night and knew exactly who that little girl was. She considered calling Maria, but something told her to stay quiet. Miraculously, Annabelle's parents never found out about her confrontation in the forest.

At City Hall, chaos brewed. "This is a circus, Regulus! A little girl stopped the logging crews. We're getting questions about bribes, and even about the murder of that lawyer. And now every idiot in town thinks these trees are special."

The Mayor wiped sweat from his brow. *What next?* The birds in the forest were acting bizarrely. Reporters were circling. The project could lose its investors. It was all going sideways.

He had no choice but to double down and weather the storm. He couldn't afford to let it fall apart—not now. "They'll love it," he muttered to himself. "Everyone will see." He had to find a way to succeed. His political future depended on it.

CHAPTER 35

Iris was becoming restless in Ezra's apartment. After three days, the walls felt like they were closing in. She decided to venture out to the grocery store with a detour to the city library. *Just a quick trip. Nothing risky.* As she drove out of the apartment complex's secure parking lot, she had no way of knowing the challenges ahead.

A siren pierced the air after she had driven just a few blocks. A police car appeared in her rearview mirror, red lights flashing, signaling her to stop. She maneuvered to the side of the road, her heart beginning to race. She wasn't speeding. She didn't run a light. *What was this about?* She reached for her registration and insurance in the glove box, fetched her driver's license from her wallet, then rolled down her window.

As the minutes ticked by, a second squad car pulled up behind the first officer. *Could this have to do with the Preserve?* The first officer approached her window, while the second, his hand hovering near his weapon, positioned himself behind her car. *I'm just a librarian, for heaven's sake, not a criminal. What is going on?*

The officer approached her window. "Registration, insurance, and license, please." Iris handed him the documents. "What is this about?"

The officer looked at the papers, nodded to the other officer, and said, "Please get out of your car, ma'am. Turn around and put your hands on your vehicle."

"Look, can you tell me what's going on?" *Is Victor behind this?* She was getting too close. She imagined the investors had gotten phone calls from reporters after Ezra had released the information from Zero to the Cottonwood Chronicle. They knew the development was in trouble. They were trying to scare her, and it was working. Her heart felt like it was going to pound right out of her chest.

"Ma'am, there's a warrant out for your arrest. Seems that you didn't show up for a court date."

"A court date for what?"

"Doesn't say here, just that there's a warrant. We need to take you in." He took hold of Iris's wrists roughly and brought them behind her back. Iris heard the click of the handcuffs around her wrists. The officer led her toward the back of the squad car.

The smell of coffee and cigarettes on his breath made her stomach turn. The handcuffs bit into her wrists. He hissed into her ear, "You're full of yourself, aren't you? You need to back the hell off the development project, lady, or they'll find you at the bottom of that river. Accidents happen in this town all of the time."

Iris's eyes got wide. She needed to breathe, but it was like her lungs had forgotten how. She needed to keep her wits about her, but the more she tried to think, the more frozen her brain became. She was hijacked by fear.

IRIS WAS BOOKED INTO JAIL. She was searched. They took her fingerprints. Her belt and shoelaces were removed and put in a bag. If they were worried about her hanging herself, she wondered why they didn't take the chain with the key and Green Tara pendant from around her neck?

"Hey, you know you're making a huge mistake. And don't I get a phone call?" Iris said sharply to the guard, leading her to a cell.

"Yes, you'll be offered a phone call." But by his tone, it sounded like that might take a long time.

Iris was led into a cell, and the door was closed. She sat on a thin mattress facing metal bars painted a sickly green. The smell of industrial cleaner burned her nose and barely covered the odor of urine and despair. She could hear someone sobbing down the corridor and the rhythmic drip of a leaky pipe. The harsh fluorescent lights buzzed overhead.

She felt nauseous. Her teeth were clenched, and her jaw hurt. Her breath was ragged. The reality of the cell made her want to cry, but she had too much adrenaline coursing through her. This was all too much. She should never have gotten involved. She started pacing the cell. *I have to calm down. I have to think.*

Iris tried to will herself to slow her breathing. *No one knows I'm here. No one is coming to rescue me.* The clanging of metal doors opening and closing echoed through the building. Guards talked in loud voices. A woman yelled expletives as she was being walked to a holding cell.

Don't panic. Keep yourself together. She took a slow, deep breath and sat down, determined to slowly relax her body from her head to her feet. After she did, she returned to her jaw and relaxed it more.

It was a stretch, but she imagined she was in a group meditation class, and a blanket of stillness enveloped her. The sounds of the jail just became part of the background. Thinking back to Joan, Iris released her burdens to the Divine, as best she could. She briefly wondered what Ella would do in this situation.

Heavy footsteps approached her cell. Looking up, her breath caught. She could hardly believe her eyes.

CHAPTER 36

The warden appeared with Valerian Rose at his side. Valerian gave Iris a conspiratorial wink as the cell door slid open.

"We're sorry, miss. There's been a computer glitch. We can't find any warrant in the system, and we're not sure what went wrong. This has never happened before." Valerian Rose stood quietly beside him, nodding, smiling calmly. He added, "You're free to go, miss. Please follow me."

Iris and Valerian walked in tandem, their footsteps echoing through the jail corridor. Iris couldn't help but steal glances at Valerian. As they approached the exit, the warden touched an electronic sensor, and the double doors slid open with a soft whoosh.

In that soft whoosh, Valerian said, "Thank the Queens, dear. And pay attention to what happens next."

The warden pointed toward the lobby exit. "You can leave through that door after you get your belongings at the window. Sorry again for the trouble. I'll call the impound lot and let them know to release your car to you. I can get you a ride there if you need it."

"No, I'll call a friend," Iris said, eager to leave before he changed his mind. Iris turned from the window with her belongings and froze. Valerian Rose was gone.

She asked the woman at the window, "Did you see where my friend went?"

Iris received a puzzled look. "I didn't see anyone in the lobby but you."

She stepped outside into the bright afternoon heat and looked in all directions. The sidewalk was bustling with men in suits and women in dresses and heels, all carrying briefcases, hurrying to court dates and meetings.

It was as if Valerian Rose had never been there. Iris felt a breeze against her face. Freedom and relief washed over her. She touched the key and the Tara pendant around her neck, closing her eyes briefly. *Thank you.*

She sat on a bench at a city bus stop, considering her next move. Calling Ezra would be easy, but he was working and had already done so much. She decided to call Joan. However, before she could punch in the numbers, a crow swooped low and was struck by a passing bus. There was an explosion of black feathers and then a heavy thud as the bird landed on the road in front of her.

Before Iris could process what happened, a man in a suit darted into the street, kneeling beside the crow without a glance at the oncoming traffic. A car honked, and he got up slowly. He waved the car on and shook his head. Then he walked over and sat beside Iris.

"Her neck is broken. It's a shame. Such a beautiful bird." He shook his head again. "I volunteer with Wildlife Rescue. On the weekends." He looked at Iris. "That was a beautiful bird," he repeated.

Everything had happened so fast, and Iris was still reeling from the past few hours. She didn't know what to say.

The man seemed to need to talk. "I wanted to be a veterinarian, but ended up an attorney. Wildlife Rescue is a great organization. I've learned a lot. But I hate losing them, you know, the animals that get brought in. We had an owl hit by a car a month ago. And now it's back to flying. We'll release it soon. There's nothing like that feeling of releasing a wild creature back to where it belongs." He fell quiet, lost in thought for a moment. "What's your name?" he asked.

"Iris, Iris Barnes." They shook hands.

"I'm William Hendricks." They both looked at the dead crow on the road. "Such a beautiful animal and such an undignified death."

Iris could only nod. It was true.

A bus pulled up and opened its doors in front of Iris.

"This must be your bus," the man said.

Iris shook her head at the bus driver, who closed the doors and drove on. "Oh no, I'm actually not waiting for a bus. I'm only sitting here. I got out of jail a few minutes ago, and I'm trying to pull myself back together. I was about to call a friend to pick me up when, well, the crow." She gestured toward the street.

"Jail? Can I be so bold as to inquire why you were in jail?"

Iris didn't feel up to this. However, once she started, she couldn't stop. She explained about Ella, the preserve, the bribe Eric refused, and the betrayal that cost him his life.

She rambled about Ivan Storic, the trunk in the attic, old photographs that shouldn't exist, and something called the Faery Investigative Society, which sounded more absurd each time she said it.

She chose not to mention how Valerian Rose appeared and got her released, then vanished. Although, in truth, it didn't matter; she already sounded beyond unhinged.

She expected William Hendricks would make an excuse to exit quickly, but instead, he said, "Well, that explains a lot. I had been wondering about how that development ever got approved."

Iris looked past him and thought she saw Valerian Rose

turning a corner in the distance. Two crows circled the scene, looking down at the fallen one below.

William stood up and fished a card out of his pocket. "Iris, please call me if there is anything I can do to help. I mean it."

"Okay, thanks," she said, surprised.

As he walked away, Iris understood the encounter was not a random coincidence. She looked once more at the lifeless crow in the street. It was time to move.

She pulled out her phone. "Hi Joan, it's Iris. I've run into a little trouble and need a ride from downtown to the car impound lot."

"Oh dear. Where are you?"

Iris gave her directions. Storm clouds gathered behind the Sandia Mountains. It looked like the monsoon season would start soon. She looked back at the dead crow in the road, its feathers at odd angles being caught by the wind.

Joan arrived in her old Toyota Camry in less than fifteen minutes. Iris opened the passenger door and thanked her profusely.

Joan waved her off. "It's no problem, Iris. I was just weeding the herb bed. What happened?"

Iris explained the situation with the mistaken warrant and the words from the arresting officer about ending up at the bottom of the river. Then a torrent of information came out about Valerian Rose and being released, the crow that was hit by the bus, and the nice attorney who stopped to help.

Joan patiently listened. "Oh my. And you think this is because of the digging you've been doing about the Preserve?"

"Yeah, probably, or it's one hell of a coincidence, but I'm starting to not believe in those anymore."

"I don't know if you saw the news, but a girl named Annabelle talked the loggers in the bosque into quitting. I guess the city is having difficulty finding another company to clear the forest after that."

Iris raised her eyebrows, "Our Annabelle?"

"I haven't spoken with her yet, but I think so," Joan said softly.

Iris was quiet. She tried to imagine little Annabelle taking on a group of burly men cutting down trees. That child seemed to always be there to guide her moral compass to true north. If Annabelle could stand up to a team of loggers, Iris knew she had to find the courage to keep going, no matter what threats they leveled at her. There was no giving up now.

At the impound lot, Joan turned to her. "You be careful, okay?"

"Yes, I will. And thanks for the ride."

"You bet."

THAT EVENING, Ezra walked into the apartment and said, "Hey, my friend at the newspaper called."

Iris looked up from reading. "What did he say?"

"They're going to run the story tomorrow. The newspaper contacted the mayor and Ivan Storic. My friend doesn't think the mayor knew about the bribe. Ivan refused to comment. I'm sure he's lawyering up. Blair and Victor are under investigation, and the attorney general is involved. It looks like Victor will be taken into custody soon for the DUI bribe scam."

Iris blinked, stunned. "Oh my God, that is great news!" She set down her book, letting the weight of it all sink in. Her breath caught for a second, then she let it out slowly. It was actually happening. All the secrets and suspicions were finally amounting to something real.

She looked over at Ezra, seeing him with new clarity. "Ezra, you did this. You got the information on Blair and Victor and got someone in the press to follow up."

"Yeah, but you got the ball rolling. You dug up all the initial information on the preserve, and you were smart enough to be suspicious about Eric's death."

"Hmm, I guess we make a good team. Hey, uhm, I had an interesting day."

"Oh yeah?"

Iris filled him in on her arrest. And the mysterious appearance and disappearance of Valerian Rose.

Ezra's eyes widened, and his voice raised with some exasperation, "Iris! Why didn't you call me? I would have come right away!"

She expected this reaction. Gently, she said, "I know you would have. But you've done so much. And I'm an adult. I need to do some things on my own." Iris saw the hurt in his eyes. He was a protector. And he was good at it. "Look, I appreciate your willingness to help, and honestly, I don't know how I would have gotten to this point without you in all of this." She raised her palm. "But, I need to be able to take care of myself. At least sometimes."

Ezra thought for a moment. "I hear you. Sorry if I was too pushy. I know you're independent. And strong."

She had said her piece, and he had responded thoughtfully, not like her ex would have. It was their first disagreement, and Iris thought it was best to change the subject. "So, I met this guy at a bus stop." She showed him the card.

"William Hendricks?" Ezra's thick eyebrows raised as he repeated, "You met William Hendricks today? I went to school with him. He always wanted to be a veterinarian." Ezra looked again at the card. "He's a lawyer now?"

"Yes, a lawyer who does wildlife rescue on the weekends."

"Huh. Makes sense. Iris, he's a good guy. I can't believe you ran into him."

"Yeah, it is kind of strange."

Ezra half-smiled. "Or not, I guess. Depends on how you think about it."

Iris nodded, understanding that the evidence of an intelligent world of helpers was piling up. "I'll call him. I already told him a lot about what's happened. Probably too much all at once, but it didn't seem to faze him."

Now that Blair and Victor were under investigation, Iris concluded she could probably go home. The thought brought mixed feelings. These past days had been wonderful, but she missed Xena and her house. "Ezra, I think it's safe for me to go home."

He nodded, then grinned. "Our domestic bliss has come to an end." Iris laughed, her eyes lingering on the room a little longer.

She packed her small bag and, at the door, looked back at the apartment, which felt alive, warm, and comforting. She would miss it. Ezra walked her out to her car. Rain was coming down hard. The monsoons had arrived. They could hear long thunder rolls, and lightning was racing across the dark sky.

"Be careful, Iris. Call me if you need anything."

Iris got in her car and smiled, nodding her head. "Of course."

She waved goodbye through the rain-streaked window. As lightning cracked in the distance, Iris allowed herself to feel hope. It wasn't over yet. But now, with the press involved and William Hendricks offering help, maybe they could win this fight.

Valerian Rose's voice came floating back to her. *Thank the Queens.*

CHAPTER 37

Sarafina's second body floated free from her broken form, lying in the street. There was no pain. The transition took her through a tunnel of shimmering light. She stepped into the Otherworld through an elegant arch formed of cottonwood branches. Though she accepted her death, she glanced back once, feeling her responsibility to the Crow Clan and the cottonwood forest. Death was a passage, not an end, and her work would continue from this side of the veil.

Her ancestors gathered around to greet her. The reunion with her parents and siblings was joyful and filled with love. Before her, a vibrant cottonwood forest glowed and pulsed with color and light.

The Fae Queen of the Forests approached, majestic and luminous. She radiated a white light with flecks of green and gold. Draped in a flowing silk gown and crowned with woven branches and blossoms, the Queen extended an elegant staff toward Sarafina.

Sarafina flew onto the staff, her body light and agile. The Fae Queen's words resonated, "Welcome, wise one. You will accompany me now. The Crows and the Humans require our support from this realm." The Fae Queen's green glowing eyes saw the future in the distance. "For what comes next."

Sarafina nodded, instantly comprehending the delicate balance between the two worlds. Her readiness to serve as a spirit ally reflected her accumulated wisdom from this life and her many previous lives.

"It is time to make a bridge," the Fae Queen whispered, "and send wisdom to those willing to listen. Together, we will restore the balance."

Back in the waking world, Sarafina's death rippled through the bosque. The air grew heavy, as though the trees themselves were grieving. The Rio Grande Bosque crows mourned the hole in their community. Sarafina's wise and steady leadership would be sorely missed. But they also knew she would guide them from the Otherworld, and they stayed alert for her messages.

Grandmother Cottonwood felt the shift immediately. She sensed Sarafina's spirit passing into the next realm and understood that her mission to protect the forest would carry on. Nothing in nature was ever truly lost.

The Queens

A shooting star streaked through the twilight sky like a long silver thread as the ancient ones gathered under the heart-shaped leaves of the Cottonwood trees. Grandmother Cottonwood's branches stirred with anticipation. A circle had formed once more at the base of her trunk, but it was no ordinary conclave. The Fae Queens of Forests, Flowers, and Mycelium were meeting tonight to discuss an important matter.

The Forest Queen arrived first, her white and green gown woven from layers of bark and leaf-cutter bee silk flowing as she walked. Her hair fell in braids of lichen and moss, and her eyes glowed softly green. Accompanying her was Sarafina, shimmering softly, half dream, half visible.

Next came the Mycelium Queen, cloaked in dark velvet streaked with glowing filaments of bioluminescent fungi. A ring of puffball spores trailed in her wake. She sneezed and then smiled. "Let's make it quick. I'm cultivating something marvelous beneath some buffalo manure.

The Flower Queen arrived last, carried on a fragrant breeze. Her dress shifted with the seasons, currently decorated with roses at the hem and lilacs at the neckline. Her face was framed with sunflower petals as she turned to look at the other Queens. "Greetings, Queens." She adjusted a yellow petal that unfurled near her eye.

Greetings were murmured as Sarafina looked on.

The Flower Queen said, "The girl, Annabelle, she is full of heart, and I find myself quite fond of her." The other Queens nodded in agreement.

The Forest Queen added, "She has won over River, as well."

Sarafina stepped forward, her voice like an echo from far away. "I chose her and she has surpassed my expectations in every way. I find hope in that. Perhaps the humans are not as far gone as I once believed."

"I wouldn't go that far," the Queen of Mycelium huffed. "They are late to the party, and if we can save nature on this planet, it will be a miracle."

"Agreed. Humans have done too little, too late to save their planet if you ask me," the Flower Queen remarked.

The Forest Queen raised her hand. "This is not the time for debate. The clock is ticking, and magic is stirring. We have work to do."

The Mycelium Queen tilted her head. "Then, shall we summon Lola?"

The Queens were in agreement. Without ceremony, the will of the Queens focused and, in a blink, Lola appeared.

"Oh, for fungus's sake," she said, brushing off a mushroom cap clinging to her sleeve. "All right. What now?" Her wings quivered as she looked around the circle. Her eyes widened when she saw Sarafina. "Oh, you're here," she said, surprised.

The Flower Queen chided her, "If you had been paying attention…"

"I get busy with… things. I can't be expected to know everything that happens."

"Let's move on to the business of the evening," said the Queen of Mycelium.

The Forest Queen leaned forward, "Lola, you are needed again. This time, to supervise the girl Annabelle as she climbs the tree. Roanoke will be there, but we think you should be there as well, just in case. We can't be too careful. A century of planning has gone into this. And it is your job to bring the keys back under faery jurisdiction."

"Yes, yes, I know. I am always overjoyed to help."

The Flower Queen rolled her eyes. "Lola, if Annabelle fails, you fail. The forest is toast, and the entire tapestry unravels. We know you care. Tonight we need you to act like it."

"Fine. But I reserve the right to complain. Because humans and crows are so, so… boring."

Sarafina stepped forward again, her form pulsing softly like moonlight on water. "Annabelle carries the key not only in her pocket but in her heart. She has the rare combination of courage, kindness, and curiosity. She is not perfect. But she is precisely what is needed."

Lola looked from Sarafina back to the Queens. "And if things don't go as planned?" she asked.

The Tree Queen answered. "Then do what you must. Call the crows. Call the wind. Call us. But do not let her fall. Not only from the tree, but from her faith. Her goodness cannot be lost." A hush settled in the circle. Then leaves whispered like a thousand tiny voices in prayer.

Lola sighed dramatically, but there was resolve in her voice. "All right. I'll fluff my wings and dust off my sparkle and go do my save-the-forest schtick. Again."

With a blink and a shimmer, she vanished.

The Queens lingered a moment. The Forest Queen turned her gaze skyward. "The star has passed, and the veil is thinning. The time is now." She turned to look at Sarafina, but she was already in flight, above the canopy, a ghost among stars.

With that, the Queens disappeared in a wind vortex of petals and leaves.

"SARAFINA? ARE YOU HERE?" Perched on a high, sheltered branch during the storm, Roanoke sensed her before he saw her—a faint shimmer in the air beside him. Her presence was subtle yet unmistakable.

"Yes, Roanoke. I am here. I will be with you. The time is now."

"Now? In the storm?"

"Yes, it must be now."

The big black crow launched from the broad cottonwood branch, his wings flapping. The wind howled through the trees, bending branches as dark clouds rolled across the sky. Thunder rumbled, a low and ominous sound that promised more than just rain. Roanoke's feathers ruffled against the force of the wind, yet he pressed on, following Sarafina's spirit through the storm.

Someone with second sight would have seen them: a glowing spirit crow gliding alongside a flesh-and-blood crow through the stormy sky, their wings flapping with urgency as they flew directly to Annabelle's house.

CHAPTER 38

$\mathcal{A}$nnabelle, reading a book, listened in her bedroom as the sound of rain pounded against the roof. Startled by a thunderclap, she looked up to see a drenched crow tapping on the window. Roanoke! She hurried to open the window.

The wet bird hopped inside, shaking off water droplets from his black feathers. "Are you ready?" he asked.

"Ready?"

"The time is now, little one."

"What do I do?" Annabelle felt the weight of her responsibility. It was finally time.

"We go together into the forest."

"I'll meet you by my bike," Annabelle whispered to him, already pulling on her boots and coat. She grabbed her box of crow gifts, hesitated, then pulled out the skeleton key and shoved it into her jeans pocket.

She climbed through the window, leaving it open just a crack for her return. Then she tiptoed in the dark around the side of the house. She couldn't imagine her parents allowing her to enter the forest in this storm. She didn't like being sneaky, but tonight she had no choice.

"Okay, I'm ready," she murmured, already on her bike. Roanoke perched on her handlebars, and Annabelle pedaled into the storm, rain soaking her as lightning carved bright veins through the dark sky.

As she pedaled, Annabelle watched the large crow atop the handlebars, a dark silhouette against the storm. Occasionally, he would stretch his wings for balance as his talons clung tightly to the metal. Roanoke wasn't just riding with her—he was guiding her, sending silent directions to her mind. The ethereal form of Sarafina flew above them, providing a thread of connection to the Otherworld.

MEANWHILE, Iris drove home slowly through the flooded downtown streets, maneuvering her car away from the deeper puddles while her windshield wipers battled the torrential downpour. Summer monsoon storms quickly overwhelmed the drainage system, transforming streets into swift-moving rivers. Finally, when she arrived home, she parked and sprinted up the steps to the porch, one arm shielding her face from the pounding sheets of rain. The short distance from the car to the front door left her completely soaked.

Inside, her home felt hollow and silent. No chirp of welcome greeted her.

"Xena?" Her voice echoed in the empty house. She searched each room, hoping the cat was merely giving her the cold shoulder due to her absence. However, there was no sign of her anywhere.

Iris stepped out onto the porch and called again. The rain poured down, water rushing along the curb. She returned inside and sat on the couch, listening to the relentless drumming of rain and wind. *Something's not right.* Iris dialed the neighbor who had been feeding Xena, but there was no answer.

"Where are you?" she muttered. She grabbed a raincoat and

waterproof boots, found a flashlight and an umbrella, and stepped back into the storm. Walking down the slick sidewalk, she called Xena's name.

The forest wasn't far, and she wondered if Xena might have wandered there to hunt for mice or climb trees. She walked toward the woods, calling for the cat, her eyes searching. Warm light spilled from the windows of nearby homes, where people carried on with their evenings safe and dry.

She reached the edge of the forest and started along a muddy trail leading to the river. She didn't believe Xena would have wandered this far from home, but something compelled her to continue. Trudging deeper into the woods, her eyes adjusted to the dim surroundings. Unfortunately, the trees offered little shelter from the rain and howling wind.

She clicked on her flashlight and froze. Someone was riding a bicycle along a parallel path, maybe a half a football field away. Was that a bird on the handlebars? It was hard to see through the trees, but that's what it looked like.

She pulled out her phone and called Ezra.

"Xena's missing," she told him. "I'm in the woods looking for her."

"If Xena is outside, won't she wait out the storm somewhere dry? Under a porch or something?"

"I don't know. I only know I need to find her."

Ezra sighed. "I'll come to help."

THE DAMP FOREST was filled with the scent of earth and green leaves. The wind had calmed a bit, and the rain lessened to a steady drizzle. Iris left the main trail to search for the path where she had seen the bicycle.

The forest was dark, and even with her flashlight, progress was challenging. Wet branches slapped against her arms and face as lightning and thunder rolled on intermittently.

Then, without warning, she tripped over a tree root and fell hard. "Ow!" she gasped, rubbing her knee. She picked herself up and continued forward, limping. She knew it was crucial to keep walking toward the person she had seen. She didn't know why this mattered. She only knew it did, and she trusted her instinct.

The drizzle had diminished to a light mist, and the forest was quiet except for the sound of water dripping from the trees. She paused to catch her breath, leaning against a tree. Her knee throbbed and was likely swelling.

Iris discovered that her raincoat was more rain-resistant than rainproof. *Note to self: buy a proper raincoat.* In the distance, she noticed someone walking toward her.

"Hey, are you okay?" Ezra called out, seeing Iris.

"Yes, just resting."

He caught up with her and asked, "Should we head back? I doubt Xena came this far."

"I guess not. But I have to keep going. I saw someone out there."

"In this storm? It's probably someone camping by the river."

"No, I think it was a girl. On a bike. With a crow on the handlebars."

Ezra blinked. "What?"

"I'm glad you came. We need to go this way," Iris pointed toward the river and walked with determination. "I feel it."

Bewildered, Ezra shook his head but followed her deeper into the forest.

THE GIRL and the crow arrived at the Grandmother Cottonwood tree, rising like a church steeple in the forest. Annabelle dismounted her bike. Moonlight filtered through the thinning clouds. She examined the tree's trunk. It was likely the largest tree in the forest. Gazing up into the branches, she couldn't see the top.

Roanoke flew to a low branch. "Annabelle, do you have the key?" he asked.

"Yes." She pulled it out of her pocket.

"There is another key," Roanoke said.

Annabelle looked confused. "Ro, this is the only key I have."

"Yes, I know. The other one should be here shortly. Now we wait."

Roanoke asked Lola to protect Annabelle and to provide her with strength. "Of course." Lola flitted around Roanoke unseen by Annabelle.

Roanoke spoke to Grandmother Cottonwood with reverence and formality, "We are here to fulfill the promise from the Crow People, Grandmother."

"Very good," the Grandmother said slowly, "Thank you and all the black-winged ones."

Iris and Ezra kept pushing through the underbrush. Iris lost a shoe to the sucking mud. She dropped down on her hands and knees to find it, then continued walking, holding the mud-filled shoe. She slipped a few times, recovering by grabbing onto low branches.

Ezra would have tried to take her arm to steady her, but in the dense forest understory, there was no space to walk side by side. Iris continued to lead the way, forging through the woods.

"Annabelle, what are you doing out here?" Iris called out.

Annabelle turned, initially not recognizing the mud-covered, limping librarian, but she recognized that voice.

"Ms. Barnes, do you have the key?"

"The key?" Iris looked confused momentarily, and then an understanding transformed her expression. "Yes, yes, I believe I do. It's an old skeleton key." She pulled it out from under her coat, slipped the chain from her neck, and handed the key to Annabelle. Iris smiled triumphantly, though she wasn't sure why.

She put the green Tara pendant, now alone on the chain, back over her head and tucked it under her shirt. A slight wind whirled around her.

Ezra watched quietly, observing the strange convergence. He noticed the large black bird perched on a nearby branch, closer than a bird would typically be to humans. Yet, everything felt right. Familiar. He scanned the air for faeries or orbs of light.

Annabelle slipped the second key into her jeans pocket next to the other one. She remembered the man accompanying Iris from the protest in the park. There was nothing about him that seemed out of place here.

Annabelle cast Roanoke a questioning glance. He spoke into her mind, "It's time. You will know what to do. Climb the tree."

Without hesitation, she grabbed a low branch and started to climb. Roanoke flew from branch to branch to stay close to her. When there was no branch to hold onto, Annabelle used the bark itself, gripping with her fingers and toes like she had done at the climbing gym.

High in the canopy, she paused. The same deep knowing she'd felt when she found Federico returned. *This was the place.* She reached into her pocket, pulling out both keys, and saw a small arched door carved into the tree.

Roanoke's voice echoed softly in her mind, "The Divine Door."

Annabelle caught her breath. She inserted the first key. It turned easily, but revealed another door behind it. She switched keys and opened the second door.

Peering into the opening, she saw a tiny room, faintly glowing. She reached into the space and her fingers brushed against something dry and delicate—parchment. The moment her hands closed around the papers, warmth spread through her. When she withdrew her hand, the arched door disappeared.

A voice, slow and old, crackled, "Thank you, child, for listening and hearing and believing. There is hope." Annabelle rested her cheek against the gnarled bark, closing her eyes. She felt the tree's aliveness. She could have stayed there a long time, but Roanoke urged her to begin her descent.

When Annabelle lowered herself to the ground from the last branch, she heard Roanoke in her mind. "Well done."

Ezra and Iris stood behind her, shining a flashlight. She held up the papers.

One was the original deed and trust for the Bosque land that Ella purchased, providing the proof Iris had searched for. The other was a record of a stock purchase by Ella Ross from 1919, for 50 shares of Coca-Cola.

Ezra let out a low whistle. "If those were never sold... that's worth millions."

Annabelle blinked. "Wait, what?"

"The power of investing over time, kid," Ezra replied, beginning to see the bigger picture.

Iris's fingers trembled as she traced the edges of the deed. Ella had done it. Across time, she had protected the land. A luminous silver thread gently connected to Iris's heart, connecting her with Ella's vision and courage through time. Now, it was Iris's turn.

A gust of wind rustled the leaves above them. Iris no longer needed to reconcile the magical doors in the tree with the real, tangible papers in Annabelle's hands. The magical and mundane worlds had collided, and both were real. There was no doubt, only a forest to save.

ROANOKE FLEW BACK to his roosting place with Delphinia. He was exhausted but stayed awake to share everything that had happened. She relished every detail and laughed at the image of Roanoke riding on the handlebars of Annabelle's bike. She nodded solemnly as he mimicked Grandmother Cottonwood's slow words. When he told her about Serafina's guidance, Delphinia's eyes widened, and she opened herself to feel the

Elder's presence with them, searching around with her consciousness. Yes, she could feel Serafina, too.

"You have been brave, Roanoke. Now it's up to the Human People. You've done everything you could."

But Roanoke's thoughts were already on the future. "There is still so much to do. We all have a job. The elders told us we need to restore the bond with the Human People so the world can return to balance. Humans have been lost without us. They need us as messengers to hear the Otherworld." Roanoke was tired, yet he spoke passionately. He didn't want his efforts to be in vain.

AFTER GIVING the papers to the grown-ups, Annabelle rode her bike home slowly through the hush that followed the storm. She slipped quietly back into the house, her parents none the wiser. She intended to return the keys to her crow box, but after checking every pocket, she found them all empty. She sighed and knew that the keys belonged to the Otherworld, the world of Lola, and the spirit of Grandmother Cottonwood.

She changed into dry nightclothes, hung her wet clothes on a chair, and slipped into bed. She had done it; she had accomplished the task she was meant to do. She fell into a deep sleep almost as soon as her head hit the pillow.

EZRA AND IRIS walked back to Iris's house. As they entered through the front door, Xena was in the living room to greet them, her tail raised. Iris picked up the big, fluffy cat and said, "Where were you? I was so worried about you!" Xena purred her loudest purr.

Iris made tea, and she and Ezra sat at the kitchen table, quietly planning their next steps. Iris was exhausted, yet her mind raced. Her goal now was to protect the forest indefinitely, as Ella had wanted. She had research to do and legal issues to understand.

Ezra wanted to share more with Iris about the faeries from his childhood and his feelings in the forest. However, Iris was focused on the work of saving the Preserve. Magic would have to wait.

Xena

In the infinite intelligence of the cosmos, it is a cat's sacred duty to vanish, create chaos, and return as though nothing happened. In the process, I saved a forest. All in a day's work.

I see Ella now, her spirit present, rocking on the porch swing with Sarafina, her partner in crime, perched on her shoulder. Ella has won—not just for herself, but for all the creatures of the Rio Grande Cottonwood forest. The silver thread held, connecting the past and the present, this world and the Otherworld. It was a team effort, and everyone played their part.

As I watch Iris and Ezra huddle over the table discussing deeds and stocks, I know it wasn't a piece of paper that saved the forest—it was the belief in the unseen, asking for help, and trusting the path. Not bad for a stormy night.

CHAPTER 39

Maria sat at the kitchen island, coffee in hand, scrolling through news on her laptop, "Nate, check out this headline- 'Bosque Bribe Results in Murder'."

Nate, rinsing his coffee mug at the sink, turned with a frown. "Huh. I wonder what the backstory is. There's so much corruption in government these days."

"Yeah, and the mayor just doubled down on developing the bosque. It looks like the main funder for the project may be going to prison, but the mayor still wants to move forward with it."

"You're kidding," Nate muttered. "That guy's unbelievable."

"Hmmm," Maria said while sipping her coffee. "Maybe don't tell Annabelle."

"Where is she anyway? She's usually up by now."

Right on cue, Annabelle shuffled in wearing sweatpants and a hoodie, blinking away sleep.

"Don't tell me what?" Annabelle asked, reaching for a cereal box in the cupboard.

Maria hesitated. "I didn't want to upset you. It's about the Bosque development. Nothing new."

Annabelle shrugged. "It's not going to happen," she said with finality. She poured cereal into her bowl, avoiding eye contact.

Nate tilted his head. "How do you know that?"

Annabelle finally met his gaze. "Because I just do."

Maria and Nate exchanged glances. Maria shook her head slightly. Annabelle returned to eating, as if the issue were settled and there was nothing left to say.

LATER THAT MORNING, fully awake and with a plan, Annabelle rode her bike to Aunt Joan's house. She needed to talk to someone who would understand. She wasn't going to tell her parents about what happened last night. She knew that sneaking out and keeping secrets from her parents was wrong. But she also knew they wouldn't believe her about Roanoke, Grandmother Cottonwood, River, and certainly not about Lola. And they wouldn't believe that she had an important role to play in saving the forest. It was better to talk with Aunt Joan about it all.

"ANNABELLE, it's so good to see you!" Joan hugged her niece. "Come in. Federico is here, too. My cup runneth over! Have some tea with us in the back garden. It's so nice there after the rain last night." Annabelle followed her to the kitchen, where water was already boiling for tea, and cookies were out on a plate.

In the back garden, the scent of wet earth and blooming lavender wrapped around Annabelle like a blanket. Hummingbirds darted between orange trumpet vine flowers.

Federico grinned when he saw her. "I knew I would see you here!"

Joan poured tea with practiced ease. "What's on your mind, m'ija?" she asked gently.

Annabelle hesitated. It was all so much. Roanoke, the River, the Fae, Grandmother Cottonwood, the keys, the divine door had all been swirling inside her, too big to hold alone. But here, she was finally able to let it all spill out.

Joan listened intently, nodding at the right moments, her face relaxed, as if nothing could surprise her. Federico, on the other hand, leaned forward, his eyes wide with excitement.

"Wait, wait- you climbed the tree? And there was a door in it?"

Annabelle nodded. "And behind the door was another door, and then a tiny room with old documents. Really important ones."

Federico shook his head. "That crow was definitely up to something."

Joan reached out, squeezing Annabelle's hand. "You did it, you did what you were meant to do."

Annabelle exhaled as the tension in her shoulders melted. "But do you think it's really over?"

Joan smiled knowingly. "Oh, sweetheart. Magic is never over. It just shifts and waits for the right moment to begin again."

Federico leaned back with a grin. "In the meantime, I want to learn to talk to crows!"

Annabelle laughed for the first time in what felt like weeks.

AT CITY HALL, Iris adjusted the strap of her briefcase and stepped into the building alongside the attorney William Hendricks.

Iris was dressed in a black pantsuit she kept for funerals. She wore red lipstick and pumps. The briefcase held everything—documents pulled from Ella's trunk and the crucial stock purchase confirmation. She'd told William she found everything in the attic. The part about the tree was... not for today.

Iris felt like an impostor, as if she were only pretending to be a grown-up. She was nervous, but this was her moment. She would rise to the occasion, buoyed by thoughts of Ella and

Annabelle and their perseverance to protect the forest. Now it was her turn.

They were ushered into the mayor's office, where they sat in blue plush chairs. The mayor smiled from behind his massive desk. "What can I do for the two of you?" Regulus asked, thinking this meeting was regarding a large donation to his campaign. That was what his assistant had told him.

"Mr. Mayor, my client and I are coming to you with an offer for the cottonwood forest that has recently been slated for development."

Regulus's smile vanished. "I'm not sure why you are here. That land is not for sale. It's already been sold. That land is being cleared for development. Development starting next week." He couldn't stop himself from automatically reciting what he had been saying for months. "We are building a top-notch development that will be an asset for Cottonwood for years to come."

Iris cut in. "Mayor Regulus, public polling on the development is running four to one against cutting down the forest. The people of Cottonwood don't want this. Not to mention, the foundation of this deal involved the murder of an innocent man, which the trial against Blair Sutter and Victor Montes will prove. We are here to offer the city a way out."

William Hendricks pulled the offer paper from his briefcase. He leaned forward to place it on the mayor's desk. "This is our offer. It is one hundred times what the developers paid for the property. This is an offer for five hundred million dollars. This is an offer the city of Cottonwood can't afford to refuse."

Regulus stared at the paper. Seconds ticked by. Then more.

Iris and the attorney looked at him expectantly. Sensing he would not receive a timely response from the mayor, William Hendricks continued, "This money comes from the estate of Ella Ross, from a very prescient stock purchase. She was the founder of the Rio Grande Bosque Preserve in 1919. This offer is contingent on an ironclad agreement that the cottonwood forest along the river will never be developed."

Regulus finally looked up from the piece of paper and said, barely above a whisper, "I will take this to the city council."

Iris and William got up to leave. Iris touched the Green Tara pendant and looked the mayor square in the eye. "There's one more thing. I want a statue of Ella Ross and a plaque, too, at the forest entrance. It should commemorate her great foresight in preserving this beautiful place for future generations."

The mayor nodded weakly.

With that, Iris and William walked out of the mayor's office. William turned to Iris and said, "I believe we just saved a forest."

CHAPTER 40

*I*ris, just back from City Hall, stood in her front yard snipping flowers for a bouquet when she spotted Joan approaching on her pink bicycle.

"How are you enjoying your summer?" Joan called out as she steered her bike toward the curb.

Iris walked toward her, a faint smile on her face. "Let's just say…it's been interesting."

Joan placed her foot on the curb and leaned forward on the handlebars. "Glad to hear it."

"I solved the mystery of the key. Well, I guess I shouldn't take credit. The mystery of the key is solved."

"What happened?" Joan squinted, studying Iris closely, even though she already knew Annabelle's version of the story.

Iris hesitated, gathering her thoughts. "Last week, during that big monsoon storm, Xena went missing, so I went out to the woods to look for her. Something was pulling me there. It didn't make sense, but I followed the feeling." Iris paused, taking a breath. "In the middle of the storm, I met up with Annabelle, your niece. She asked me for the key. And the key opened a door high up in a tree, and inside were some documents. Ella's documents. This space inside the tree contained the deed and the purchase agreement for the Bosque Preserve. And a stock receipt that was worth… well, a fortune."

Joan's face softened, her eyes twinkling. Iris continued, "I'm not sure where Annabelle got her key. And she was amazing, climbing that tree."

"She's a remarkable child," Joan said. "She's connected to the Crow Clan. I've been watching her grow into her purpose for years."

Iris hesitated, feeling the enormity of what had happened settling deeper inside. "It feels surreal. But in the end, we went to the mayor with the documents, and Ella's stock purchase from a century ago ended up saving the preserve. The forest won't be developed."

Joan's eyes misted. "That is wonderful news, Iris. Truly."

"It's like Ella planned for all of this. It's as if a hundred years ago, she knew developers would eventually come for the bosque. She made sure the key was handed down to me by everyone who's owned this house. And that key opened a door in a tree containing the documents I needed. And I ended up there because my cat disappeared in the middle of a storm." Iris pressed her fingers to her temples. "I know I sound crazy. I'm still trying to understand how all this could be true. But it happened." Iris shook her head. "Even as I'm telling you all this, Joan, it doesn't feel real. How could Ella have known what was needed in the future, and why me?"

Joan's gaze was steady and full of understanding. "Yes, why indeed? We all have a purpose. And when we trust in the unfolding of things, the right path appears. You followed the signs. You listened. That's rare." Joan paused and looked at Iris with warmth. "I want to thank you on behalf of the city of Cottonwood for saving all those trees and preserving that land. You stepped out of your comfort zone, and you did a very wonderful thing."

Iris gave a short laugh. "Yes, yes, I did step out of my comfort zone. That's for sure. I wanted to drop it, but I couldn't. There was that guy who was murdered. It was just wrong, all the greed. And Annabelle, well, she was so heartbroken and then with those loggers in the forest... I still can't believe that. She was like, I don't know, Joan of Arc or something. Anyway, I have to say it has been an interesting summer so far."

Joan smiled knowingly. "And you survived it."

"Yeah, I did."

Joan's expression turned thoughtful. "But this is just the beginning. The bosque needed saving, but there are other battles ahead. We live in interesting times. You've shown you have the strength to face challenges. The work isn't over."

A gentle breeze stirred the air, carrying the scent of flowers. Joan's eyes sparkled mischievously. "Speaking of help, if you see Ezra, tell him my bees are acting up again."

Hearing Ezra's name brought an involuntary smile to Iris's face and a slight flip of her heart.

Joan smiled. "Ah, I see."

Iris sighed, shaking her head. "You see too much, Joan." As Joan pedaled away, Iris couldn't help but wonder what was in store for the rest of her summer.

CHAPTER 41

Federico was busy turning his Adopt-A-Tree website, Forest Friends, into a reality. In the library, he, Ezra, and Joey sat huddled over a screen, finalizing the website. The forest service had donated a drone, allowing them to map the entire bosque. Every tree had a number and soon a guardian.

The three had become fast friends. On the first day they met at the library, Federico shared with Ezra and Joey the vision he had when he fell from the tree.

Ezra remarked, "Man, that was an initiation."

Federico looked at him quizzically. "What do you mean?"

"A long time ago, less so now, young people would go on a quest in the wilderness for a vision to find their purpose. They would get in touch with their spirit guides in dreams. But what happened to you? It's a modern-day version. Your experience was a bit more haphazard and dangerous, but it served its purpose. Falling out of that tree gave you a vision and brought you to a calling, a purpose. It changed you."

Joey chimed in, "I think I had an initiation, too. When I got shot. I wanted to change course, and Federico helped me. And really, the shooter helped me too in a super weird way." Joey playfully punched Federico's shoulder, and Federico smiled.

Joey designed the logo for Forest Friends. And with Ezra and Federico's help, he was beginning to realize that his drawing skills were special and that he could do something with them that made a difference. It felt good. He knew he was a work in progress, but that day at the park and spending time with Federico in the hospital were turning points toward a new life.

Federico responded to Ezra, "Huh. I never thought of it that way. It's true, though. That beautiful lady with the blue cloak gave me a message. I can't ever forget the dead forest I saw. And I guess that did change everything." Thinking about it more, Federico said, "Flying the drone opened me up to it. It made me feel small, and all my problems felt smaller, too. When I wasn't always thinking about my problems, I had more room in my head for other things. And that turned out to be Forest Friends."

Ezra looked fondly at Federico. "And your vision made you realize how important the forest is. And then you didn't take it for granted."

"Yep. I thought about how it's all interconnected. Trees make the oxygen we breathe. Did you know that?"

Ezra replied, "Yeah. You know what else? They sequester carbon, which means they slow down climate change."

"Huh. That's cool. And there's medicine in the forest. I read that most drugs come from plants."

"Shrooms are where it's at, man," Joey said.

Ezra smiled. "Federico, you've been doing your research."

"Yeah." The fear and doubt that had so often crept into his thoughts now seemed self-absorbed and small. He was done with that life.

After weeks of work, Federico, Joey, and Ezra worked together on the website's last line. It read, "Our humanity is enhanced by protecting the earth, protecting the forests, and connecting to nature. Adopt a tree today and become a part of the forest. Proceeds go to forest preservation."

Ezra and Federico looked at each other. It was finished. It was time.

"It's all yours, Federico, take it live."

Federico's finger hovered over the publish button. Then decisively, he pressed it. Joey high-fived Ezra and Federico. Then everything was still for a few moments as they watched the screen.

Within minutes of posting the website, adoption requests began pouring in. So many people in Cottonwood loved their forest and wanted to save it, and they were happy to do anything to help. Ezra had made sure that before they finished the site, his friend at the newspaper interviewed the kid who had fallen from a tree, had a vision, and was now building a website to save the forest.

Far above the city library, black wings stirred the air. Crows cawed softly to each other in words not understood by most humans, but they were a blessing on the unlikely human champions of the forest. The threads between the worlds, once frayed, were weaving themselves whole again.

Federico's idea spread like a mycelial web around the world. Kids started creating websites similar to Federico's for their local forests, putting pressure on local governments to preserve them. It's hard to know how many forests were saved by this effort. However, the net number of forested acres worldwide increased instead of decreased, and forests started to heal.

IRIS WALKED toward the sunlit corner inside Trifecta. Her mood and spirit matched the buoyant, high-ceilinged, light-filled coffee shop. While she waited for Ezra, she sat at a wooden table holding her warm mug. As she sipped her latte, Iris had to admit that everything that happened in the forest that night and talking to the mayor this morning was miraculous on an order of magnitude that she had never experienced. She felt a deep sense of awe and gratitude. Something beyond logic made the world turn and connected past and present and life and death in ways she'd never entertained.

Ezra, wearing a black Scooby Doo T-shirt, walked in the glass door entrance, and his eyes landed on her immediately. His smile radiated warmth as he sat down across from her. "From your expression, it looks like it must have gone well with the mayor."

Iris reached out to lightly touch Ezra's forearm on the table. "It did, I think he'll take the deal. I just want to tell you, I've been thinking, and so much has happened, and it's been so much to process."

Ezra looked at her with affection. His hand turned, fingers lacing through hers.

Iris smiled and looked down. "You know, when you spoke to me about magic and its relationship with the Otherworld behind the veil?"

Ezra smiled, and his eyes danced. "Yeah."

"Well, you're right. I know it now, too. And I know Ella has been part of this whole thing and…I know you saw faeries. And those skeleton keys that opened the door in the tree were from the Otherworld. You knew."

Ezra's phone buzzed, and he looked at it. "Sorry- I don't want to, but I have to go. Someone's locked out. Stay here. I'll be back soon." He squeezed her hand and got up to leave.

MAYOR REGULUS, flanked by city council members, stood at a press conference at the edge of the cottonwood forest.

The press thought they were there for the groundbreaking ceremony of the river development, but there were no shovels or equipment.

Instead, at the podium, Mayor Regulus looked around at the

crowd and said, without his usual smiling and bluster, "After much consideration and thoughtful listening to my constituents," he looked up as cameras flashed, "I have decided to preserve the Rio Grande Cottonwood Forest for future generations."

With microphones pointed at the mayor, the press corps yelled questions above the crowd's murmur.

"Why the change of heart, mayor?"

"Do you have a comment on the murder trial?"

"Did you know Ivan Storic tried to bribe Eric Sutter?"

The mayor's assistant shielded him from the reporters and ushered him to a waiting car. She turned and said to the crowd, "There will be no questions."

NATE WALKED into his lab and was greeted by his interns: three excited PhD post-docs. He quickly read their faces but tried to dampen his hopes.

"Nate, this strain is working even better than we thought it could!" one of the interns said while the two others vigorously nodded their heads. They all had grown up during a time of utter despair about climate change and were determined to take action. Nate's openings for interns were always competitive because his research lab was regarded as cutting-edge.

Nate sat down at a computer and scanned the report, his pulse quickening. The interns nearly tripped over one another as they showed him the data: measurements of soil water retention, tree uptake of soil nutrients, and tree health. He was amazed. This new mycorrhizal network was spreading quickly and proving to be very efficient. The trees were connecting to it rapidly in their test plot, and they were already clearly benefiting.

He understood the immense capacity for self-healing inherent in a complex system like the cottonwood forest. He recognized that this mycorrhizal network could serve as a tool to alleviate the stress of climate change for these trees.

Nate couldn't help but feel a surge of pride as he read through the findings. After years of working in quiet frustration, this breakthrough was everything he had hoped for. It was a victory not only for the forest but also for his own belief in the power of science to meaningfully help the world.

"Amazing work, guys. I think we just saved a forest. I'm going to go make a few calls." This was the moment he had been waiting for; there was no time to waste now.

He called the county extension and reached his contact there, a PhD biologist who had been following and encouraging Nate's work.

"John, I think we're ready," Nate said. "We have a mycorrhizal strain that is ready for forest inoculation. And I think it can save the bosque."

Iris, still sitting at the coffee shop, took a sip of her second latte, topped with a frothy milk heart design. When she looked up, she saw Ezra walk back in, smiling ear to ear. Iris reflected on how Ezra had been her constant throughout the chaos, always there with support and good humor. Unable to contain herself any longer, she got up from the table.

They met in the center of the coffee shop. Iris wrapped her arms around Ezra, hugging him and resting her head against his chest. Ezra placed his fingers under her chin, lifting her head to kiss her. They kissed for a long time, unaware of the other coffee shop patrons, all smiling.

"Finally!" one of the regulars yelled.

"Yeah, get a room, you guys," the barista grinned.

Xena

The beginning is the end, and the end is the beginning. This is only the beginning for Iris, Ezra, Annabelle, and Federico. It is the end of a long trajectory for Ella's influence on this world. Joan is closer to the end than the beginning, but she still has work to do in this world.

You might be thinking it would sure be nice to have a bodhisattva like me to help you on your path. I'm sticking with Iris for the future, but I can tell you that you have more help than you can imagine. The forest has always heard you. The crows have always watched. The river remembers you. We live in a universe overflowing with spirit allies. Simply ask, and you'll see. And be alert for the magic, dear reader. It's all around you.

ACKNOWLEDGMENTS

I want to extend thanks to those I consider my best teachers: Sean Esbjorn-Hargins for opening my mind to all things exo and subtle sensing, Aiden Wachter for bringing practical magic into my life, and Dara Saville for sharing her deep knowledge of the flora of the Rio Grande Middle Valley. The book in this form would not exist without them.

I offer my gratitude to my early readers and all their kind feedback. I especially thank Camille McLearn, for entering the world of Cottonwood with me and making this book better in every way. And I give my most profound appreciation to my husband, Alexander Smith, for his unflagging support and confidence in me.

ABOUT THE AUTHOR

Lisa Page spends her days writing and reading fiction, crafting practical magic, and communing with the natural world. A life-long student of mystery and meaning, she weaves together her passions for the magical, the ecological, and the everyday sacred into stories that explore the hidden forces shaping our lives. She lives in Albuquerque, New Mexico, with her husband, various four-leggeds, and a garden that bends toward chaos. *Saving Cottonwood* is her debut novel. You can learn about updates and new releases at her website: lisapageauthor.com

If you enjoyed *Saving Cottonwood*, consider leaving a review on Amazon. It helps this book find its people.

www.ingramcontent.com/pod-product-compliance
Lightning Source LLC
Chambersburg PA
CBHW030002010826
48973CB00007B/2129